THE BOOK OF JOBS

A COLLECTION OF HELEN WU AND AMY DRESDEN STORIES

M.L. Grider

Copyright © 2022, M.L. Grider

Published by:
Thursday Night Press
an imprint of
DX Varos Publishing
7665 E. Eastman Ave. #B101
Denver, CO 80231

Book cover design and layout by, Ellie Bockert Augsburger of Creative Digital Studios.
Cover design features:
www.CreativeDigitalStudios.com using Asian woman and gun by pongimages; Attractive slim woman walking, isolated vector silhouette by michalsanca

ISBN: 978-1-955065-54-2 (paperback)
ISBN: 978-1-955065-55-9 (ebook)

To my children's college tuition,
where all the profits of this work are going.

Table of Contents

Introduction

In order to make a reader care about a fictional character the author must make that character real. To do that the author must know the character intimately. This was once summed up for me by another author with what he called "the ice cream test." The writer must *know* their character's favorite flavor of ice cream. Not merely assign it like ticking off a box on a statistics sheet but understand what that person would like about Caramel Ripple as opposed to Mint Chocolate Chip. If a writer's characters are not that "real" to them then it is unrealistic to expect the character to be "real" to the reader. And if that happens the reader simply will not become invested in the story.

To this end, I had to better understand who Helen Wu and Amy Dresden are. I had to "know" all of the formative events in their lives that shaped their personalities and their decision making processes. Even if many of these things are totally mundane and irrelevant to the story at hand, *I* had to know them. In the processes of exploring their backgrounds I discovered many things, some only interesting to me, like

Helen was on the swim team in high school and likes cinnamon buns; or Amy's younger sister was so jealous of her sibling that she had a one night stand with Ted and slept with all three of Monk's Raiders.

A few of these things turned out to be interesting enough to become actual stories. And that is what this book is. All nine of these stories take place before they met and are mostly concerned with why they both left their previous careers and opened retail shops. For what happens when Amy met Helen, look for my first novel "Bitter Vintage" or its upcoming sequel "Bitter Sacrament."

M.L. Grider

The Second Story Job

1982

At last the house was silent. Helen opened her door and gazed down the long, dark hallway. She put on her Cookie Monster slippers to soften her already light footfalls. Even though she was barely eighty pounds, trying to walk down the hall was like tap dancing on a xylophone. Lynn was a notoriously light sleeper, and the slightest creak would bring her down all over Helen. Helen had been waiting forever for Lynn to finally settle down and go to bed. She must have been banging around in her room for hours. Doing what, God only knew.

Their father and mother had gone to Vegas for the weekend to celebrate their twenty-fifth wedding anniversary and left the sisters home alone for the very first time. That left Lynn, sixteen, in charge, and she was taking her responsibility way too seriously. Helen had wanted to invite her best friend, Holly, to sleep over, but Lynn was being a real bitch about it.

"Mom and Daddy said, 'no guests.' They're trusting us, and I don't want to let them down," Lynn had said. "Holly is a bad influence on you and you know it. That girl has a mouth like a drunken sailor and the morals of a skunk. The minute she finds out our parents are gone she'll call a bunch of boys, throw a wild party, and end up burning the whole house down." Lynn was such a goodie-good, Little Miss Perfect. Like Holly always said, "That bitch wouldn't say shit if she had a mouthful." It drove Helen straight up the walls.

Lynn just couldn't seem to grasp that Helen was fourteen now and not a little kid anymore. In fact, Helen was surprised that Lynn didn't insist on an 8:00 bedtime and try to read her a chapter of one of those cloying Nancy Drew Mysteries she still gave Helen for Christmas and birthdays, even though she hadn't read one in years. These days all Helen read was true crime stories like *The Stranger Beside Me* or *Badge of the Assassin*. Granted, Helen did not look her age, a fact she hated now, but would grow to love when she still looked thirty at sixty.

At the age of fourteen, Helen Wu was totally dissatisfied with her appearance. She had already reached her full height of four feet and eleven inches, and as her mother had so discreetly put it, all the plumbing had come in the year before. Worst of all, to her unending embarrassment, she had filled out as much as she was ever going to. A fact that the other girls at school never let her forget.

Tonight however, in spite of her childish appearance, Helen had her sights set on some "adult entertainment."

4

When her brother, Garrett, had been back from A&M for spring break he left his copy of John Derek's *Tarzan, the Ape Man*, hidden in his room. Helen had run across it when she was raiding his stash of magazines.

Helen had seen the beginning of the film with the rest of her family when it was broadcast on the pay channel. But as soon as Bo Derek's clothes began to come off, her mother had turned Bo off. Finally Helen was going to get to see all of it. All she had to do was sneak past Lynn's bedroom door. Then slink downstairs to the den and the VCR, and she would have Bo Derek all to herself.

Helen began the tedious trek along the hallway. It was not the first time she had snuck out of her room when the rest of the household was fast asleep. Over the years she had become well acquainted with the floorboards. But tonight, something was telling her to be extra careful.

Lynn must have felt it too. All night she had been even more uptight than usual. She insisted they eat early. Right after dinner she showered and washed her hair. It struck Helen odd because their mother was convinced if they went to bed with wet hair, they would contract pneumonia in the night from the damp and be dead by morning. It was the closest Helen had ever seen Lynn come to disobeying their parents. Whether or not Lynn agreed with them, she always did whatever her parents told her to do. No matter how ridiculous or restrictive they were, Lynn always followed the rules. Helen was particularly annoyed by this because Lynn spent almost an hour blow-drying her long hair, which interfered with TV reception. Helen had had to watch *The Love Boat* through the static. Worst of all, it was the episode with Linda Evans as a gold-digger trying to snare a rich husband.

When Lynn was done she came downstairs dressed in her long, pink, fleece robe and a splash of perfume. Helen wondered where she got the perfume. Neither one of them were allowed to wear any cosmetics. Lynn passed it off by claiming the scent was from her new shampoo.

Lynn talked incessantly about how tired she was after such a long day. "Aren't you tired too, Helen? There's nothing but reruns on TV tonight, and it was such a long day. Maybe we should make it an early night tonight. How about it, *Meimei*, ready to hit the old hay? Daddy left us some spending money so we could go out for some ice cream tomorrow if you're a good girl."

Helen was only too happy to comply with Lynn's suggestion. After all, the sooner Lynn was in bed asleep, the sooner Helen could slip off to Africa with Bo. She had heard so much about the movie. Holly had told her that the ratings board had originally wanted to give it an X-rating. The thought of Bo Derek in a nearly X-rated movie made Helen's heart race. She only wished Holly could watch it with her.

Helen had memorized the pattern of creaky floorboards. She stopped. There was something amiss, something different tonight. The hallway was always dark, illuminated only by a dim nightlight in the bathroom. But tonight it was darker than usual. *Why?*

Lynn's bedroom door was closed. Lynn never slept with the door closed. But so much the better; with the door shut, she could get by easier. Still, just to be on the safe side, she stopped at the closed door and pressed her ear to it to listen.

There was music softly playing, Lynn was listening to one of those horrid, candy floss pop Air Supply albums of hers. Russell Hitchcock was whinnying on and on about being all out of love. Helen hated pop music, especially the artless, generic, girly crap Lynn listened too. She preferred talented musicians with something to say, like Charlie Parker.

But it was none of Helen's business if Lynn was playing records. In fact the music, if you could call it that, would cover the sound of her movie. Quiet as a cat she scampered past the door. At the stairs she sat sidesaddle on the banister and slid down, not wanting to risk a squeaky step. On silent feet she went to the family room. Careful to make sure the volume was all the way down, she turned on the television.

Outside, it was a quiet October night. The Santa Ana winds had not started for the season yet, but there was something rustling in the shrubs outside. The branches on the old oak were tapping on the picture window. Light from the streetlamps cast a twisted latticework of shadows through the thin cotton drapes.

Helen pulled her robe tighter around her and came to the edge of the window. Hiding behind the window frame she peeked around the edge into the front yard. The street was still and silent. But the branches were moving.

She pulled the drape open more for a better look. Something was hiding in the hedge that separated her mother's flowerbeds from the house.

Something moved in the bush. Helen stared, straining to hear the slightest sound. She jumped back when the branches exploded outward. A bright yellow tomcat lunged out. It indignantly charged through the flowers and across the front lawn.

Helen hated that cat, but then she hated most cats, mainly because they hated her. But she hated this cat in particular. It belonged to the people across the street and they refused to have it fixed. So it was always prowling around Helen's house trying to get at Lynn's cat, even though Sandy was spayed and never allowed outside. For a moment she imagined tossing Sandy out the back door on her fluffy butt just to see how she would handle the amorous advances of the big, yellow tomcat. Helen never understood why people went to all the time and trouble of taking care of pets. It all seemed like a lot of unnecessary work for no good reason to her.

The cat came to an abrupt stop at the curb and attempted to regain his dignity by licking between the toes of his back paw. He looked up at Helen and seemed to be daring her to challenge him. He gave it a second thought then turned his back on her. With his tail held up as rigid as a flagpole, he jumped up onto the hood of an orange Datsun wagon parked in the street directly in front of the house. She watched as the cat circled around three times and settled down on the hood of the ugly car.

Helen had seen that old car before. She couldn't place where, but she had seen it. It stuck in her mind because of the horrible black vinyl roof that made it look like a pumpkin. She decided that it must belong to one of the high school kids that lived in the neighborhood and turned her attention back to Bo.

Before she slipped the tape into the VCR she checked the reels and saw that it was already three quarters of the way into the movie. Garrett must have stopped at the good part. To be sure there was no trace of her "borrowing" the tape, she marked the position of the spools on the clear plastic window with a dry erase marker. Helen wanted to savor the entire movie. She didn't want to miss one second of Bo. Without looking at where Garrett had left off she pushed it in and hit the rewind button.

While the tape was rewinding, Helen went to the kitchen for a snack. She pulled out the two bottom drawers by the kitchen sink and used them as steps to reach the bag of Milano mint cookies her mother had hidden on the top shelf. Just as her fingertips reached her prize there was a soft tapping against the den window glass. Helen froze. *There is no way Lynn didn't hear that.* Lynn would be down in an instant and her evening would be ruined. She held her breath and waited to be busted. But Lynn never came. Gradually, curiosity began to overtake the fear of getting caught. *What was that tapping anyway?*

Helen climbed down from the counter and dashed back into the den. In the silhouette of shadows on the drapes she was sure she saw a person climbing the tree outside. She dropped her precious mint cookies on the soft carpet, rushed to the window, and tore the drapes open.

A Topsider sticking out of stone-washed jeans was disappearing above the top of the window. Helen dropped down to her knees for a better angle and looked up at a big white guy climbing the old oak. The thick branches bowed under his weight. *This guy is huge.*

Helen's mind instantly started calculating. From years of playing tag and hide-n-seek with her siblings she knew that that tree went straight up to Lynn's bedroom window. Helen had used that route many times herself to elude being made "it" by bigger, stronger siblings. There could be only one thing on that ape's mind, only one purpose to make him climb that tree, only one thing he could possibly be after. He was coming to *tag* Lynn... and then her.

9

Helen jumped to her feet and ran to the phone to call the police. But as soon as her hand was on the cradle her mind began to race again, weighing all the possible outcomes.

If she called the police, it would take them half an hour or more to show up. By that time, The Great White Ape out there could have already played *me Tarzan, you Jane* with Lynn and moved on to making Helen into Cheetah. The arrival of the police would only further enrage him and make him kill them both on the spot if he hadn't already. Or it could make him try to use one of them as a hostage, like a human shield. He might even try and kidnap one of them. After a shootout with the inept cops the brigand would drag her on an interstate killing spree like Charlie Starkweather did with Caril Ann Fugate back in the fifties in one of her true crime books.

If she called the police, all they would do is tell her to hide until they could find time to get around to her. Could Helen hide somewhere while a burglar ravished her helpless sister? Would she be able to live with herself after letting her sister get mauled and defiled. How could she ever be able to look Lynn in the eye knowing she had cowered under her bed like Cora Amurao while Richard Speck—another true crime story—tortured, raped, and murdered eight student nurses one by one in the next room? No, she had to take matters into her own hands and save Lynn.

She reasoned that if she called the police then went to help Lynn, it would complicate things for her later. It showed premeditation. If she called the cops first then dispatched the intruder herself she could end up facing a trial. Manslaughter or even murder. With the courts as ass backward as they were in L.A. she would most likely end up in jail for saving her sister from getting raped by some psycho. Besides, Tarzan had probably already cut the phone lines. That was the first thing Tex Watson did at the Tate and LaBianca houses. She would call after she had dealt with the intruder herself. Now she had to move fast.

Helen streaked through the living room with her robe trailing behind her like a superhero's cape. That was how she saw herself, rushing to her sister's aid in the nick of time. Beyond the formal living room was Daddy's home office, and in the closet of Daddy's office was Daddy's safe. That's what Helen needed now.

The safe was about the size of a steamer trunk. Afraid to risk a light, she crouched on her knees in the darkness and felt the engraved numbers on the dial. Daddy didn't know that she had figured out the combination a long time ago. It was so simple to guess. Start at 62, the year Garrett was born, then turn to the left past zero back to 66, the year Lynn was born, then right to 68 her own birthday. Daddy was too sentimental for his own good.

There was a soft click and the door popped open. The safe was cluttered with important family documents. Tax returns, Mom and Daddy's marriage license, the birth certificates of her and her siblings, the mortgage papers on the house, insurance papers, all the usual documents of the typical middle class suburban family. But there were also Daddy's guns.

The actions of three pump shotguns leaned diagonally across the opening. But she was not interested in shotguns. Daddy always said that tactically a shotgun is a good choice in close quarters, like inside a house. But all of Daddy's guns were fowling pieces. That meant they all had long barrels, 28 to 32 inches. Even though she knew exactly where

Daddy hid the barrels, they would be too cumbersome for someone of her diminutive stature to handle in the confined space of the house. And they all had plugged magazines, so even with a round in the chamber that meant only three shots. Her fertile imagination had convinced her that there were at least five intruders in the house now. Maybe even a cult of maniacs like the Manson family. When this was over she would be a famous hero for fighting them off all by herself.

She had to make a choice and make it fast. Time was running out. She had to get moving soon, or they would find her helpless on her knees in the closet. She needed a handgun to do this properly. Daddy had taken her shooting many times and taught her how to handle all of the guns in his safe. Starting at the age of ten, he had begun to teach each of his children to shoot.

Garrett was a competent shooter but not great. In fact, to his mechanical turn of mind, Garrett was more interested in how the guns worked and how they were made then actually shooting them. Their father could always enjoy an informed discussion about the technical aspects of any number of makes or models with his son, but Garrett had little interest in going out to shoot with his father. Their father was a little disappointed in Garrett's lack of interest in guns, but he accepted it as a fact of life.

Lynn was just too girly to be remotely interested in shooting. On trips to the range she would complain about the noise and dirt and the smell. But she would dutifully load all of his magazines, pick up his spent brass, and lay out their picnic lunch. When it came time to actually shoot, it all went wrong. She would absolutely not hold any weapon properly, no matter how patiently or how many times he demonstrated the correct way to her. With each shot she would close her eyes tightly and dramatically exaggerate the recoil nearly dropping his guns, even his prized model 59. If he tried to give her a shotgun she would actually fall down with each shot. Being a good father he took the hint and simply stopped making her go with him.

But shooting had become a special connection between Helen and Daddy. It was their thing. Helen was a natural at it. By the time she was eleven, she could shoot a 3-inch group with a 9mm at one hundred feet. Time spent on the shooting range was their bonding time. It was a precious time to Helen because not only did she truly love everything about shooting, it brought her closer to her father. Even as a small child Helen realized that she had a hard time getting close to anyone, even her family. She had no real interest in playing with other children. She found most of them to be tedious and annoying. She was always happier on her own. So when she found a common interest with her father, it became one of her most cherished childhood memories.

A thrill ran through her as she contemplated her choices. Helen had never felt so alive. Everything felt more real now. But there was no time to waste. There were three handguns in Daddy's safe. An old, well-used Colt Woodsman that her grandfather had given her father when *Yeiyei* had returned from World War II. It was the gun that *Yeiyei* had taught Daddy to shoot with, and in turn Daddy had taught her to shoot with it. It was a great target gun and would eventually become a prized collectors' item. Revered for its accuracy and non-existent recoil Helen almost never missed with it. But it was chambered for a .22 Long Rifle, and underpowered. A fact New York cop Frank Serpico had

13

proved in 1971 when he had been shot in the face at point blank range by a Woodsman and lived to tell the tale, and quite a few other tales as well. As big as Tarzan was, if she shot him with the Woodsman, it would only piss him off.

Next was Daddy's baby. His Smith and Wesson model 59 9mm. It was a beautiful weapon, deep blue finish with aftermarket stag horn stocks. It featured a double action/single action trigger and a 15-round high-capacity magazine. It would be just perfect for this type of situation, except for one flaw. The flaw was not so much with the large gun as it was with Helen's small hands. The extra width added to the frame to accommodate the dual stack magazine and the extended gate of the double action, made the trigger pull too long for her undersized fingers to reach properly. That left only one choice.

Wrapped in a battered old leather rug was *Yeiyei's* .45. It had been issued to her grandfather in 1944 when he was promoted to sergeant in the 14th Air Service Group and sent to Burma as part of the support group serving the famous Flying Tigers. *Yeiyei* was trained as an aircraft mechanic and eventually landed a high paying civilian job at Boeing after the war. That was the beginning of the Wu family tradition of engineering. *Yeiyei* often joked to his grandchildren that it was good to be a Chinese engineer, as long as railroads weren't involved.

It was a family legend that *Yeiyei* had used this very gun to kill a Japanese fighter pilot that had been shot down over Burma. The pilot had evidently walked into a village close to the airbase where *Yeiyei* and his buddies were having a drink in a bar. When the pilot saw the Americans he tried to attack *Yeiyei* with a *wakizashi* sword. Proving the old adage yet again, never bring a knife to a gun fight.

Helen unzipped the rug and gently caressed the cold steel of the slide. It was a thing of beauty. Colt 1911/1A1, .45 ACP semi-automatic built under contract to Colt by Remington Rand in 1940. This one had a Parkerized metal finish instead of bluing, and showed a number of scars from long service. It held only 7 rounds, but they were .45 ACP rounds. So unless Tarzan had seven buddies with him Helen was not worried about running out of ammo. Even though the gun was a larger caliber then Daddy's model 59 the frame was flatter and fit her hand better and being single action it had a much shorter trigger pull.

Reverently, she ejected the magazine and began to load Winchester 185 grain Silvertip cartridges into it. The jacketed hollow points would settle any argument. Once she had the seven cartridges in the magazine as gently as she could she pulled the slide back until it locked open. With the gentle touch of a lover she placed an eighth round through the ejector port and into the chamber. She took a deep breath and pressed the slide release lever and the action snapped shut with a sharp metallic clank. She slammed the magazine into the butt of the gun and jumped to her feet.

Sure that the burglars heard the slide clank home, she stood, feet apart, with the weapon in both hands leveled at the door. The gun felt good in her hands, like it belonged there, like it was a part of her. With it, she was no longer the tiny helpless little girl; she had the power of life and death at her fingertip. She was in control, and she liked it.

She stood without so much as blinking for almost a full five minutes expecting, hoping, that an assailant would kick open the office door. She could see him now, huge, over six feet tall, long shaggy blond hair and a slight German accent.

He would have a Heckler & Koch MP-5 with a folding stock in his hands. But he wouldn't be fast enough. Helen would drop him before he ever saw her. She felt like an overanxious child waiting for Christmas morning. But no madman came crashing in.

Helen slowly raised the muzzle of the pistol and went to the door. She pressed her ear to the door and listened. Silence. This was just like one of the true crime novels she devoured. Maybe someday, Robert Tanenbaum would write a book about what Helen was going to do tonight. She realized for the first time she was disappointed not to hear chanting or maybe a chainsaw. She slipped through the next room as silent as a phantom.

A quick reconnaissance of the first floor proved the gang—by now she was sure it was an entire motorcycle gang—was still upstairs. She stood at the foot of the stairs and tried to see through the gloom above. The stairs were risky. Her head would be an easy target to anyone on the landing above long before she would have a chance to see them.

Maybe the tree. Nobody would ever expect me to go outside, climb the tree, and come in through the same window he had used. No, too risky. The gang most likely has a driver waiting outside, and that would give me away. It has to be the rickety, old stairs.

To avoid making noise on the creaky staircase Helen balanced on the molding along the edge of the steps and held the banister with her left hand, slowly inching her way up.

At the top of the stairs, she froze in place at a faint scratching sound. She crouched down at the top of the stairs and waited. Rhythmic and steady it began again. Helen put her back to the wall and composed herself. It seemed strange to her that she could be so calm yet so exhilarated at the same time. She was not in the least bit afraid. In fact, she was almost looking forward to the confrontation with Tarzan. She pivoted around the corner and leveled the gun down the hall, sweeping left and right for targets.

She was disappointed again. The only other living thing in the hall was Lynn's stupid cat. Lynn's door was still closed and Sandy was alternating between scratching at the foot of the door and reaching her paw under the door to try to pull it open. Sandy looked up at Helen, hissed and scampered down the hall. Nothing unusual in there, Sandy always reacted to Helen like that. What was out of the ordinary was Sandy was outside of Lynn's room. The cat followed Lynn everywhere, from room to room all day long and always slept on the foot of her bed at night. That meant Tarzan must still be in there with Lynn.

Helen padded her way along the hallway, scrupulously choosing the stable floorboards to avoid any squeaks that could give her away. There was no sound of any of the other rooms being ransacked for valuables. No hushed whispers of other gang members creeping through the rooms looking for more victims. No telltale shadows of assassins waiting to leap out of hiding at her. She would have to be satisfied with rescuing Lynn from just one assailant. Unless they were all still in Lynn's room. Deciding which would have the honor of going first. That would of course all depend on their ranking in the gang, which could lead to infighting. If Lynn was smart, she could play one against the other to buy time for Helen to rescue her.

If there was more than one, she would have to put them all down fast; that meant head shots, fast and clean. But she would save the leader for last. So she could exact a

17

little bit of payback. First one to the groin. That would give her a moment to go make sure of the others. Then one in the forehead.

Helen pressed her ear to the door and listened. Air Supply was still whining on and on. She could hear the bedsprings going pretty good. There was definitely a man's voice in there. Grunting and panting but not saying anything intelligible. Lynn was moaning and groaning too. Helen had been too slow. Tarzan was already raping Lynn.

She tried to push the door open but it didn't budge. How could that be? Their parents had never allowed them to have locks on their doors. The rapist must have barricaded it. Helen put her tiny shoulder to the door and gave it a quick but firm push. It budged. It wasn't barricaded, it was just wedged with the door jam. Lynn often used it to fix the door open just far enough to let Sandy come and go.

Helen fixed her shoulder to the door and steadily pushed it open. She crept in with the .45 up and ready to kill anyone over five feet tall.

The room was in semi-darkness, illuminated by dozens of fragrant candles in every nook and cranny. The half-light was enough for Helen to see everything clearly. She was ready for any manner of depravity and brutality but she was not even remotely prepared for what she saw next.

Lynn was only five-foot-two, and it was obvious she and Helen were siblings. But unlike Helen there was no mistaking Lynn for a boy. She had developed in ways Helen never would. Lynn's naked body glistened in the candlelight. She straddled Tarzan like a wild bronco rider going for the rodeo championship. She clung to fistfuls of Tarzan's curly blond chest hair and swung her head from side to side, flinging her glossy hair around.

Helen had been right about one thing, the guy was enormous. He had his meaty hands around the entire circumference of Lynn's waist. He looked a little familiar but in the darkness Helen couldn't make out much more than he was blond, had massive shoulders, and, as best as she could tell from this angle, well over six feet tall.

For the first time, it crossed Helen's mind that Lynn might not be totally impartial to Tarzan's ardor. In fact, she did seem to be rather enjoying it at the moment. *But that is impossible.*

There is no way Lynn could be a willing party to this. She's such a goody-two-shoes. Before she could ever even think of sleeping with some guy she would have had to pull the stick out of her ass. Helen could never imagine her doing that because without the stick up her ass Lynn wouldn't have a spine. They weren't even allowed to talk to boys without a chaperone, let alone actually have one on the premises. That would mean that Lynn had broken rules and lied to their parents. No way was that possible. There was no way on Earth little Miss Perfect of 1982 could be a secret slut.

But she did seem to be having a good time. Tarzan didn't look like he had any kind of a weapon, and he wasn't exactly holding her down and forcing her. Maybe it was the result of Lynn's years of sexual repression suddenly exploding.

Yeah, that's it! It's like...it's like...Stockholm Syndrome. Like what happened with Patty Hearst. Maybe she thought if she went along with him at first, he wouldn't hurt her. Maybe Lynn's doing it so he won't want to rape me too. Then she got all caught up in it. Just like Patty Hearst did with that Willie Wolfe guy. Maybe she's trying

19

to gain his trust so she can stick a letter opener in his back the first time he lets his guard down. Well it's down now and I have a little surprise for him, and it's not a letter opener.

Helen moved sideways into the room for a better angle. From her original position Lynn was in the crossfire. Lynn and Tarzan were too engrossed to notice her. Helen considered kneeling down quietly by the bed and blowing his brains out. But again that would be too quick and merciful for what he was doing to her sister. Maybe she could put the gun to his temple and whisper in his ear what she was going to do to him. No, that was too Hollywood. Besides sticking the muzzle of a self-loader against something, like a person's head or into their ribs could push the slide back and cause the gun to misfire. And as big and strong as Tarzan obviously was she didn't dare risk getting close enough for him to grab her.

"Take your stinking rotten hands off my sister," It was not exactly a shout, but she spoke loudly enough to be heard over the couple's own voices. Helen's voice was calm and level, there was no sound of fright, or anger. That was what made it so menacing.

Lynn snapped her face to Helen and screamed. She covered her chest with her hands and jumped off Tarzan. When Lynn suddenly pulled off of him, Tarzan's eyes popped open and he saw Helen for the first time. "Jesus H. Christ! What's—"

"Shut up, and let my sister go before I wet her sheets with your brains," Helen said, now more quietly, but still with that strange calmness that suggested it did not matter much to her whether she shot him or not. Either outcome was perfectly acceptable to her.

"Helen, put the gun down before you hurt somebody," Lynn said desperately.

"Let's all just try to keep calm and talk this over like adults," Tarzan said in a condescending tone.

"I am calm, that's why you're not shot. If you expect to stay that way, you will shut your pie hole and do exactly as you're told. Now stand up and put your hands on the top of your thick skull"

Clearly humiliated about having nothing on but a pair of dark blue socks, Tarzan stood up and up and up. He was around six-foot-three and well over two-hundred pounds, all of it muscle.

"My, you're a big one," Helen said mockingly.

"Helen, sweetie, just put the gun down before somebody gets hurt," Lynn said again, her voice quavering.

"Too late for that. Did you really think you could break into my house and rape my sister and get away with it?" Helen was beginning to enjoy herself. She liked having this monster helpless and sniveling. Having total control of the great ape was exhilarating.

"What, wait...I didn't rape—" Tarzan began to stammer.

"Don't try to claim innocence with me. I caught you in the act."

"He wasn't forcing me!" Lynn gasped and threw herself in front of Tarzan.

"Lynn, you don't need to protect him. He can't hurt you anymore. In fact when I'm finished with this soon to be dickless housebreaker, he won't be able to hurt anybody ever again. Now get out of the way."

"He wasn't hurting me, and he's not a housebreaker. He's my boyfriend!"

Helen's brain locked up. This did not compute. She could imagine the word "TILT" suddenly blinking on and off on her forehead. Her sister did not sneak boys into her room late at night to *get laid*. Lynn did not get laid, she could not get laid. That was against the rules.

Lynn's head would explode if she caught Helen eating breakfast cereal straight out of the box without milk. Lynn would fume for days if someone changed the order of the shoes by the front door. Lynn would call the FBI if someone tore the tag off of a pillow. Lynn was incapable of breaking any rules, no matter how small, let alone the biggest rule of them all.

But Helen recovered quickly; a smug, self-satisfied smile crept across her face. Slowly, she raised the gaping maw of the .45 to the ceiling and gingerly un-cocked the hammer. A dangerous and difficult task for someone with such small hands.

"What's Daddy going to think when I tell him his sweet, innocent, little baby girl was up in her room screwing some boy's ears off? And a white boy at that?" For the first time in her life, Helen had something on Lynn, and she was not going to waste the opportunity.

Lynn's face contorted with anger, "At least he is a *boy!*"

"I can see that." Helen said as she switched on the bedside lamp with a slight chuckle. She had Lynn over a barrel now, and she was enjoying it. "Oh look, the last chicken in the shop."

"Don't be vulgar, Helen. It's not very ladylike," Lynn scolded automatically.

"Not ladylike? And I suppose what you're doing *is*?"

"It's not like that! We're in love! We're going to get married someday," Lynn whined.

22

"As soon as I finish dental school," Tarzan added.

"You're not going to finish anything if Daddy finds out about this. I mean it's none of my business if Lynn bangs a truck full of drunken Indians, but if our Daddy finds out she's been so much as holding hands with a white guy there won't be enough of you left to bury."

"Daddy doesn't ever need to find out, does he?" Lynn pleaded.

Helen just stared at Lynn for a moment, her face was a complete blank, her eyes were expressionless.

"I don't know. 'It is my responsibility to tell our parents if you're doing something that could get you hurt,'" Helen said, quoting the excuse Lynn used every time she told on her siblings over the years.

"Hurting Lynn is the last thing I would ever do," Tarzan started to say. Helen brought the gun back down and pointed it at his face.

"*The very last* thing you would ever do."

"Helen, please don't point that thing at him. It might go off," Lynn said.

"It might," Helen said coolly, even though she knew that without re-cocking the gun there was no chance of that. She looked deeply into Tarzan's bright blue eyes for a long time with that unnerving dead stare of hers. Finally she said, "You look familiar to me, but all you round eyes look alike to us. Do I know you?"

He coughed and tried to speak, but Lynn cut in. "He's Steve Dziubinska."

"*Gesundheit*" Helen said.

"Steve's one of Garrett's old high school buddies. He was on the *jai alai* team with Garrett before they graduated.

You've met him lots of times. He used to come over to hang out with Garrett all the time. That's how we met."

"So you figure while the cat's away, huh? Some friend you are. Do you go around seducing all your friends' kid sisters?"

"This is no one night stand—" he said.

"Oh, so you've screwed my sister before?"

"We're not 'screwing.' We're in love. We have been going together for two years," Lynn insisted.

"Two years? You have been doing it to my sister since she was fourteen? I should plug you just for that, you pervert."

"No!" Lynn shouted. "It's not like that at all. It's not all dirty and nasty. It's beautiful. We're in love. Steve didn't make me do it. The first time it was my idea, and we'd already been together a whole year."

"I'm supposed to believe that all of the sudden you just decided to boink Mister Wonderful here, all on your own? You've been doing this big nose since you were fifteen? *Wow, you are a slut!* How many other guys have you been with? Never mind, I don't think I want to know. One's enough to break Daddy's heart. So just what's to stop me from telling Daddy Little Miss Perfect is nothing but a common tramp? It will kill him when he finds out what a slut you are."

"She's right!" Lynn sobbed into Steve's chest. "I'm nothing but a tramp." Steve pulled her aside and took a step toward Helen with his fists clenched.

"I don't fucking care if you are her little sister, you can't talk to her like that."

Helen cocked the gun, and Tarzan stepped back.

"I can't?" Helen said with a raised eyebrow. She was perplexed. Steve's reaction was anything but what she was expecting. Helen would be quite happy to shoot Steve, it might even be fun. But he was willing to die rather than let Helen insult Lynn. Willing to lay down his own life to protect her. He wasn't just trying out a little foreign cooking, he really cared about Lynn. What would it be like to have someone care that much about you? Or to be able to care that much about someone else?

"Mister Dziubinska, you may have just saved your own life," Helen smiled at him sweetly, ostentatiously un-cocked the .45 and put it into the pocket of her robe. "If you're willing to catch lead for my sister's honor, then I don't believe you have soiled it. Lynn and I can come to an agreement about how much she wants Daddy to know later, when we're all dressed a little more appropriately."

"What?" Steve's mouth dropped open at the change in Helen.

Helen shook her head, "Blonds, they're pretty, but they're dumb. If you're willing to get shot to protect her, even from me, you must really love my sister. So until someone better comes along I guess you'll do…for now." Helen began to walk to the door. She stopped and turned back. "But if you ever hurt my sister…" a smile spread across Helen's face and she shut the door.

The next morning, after Steve had gone for the day, Lynn and Helen came to an understanding about keeping secrets. It was a new intimacy between them. Having a secret to share created a strange bond of trust that brought them much closer than they had ever been. Helen never told their parents about that night. Later, when Helen and Holly had their falling out in high school, Lynn helped her little sister keep the embarrassing intimate details from their parents' ears. When Helen moved out of her parents' house at the age of twenty to share an apartment with Bridget, her "college friend," Lynn never pointed out to Daddy that the two co-eds had to share one bedroom.

Although she never talked about it with anyone, Helen always attributed one of her reasons to eventually become a police officer to that night. The taste of personal power and total control over another human being captivated her. She wanted more of it... needed more of it.

Six years later, Steve made good on his promise to marry Lynn in spite of her father's disapproval. Helen and Lynn remained close over the years. In the end it was Helen that convinced him to come to accept Steve's and Lynn's marriage and get to know his two beautiful grandchildren.

Don't Give Up Your Day Job,

1988

Ted "The Monk" Moakler's juvenile insecurities were getting out of hand. At first Amy found his jealousy sort of flattering, but now it was turning into paranoia. God knew that Amy had never given him anything to be jealous of. It wasn't like she was out hitting on other men. She wasn't interested in other men. She was hardly interested Ted. That was the problem.

Ted's insecurity wasn't too bad until they moved to L.A. Back home in Chicago, Ted had been a big fish in a small bowl. In addition to being a great bass player he was handsome and charismatic. His band was booked every weekend in the hottest rock clubs. In spite of his diminutive stature, pretty young girls threw themselves at him all the time. If anyone had cause to be jealous, it was Amy.

Back then, Ted went out of his way to show her off. He even encouraged Amy to dress the part of the rock and roll party girl. It bolstered his ego when she showed up at his gigs in fishnet stockings and tiny black leather miniskirts. She was the hottest chick on the scene, and she was there to see him. It didn't threaten his masculinity that she towered five inches over him, even in flats. He was the rock star, and she was the gorgeous blonde ingénue on his arm.

They had met through the Chicago Amateur Dramatic Association. Ted's mother was overwhelmingly involved in the association, and she felt that, at the ripe old age of twenty-two, Ted needed to develop an interest in culture and stop wasting all his time with that lewd rock and roll. So with the threat of cutting off financial support, she pressured Ted into arranging the background music for the Dramatic Association's production of Lillian Hellman's *The Children's Hour*.

That was when Ted first saw Amy Dresden. She was the rising star of the Dramatic Association. Even though she was only eighteen at the time, she was cast in the much more mature role of Martha Dobie. She was more than just beautiful on the stage, she had presence. Ted was enraptured by her.

Amy was a tomboy growing up, just one of the guys. Tall and skinny, she was usually a head taller than the other girls in her grade, and she was built like a stick. She was all straight lines and sharp corners, with no curves at all. Then at the age of thirteen the hormone fairy came to call, and by the end of that summer Amy was no longer the first one the boys picked to play soccer or basketball. They still picked her first but they had other games in mind.

Before her fifteenth birthday she learned two hard facts of life. First, whether it is true or not, boys believe that all blondes are dumb, and second, if the blonde in question just happens to have big boobs, that means she's dumb and an easy lay. Even the boys she had played soccer and basketball and rode skateboards with since they were kids all treated her differently now. Not just as if she was a different person, but as if she was from another planet. It was really embarrassing when guys she had hung out with for years couldn't look her in the eye anymore because they were staring at her chest, even if she was in baggy sweatshirts and lose jeans. Even worse was when the same guys deliberately fouled her on the court just to cop a feel or turned every word she said into a crude double entendre.

The girls were no better. They all became rude and catty about her. They gossiped about who she might be sleeping with this week or what bleach she used, or how much she had paid for the add-ons.

Even as attractive as she was, Amy didn't date a lot. Not for a lack of offers, but more from a lack of interest. Up till then, she had only dated a few guys she went to high school with or one or two from the drama program at Chicago-Kennedy-King College. She almost never had a second date with any of them, because all they seemed to be interested in was getting into her pants.

When she did date, she had a definite type. She always went for the bad boy rock and rollers with the long outrageous hair, spiked leather jackets and tight pants. Eddie Van Halen and David Lee Roth were her dreamboats, not pretty boys like Tom Cruise or Johnny Depp. But that was not all that made Ted her type. Amy saw tremendous potential in Ted. To her he wasn't just a short guy with big dreams. To her he was the next Stevie Ray Vaughan. All he needed was a little refinement, and she was just the person to give it to him.

Ted was also different because he was in no hurry to get her into bed. He didn't push her at all. Part of it was his tremendous ego. Most of the guys she had dated saw her as a goal, a trophy to capture. She was Mount Everest, tall, mysterious, ominous, the mountain with the biggest tits. But Ted could take her or leave her. He had been with girls just as beautiful as Amy, and he could be again. He could have groupies two at a time if he wanted. He *knew* he could have any girl he wanted, no matter how beautiful. So it was flattering to Amy that he wanted her exclusively. He had seen something more than just long legs and great gazongas. She was more than just a hot-looking chick to him, she was an entire human being.

Ted didn't even try to make the move into the bedroom, he left that entirely up to her. They had been dating for almost six months before she decided to "spend the night" at his apartment. It was a short time after that that she moved in.

Then there was the tragedy that changed everything.

Ted lived fairly comfortably on the income from royalties his family received from some widget his great-grandfather had invented back in the twenties, and with paying gigs rolling in every weekend, money was not a problem. So for Christmas of 1987 Ted bought himself a present. His first ever brand-new car. It was a pearl-white 1988 Chevrolet Corvette convertible. His ego insisted that he had to drive it to all his gigs, instead of riding in the old Ford panel van that the rest of the band used to haul their gear.

At about six o'clock on the morning of January 1, 1988, Monk's Raiders were on their way home from a New Year's Eve gig. Ted and Amy went straight back to their apartment in his new Vette. But the rest of the band had to take the long way home in the snow in the old van.

They were crossing the Jackson Boulevard Bridge when two street racing teenage boys tried to pass the van doing ninety. The driver on the left tried to make his move and crowd the other one out. The little Honda smashed into the rear left fender of the van at full speed and propelled it through the guard rail into the murky river below. The driver of the Honda was killed instantly. Monk's Raiders weren't so lucky. All four were trapped inside and drowned when it hit the frosty water below. The other driver was never caught.

Ted was emotionally destroyed by the accident. They were more than just his band. He had grown up with those guys. They had all learned to play together, that's what made the Raiders so great. They had been buddies from grade school, more than buddies. They were like brothers. What a way to start the New Year.

Ted was wracked with survivor's guilt. If he hadn't bought the Vette, he would have been in the van with his band where he belonged. Four funerals in two days was just too much for him. He went on a month long bender of guilt and remorse fueled by alcohol and cocaine. Only the threat of Amy leaving him had pulled him out of the self-destructive spiral.

After he dried out a bit he didn't have the strength of will to form a new band. It felt like betraying the memory of his friends. He couldn't face the idea of a solo act either. Haunted by the ghosts of the guys, everything was the past to him with no future. Ted needed a new start, a new beginning. So he and Amy pooled their savings and packed up all their belongings to make the move to the big time. They moved to Los Angeles.

But Los Angeles was not the fresh start that Ted was counting on. In Chicago, Ted had been a big fish in a small bowl. In LA he was still a big fish, like a tuna, in a school of other tuna swimming in an overcrowded shark tank at feeding time. It had never occurred to him that he would have to audition to get into someone else's band. Or that after an audition he might not get the gig. He just assumed that he would form his own band in a couple of weeks and start booking clubs. But the work was slow in coming. And everything in LA was so expensive.

It didn't help his bruised ego that Amy was doing better than he was. Things started to go really wrong their first week in LA when Amy met Rachel. Amy found an ad in a trade paper for open auditions for a low-budget horror movie and went to read for the part of Kennedy Montfort, the plucky honor student that is chosen to be a virgin sacrifice by the evil cheerleader-vampires.

She sat out in the lobby of the producer's office for two hours with ten other girls waiting for their chance to read for the part. Across from Amy was a stunning redhead in blue jeans and a tight t-shirt. She was openly staring at Amy and making her more than a little uncomfortable. After about fifteen minutes she finally spoke.

"Are you reading for Kennedy Montfort?" she said without preamble.

"Uh, yes," Amy said a little embarrassed to be interested in such a shallow role.

"I figured. You're too vanilla to be any of the vampires," she said.

"Thank you, I think," Amy said.

"I'm reading for Kennedy's bad-girl best friend. Hey, maybe we could help each other out. I hate to go into a reading cold. Would you like to run some lines with me?"

The idea seemed safe enough to Amy, so she agreed. The dialogue was so campy that by the third reading it was becoming funny.

After they had both read, they were told that the parts had already been cast, but there were still some parts open for the vampire cheerleaders in the orgy scene, if they didn't mind doing a little tasteful nudity.

Frustrated, they decided to commiserate with one another over lunch. Rachel Langdon and Amy hit it off at once and remained friends for years. Rachel turned out to be a free-spirited native of the Land of La. She had been a fashion model from the age of twelve, but when she began to fill out, the jobs dried up, and she decided to try acting. When they finished lunch, Rachel took Amy over to the modeling agency she used. After a quick interview Amy was told the agency would represent her, but she would have to provide them with a professional quality portfolio, not just some pretty snapshots.

Rachel helped Amy get her portfolio together, and after three months Amy was booking paid work through the agency. It was nothing exciting. She wasn't getting rich, or on the cover of *Vogue* or flying off to Rio to do a shoot for the Swimsuit Issue of *Sports Illustrated*. But by the end of that year, Amy was getting paid to walk down runways—*with her clothes on.*

Ted didn't like Rachel one little bit. He called her Carol Chameleon behind her back because her hair changed color so frequently. He thought she was nothing but a party girl and though he would never say it out loud, he was offended that she was dating a black guy. The other thing he would never say out loud, or even articulate to himself, was he thought Rachel might want to be a little more than friends with Amy. But the real source of his dislike for Rachel was that she took so much of Amy's time and attention away from him.

In the meantime, money was getting tight. Ted had not had any paying gigs in a year. Amy was out all the time working or doing photo shoots with one pervert photographer or another. He was sure that half of these guys were only trying to get her out of her clothes. One actually had her meet him in Griffith Park and spent the day climbing around on the old trains in a pair of Daisy Dukes with a six-shooter. A week didn't go by that she didn't get asked to go down to the beach to do a bikini shoot.

But things really got bad when Rachel hooked Amy up with Streckfus Gibson. Gibson was Rachel's personal trainer at some gym or other. For the last few months, all Ted heard from Amy was Streckfus says this and Streckfus says that. He even got her started on a health food kick that was driving Ted nuts. If he opened a bag of chips, he got a lecture about trans-fats and cholesterol. God forbid he popped a top on a brewski.

If Amy wasn't out catting around with Rachel, she was at the damn gym. Ted asked her once how they could afford to pay for the gym fees, and she told him that Streckfus had "worked a deal" with her. Ted knew what that meant. Amy insisted it was nothing like that. All she had to do was teach a couple of aerobics classes at the gym, and Streckfus waived her membership fees. Before Ted knew what was happening, Amy was at the gym three times a week, wearing next to nothing, and shaking her ass in Streckfus' aerobics classes. Ted was sure she was fucking the guy.

Then she started to hang out with people she had met in the gym. She told Ted that some guy named Don Moorhead had offered her a part-time job at his antique shop in North Hollywood. So all day Saturday and Sunday she was working in this Don dude's shop, selling used junk. It was working on Ted's nerves, so one Wednesday afternoon when she was teaching a class, he hopped in his Vette and cruised down to the Family Fitness Center to take *his girlfriend* out to lunch. *Guys did that with their girlfriends, right?*

The front desk was being worked by the single-most flamboyantly gay man Ted had ever seen. He had Paul Lynde's sarcastic attitude and looked like Andy Warhol. He looked Ted up and down and smirked.

"Oh…Our first time to the gym, I see," he lisped.

"I need to see Gibson. Is he available?" Ted demanded.

"Streckfus is most *certainly not available*, and he's busy now, too."

"Look, Tinker Bell, I said I want to talk to Gibson. I'm not in the mood for any hissy bullshit."

"Only paying members, or their guests, are allowed beyond this point. Why don't you leave a message with me, and I'll see he gets it."

Ted was furious; he had come here to have it out with Gibson, man to man. Not to be stopped by a ninety-eight pound homo. He tried to storm past, but the fruit was fast on his feet. He got in-between Ted and the doors to the locker-rooms.

"Oh, aren't we butch? I'm just shaking in my tights. Now you and your *nineteen eighty two* C.C. DeVille hairdo go find yourselves a barber to pester before I call the cops."

Ted didn't like to fight for fear of damaging his precious hands, but this little poufter was asking for it. Still, there was no point in unnecessary risk to his priceless fingers by striking anything hard. Ted drove a fist into the receptionist's soft belly. It was the first time since the third grade that Ted had actually hit someone, and he got the same results now as he got then. Dean, the receptionist, collapsed and gasped in amazement,

"You hit me!" he said with tears running down his face.

There was no turning back for Ted now. Ted wasn't sure whether or not Gibson had actually done it or not, but now he was committed to kicking Gibson's ass for trying to steal his girlfriend. As Dean had pointed out, Ted had never been to the Family Fitness Center and had no idea about the layout. He started to rush through doors completely at random, searching for Amy and Gibson.

The next thing he knew, he was striding along between two rows of lockers. The last thing he remembered thinking, before everything went completely mad, was that this was the best smelling locker room he had ever been in. He turned the corner at the end of the lockers and walked right into five screaming women in various states of undress. It wouldn't have been so bad if they had all been strangers. He could have at least tried to run out of the lady's locker room and escape. But Rachel was one of them, and if that wasn't bad enough, Amy was there too.

He remembered women screaming and scattering. He tried to turn and run away, but he heard Amy's voice clear and distinct in the chaos.

"Theodore Benjamin Moakler! Have you completely lost your mind?"

Ted froze. He didn't know why, he just froze. A heavyset black woman in neon green panties and bra snatched something out of her locker and came at Ted screaming about Peeping Toms. She emptied a full can of pepper spray into his face. Then she kicked him in the groin, for good measure.

Ted doubled over lost in a mist of agony. He was vaguely aware of being roughly picked up by the seat of his pants and carried. He was banged head-first into several doors, and he could hear Amy pleading with someone not to hurt him. Then he was lying on the sidewalk in the sun getting kicked in the ribs. He could hear Amy begging his assailant to stop kicking him.

Someone turned a hose on his face, and the pepper spray began to disperse.

"That's him, Sweetie! That's the brute that attacked me!" the little queer from the front desk was shouting.

The icy water hit him in the face again with unnecessary force and began to flush out his burning eyes. Ted was on the sidewalk in front of the Family Fitness Center. Most of the women were gone now. Someone had carried him out of the women's locker room and dumped him on the sidewalk like so much garbage. He could still hear Amy shouting at someone. As his vision cleared he looked up, and up, and up, at a Greek God of a man. This guy was huge; his shoulders were probably as wide as Ted was tall. He was wearing white gym shoes and half-sox with pink pompoms on the back, tight black work-out shorts and a white golf shirt, with his name, "Streckfus" over the pocket in cursive.

"Please don't hurt him, Streckfus, He's not a pervert, he's just a little confused. He's been having a hard time adjusting to the move to LA. Let me take him home, and he'll be fine. Nothing like this will ever happen again, I promise," Amy was saying to the big guy. Rachel came running out of the front door and wrapped a towel around Amy. It finally dawned on Ted then that Streckfus had dragged him bodily out of the woman's locker room like a bag of dirty laundry. Streckfus had been so angry, that Amy obviously forgot she had just stepped out of the shower, dripping wet, and chased them outside to prevent the muscle-bound Gibson from stomping Ted's head into the ground. Only as the other women began to pour out of the gym with hastily thrown-on clothing did Amy realize she had run through the gym like Lady Godiva.

"Amy, go inside and put some clothes on, before you get arrested too," Streckfus said through gritted teeth. Ted tried to stand up, but Gibson turned the water back on his face. "The cops are on their way. If you try and move, I will break every bone in your perverted little body, you lousy peeping midget." He looked as if he would have a good time doing it, too. "The only thing that keeps me from beating you like one of Ricky Ricardo's conga drums is Amy would get stuck with the bill for your trip to the E.R."

It was a long night for Ted. He spent the night in jail before Amy, against Rachel's advice, was able to get his bail together. One of the conditions to get Gibson not to press charges against Ted was neither Ted, nor Amy could ever return to the Family Fitness Center. The State of California, on the other hand, was not so forgiving.

Because it was a first offense, and Gibson had agreed to drop charges, even though Dean was his boyfriend, the sex offender charge was reduced to trespassing. But Ted was put on probation for three years and had to attend state-approved anger management counseling for the next year. Ted thought his wife-beating class was a waste of his time, but he did get something out of it in the end.

Alan Preston had been charged with assault after he had slapped his ex-girlfriend for flushing his stash. Ted and Al saw eye-to-eye from the start. Al was a small time dealer that specialized in selling weed to rockers. With Al's contacts, Ted managed to pull a new band together in no time.

With a new band there were a thousand little details to iron out. Between rehearsals, trying to write new material, and the occasional "job" with Al, Ted was too busy to obsess over Amy.

To Amy, he was the old charming Ted again. It was like it had been back in Chicago before the accident, only better. Ted had his music again and threw himself back into his work with the old passion. Amy took the job at the antique store with Donna Moorhead and still had modeling jobs trickling in. It was better now for Amy because she had her work too. She had her life with Ted, instead of Ted being her life.

The Odd Job

1989

Sometimes my conscience still bothers me about that one, but the money the *Enquirer* was offering for the cowboy shots was just too damn good. Besides, I didn't do anything unethical. I have a model release in my files, all nice and legal. I own the rights to all the photos I took of her, clear and aboveboard. They are mine, and I can use them in any way I like. It's not like the photos I sold were nudes or anything compromising. *Penthouse* would have paid twice as much for the nude shots. But I didn't really take those did I? Besides, I destroyed those in '89. They were bad karma.

I did have pictures of her with a gun in her hand, and the tabloids were eating that up with a fork and spoon after what happened to her up in Carmel. I should have called Amy first and let her know I was planning to sell the photos, but after that weirdness on our last shoot together she still refuses to take my calls.

The last time I worked with her was nearly nine years ago now, toward the end of 1988; back before I was married. One of the *uber*-rich had bought the old Harryhausen Hotel and was planning to demolish it at the end of the month. The Harryhausen had been an L.A. landmark for over ninety years. Built in 1899, it was used in dozens of movies, and had been the playground of the in-crowd between the world wars. Now it was just in the way. To make way for more antiseptic chrome and featureless glass, they were going to pull down all that history; destroy the Victorian grandeur for the sterile *nouveau riche* modern architecture.

I had always wanted to do a glamour shoot in the elegant old place but had never got around to it. This would be my last chance to capture a bit of old Hollywood before it went under the wrecking ball.

I would have to pay for props and wardrobe and a suite at the Harryhausen to use as a base of operations. That meant it would have to be a TFP shoot, a Time for Prints shoot. In other words, the model didn't get paid in cash; but in exchange for her time she would get prints for her portfolio.

I needed a model that had some distinctive qualities. She would have to have a timeless style, she had to be tall and elegant like the hotel, and she had to have presence. I also wanted to use a girl I had worked with before. One that knew how to follow instructions. One that I could count on to be on time, well almost on time. Lastly, she had to be blonde. Really, really, blonde.

The blondest woman I knew was Amy Dresden. I had met her a few months before when she came into my studio looking for some headshots for her portfolio. After the headshots were in the can, and I had convinced her that I was not some sort of pervert, I talked her into doing the Wild West shoot with me up at Travel Town in Griffith Park.

We met at the park the next week and spent the day with her dressed as Jesse James' hot sister robbing the antique trains. It was a good shoot. She grokked what we were doing and played the part well. She followed instructions and even had some creative ideas of her own for the shoot. In the end, we both got some beautiful images for our portfolios. After that shoot I put Amy on FBS, Favorite Blonde Status. So, when the Harryhausen shoot came up she was the first person I thought of.

***

Three days later I was at the Harryhausen in suite 458. Amy was late. So far only half an hour late, which was not unusual for TFP shoots. I busied myself with the last minute details. I hung all the clothing I had brought for the shoot in the bedroom closet and chose the first outfit I planned to use. I picked a little red cocktail dress from the twenties I had found in a thrift shop some time ago. It was a chic little thing made of iridescent silk. While it was completely opaque, the way it shimmered in the light would give the illusion of transparency, without giving anything away. However, it would also show every wrinkle.

I hung the dress on the steamer and switched it on. Now the steamer is not all that complicated. It has no moving parts. It's just a jug of water with a heater about the size of a toaster that forces steam up a long hose like a vacuum cleaner's. There are only two control settings, on

43

and off. So, you can imagine I was surprised when it just stopped on me.

My first thought was that the heating element was burned out, but when I looked at it, I discovered that the problem had been operator error. Somehow I had accidently hit the toggle switch and turned it off.

I kicked the switch back to the on position and saw the little amber light come on to tell me it was working, but it would still take several minutes for it to heat the water back up. So, I went into the sitting room of the suite to double-check my camera gear. I put fresh batteries in my Nikon F4, and both radio slaves, and gave my lenses a quick wipe, whether they needed it or not.

Still no sign of Amy, so I went back to the bedroom to finish my steaming. But the steamer was off again. I bent down and tried the switch with my hand this time. It clicked on and the little light blinked to life. Before I could give the matter much thought there was a knock at the door. Amy was here and it was time to get to work. In case there was a short or something I flicked the steamer off, and just to be on the safe side I pulled the plug.

Amy was all smiles when I opened the door and found not one, but two magnificent blondes.

"This is my friend Rachel Langdon. I hope you don't mind that I brought her along. She's going to help me with my make-up and hair." Translation: she's here to make sure you don't try anything funny. There was nothing unusual about models bringing people along on shoots, boyfriends, pals, siblings, parents, or even other models. I couldn't say as I blamed her. Even though we had worked together twice before, and I had demonstrated that I was harmless—well mostly harmless. I was still asking her to meet me in a hotel room.

What was unusual was Rachel herself. She was a genuine five-alarm hottie. Tall, with long legs, and strawberry blonde hair with dark red highlights. She was definitely a knock-out, but in a more obvious way than Amy. She had more of an in-your-face, Jayne Mansfield vibe compared to Amy's more refined, Audrey Hepburn presence. If I played this right, I might even be able to get her in front of the camera, too. The two women together would be a great contrast of types.

Amy had a wholesome all natural quality, a girl-next-door sort of a feel. She had pale blue eyes as big as dinner plates and the most amazing platinum blonde hair. She was also tall and leggy and had...err...well...she was tall and leggy, and even the most casual observer could see it was all original equipment.

After the introductions, and a little getting acquainted, Rachel asked me about how I wanted Amy's make-up and hair. I pulled a book out of my bag, *Stardust Memories*, by Terry Leech. It is a compilation of dozens of photographers' work with movie stars going back to the early teens. I opened to a full page head shot of Regan Ryan-Reilly from 1921. The fact that Amy looked remarkably like this actress was probably why I had thought of her first for this shoot. I ushered the girls into the dressing room to get started on Amy's make-up.

"*Ooh La La!*" Rachel called out, as she entered the bedroom. She snatched the garment hanging on the steamer and did a spin holding it up in front of her. "Where you expecting her to tidy up the room first?"

I was shocked to see that she was not holding the red cocktail dress I had picked. Instead, she had a little French maid's uniform I had only brought as a backup.

"Lewis, I thought you said you wanted me dressed like a flapper," Amy said. "There's no way in Hell you're getting me into…that."

I thought Rachel had pulled the maid outfit from the closet and I expected to see the red dress still on the steamer. I took the uniform from Rachel and opened the closet to put it away.

"Where did you find that? I don't know what this is doing here. It's from another shoot entirely. I must have gotten the clothing mixed up by mistake when I was packing," I said, not too convincingly. "I was planning to use this one." I pulled out the red dress and laid it out on the bed. "See? Just like the dress in the book. Why don't you get started with the makeup while I steam the wrinkles out of this?

"I want to be as historically accurate as we can. I got this in an antique shop. It's really from the period. So, you can't wear any modern undergarments with it, this thing will show every strap and panty line," I said, as business-like as I could, while telling a woman to take off her underwear. One of the strange anomalies about models is their attitude about underwear. A girl won't think twice about wearing a bikini that's nothing more than three postage stamps held together by some dental floss, or even shooting completely naked. But the same girl would never consider going without a bra, even in a turtle-necked sweater. I opened the closet and my stomach contracted to the size of a golf ball. I sorted frantically through the clothing. But the pale pink romper I had brought was gone.

"Lewis, I'm not at all comfortable with this. I'm not going commando. So, don't even bother suggesting it."

"No, no, of course not." I said, as I desperately sorted through the dresses a second time. They seemed to have rearranged themselves since I hung them. "I have something that flappers really wore back then." I knew the romper was there. I put it in there myself. Without the romper there was no way we could use the red dress. Without the romper under the dress she wouldn't look like a glamorous movie star, she would look like an expensive call-girl, trying to look like a glamorous movie star.

"Maybe I left it with the stockings," I said trying to buy time and not look too much like an idiot. I rechecked the garment bag I had brought the clothing up in and found the pink romper wadded into a tight ball at the bottom.

"Here it is!" I said with relief. On its own, the sheer romper would leave nothing to the imagination, but under the silk of the cocktail dress it would make the subtle difference between sexy and slutty. But after being crushed in the bag the wrinkles were so deeply set it looked more like an inner city road map then delicate lingerie. "Sorry about that, I'll steam it out for you."

In my haste to downplay the maid's uniform, and find the romper, I didn't notice that the steamer was turned on, and hot, again. I grabbed the hose to steam the lingerie and it spat boiling water down my arm, scalding my hand and wrist.

Cursing, I rushed into the bathroom and ran cold water on the burn. It wasn't too bad, I decided. It would be red and tender for a while, but no real damage was done to anything but my pride. I turned off the tap and dried my hands. I ran my fingers through my thinning hair and looked into the mirror. Things were getting out of hand and if I did not take back control this entire shoot would blow up in my face. *Just take a deep breath and count to ten. Nice and slow and everything will be okay.*

But I never got to ten. At about six both girls screamed in the bedroom. I threw the door open and found the room was pitch black. They had pulled the heavy drapes for privacy so the only light in the room now came from the open bathroom door. There was a strong smell of ozone in the room and the light fixture in the ceiling was smoking.

Amy was still seated at the vanity table where Rachel had been doing her face. Rachel was fumbling for the drapes.

"What's going on in here?" I asked. "What's all the screaming?"

"You tell us!" Rachel snapped. "What's with the lights?" She threw open the drapes, and late afternoon sun light poured in.

"Beats me," I said. "Could it be a fuse?"

"No way! The lights exploded!" Amy said.

"I started doing her hair. When I plugged in my curling iron, POP! There was this flash and then all the light bulbs just exploded."

"It must have been a power surge," I said. "Are you guys alright?"

"We're fine," Amy said, with a nervous chuckle.

"It is an old building. The wiring must be a little twitchy."

"Twitchy isn't the word!" Amy said. "It's a good thing you brought me a change of underwear."

I went into the living room and got a of couple power strips from my head case. I always use them with my studio

48

heads when I'm on a location to prevent just this sort of thing.

"Here, try plugging your curling iron into this. It has a built-in surge protector. This is an old building. The electrical system is probably a long way from code. That would explain why the steamer was acting up too."

I switched off the broken lights and went to plug the steamer into a power strip only to find it had already been unplugged. I thought one of the girls did it because of the power surge, so I just went about setting up again. That's when I realized that the maid's uniform was hanging on the steamer...again.

"Very funny," I said, assuming that one of the girls had done it to embarrass me. I took the uniform and put it back in the closet. But the romper was gone again. I went through all the clothing two more times before I admitted to myself that it just wasn't in the closet. I stepped out and looked around the room.

"Where did you put the slip?" I asked. The girls just looked at me like I was speaking Zulu. "Okay, very funny,"

"I don't know what you're talking about," Rachel said. Amy gave me a long, hard stare, cold and calculating.

"I don't know what you're up to, Lewis," she said. "But I don't like it. I don't do those sorts of pictures."

"I don't do that sort of work either."

"Maybe we should reschedule this shoot," Rachel said, as she picked up a cotton ball from the vanity top and tossed it in the wire wastebasket at her feet. I watched it drop into the basket. I knew if I let them walk now, Amy would never work with me again. The white cotton landed on a pink mound at the bottom of the basket.

"We can't reschedule this shoot," I said, staring at the basket. "They are going to tear this building down in a couple of weeks. This is our last chance to ever shoot here." Then I realized what I was looking at. It was the romper, in the bottom of the wastebasket.

"Well, I'm not shooting without anything under that dress," Amy insisted.

"Don't worry," I said, as I pulled the romper from the basket and held it up. "I have it under control."

I was beginning to suspect that Rachel might be trying to sabotage the shoot for some reason of her own. I couldn't possibly guess what that reason might be, but there was no other explanation. Maybe it was jealousy. Perhaps she resented Amy—it was not unusual for really pretty girls to be competitive about their looks—or maybe it was personal. Maybe Amy was seeing Rachel's boyfriend behind her back. Who knew? But I decided that I should keep an eye on Rachel from then on.

I turned the steamer on again and worked the wrinkles out of the garment. This took a little time because the wrinkles were set pretty deeply, some were actually heavy creases. By the time I was done, Rachel had finished with the long platinum ringlets in Amy's hair. I had to admit she had done a great job. Amy looked as if she had just stepped off the silver screen.

I handed her the still warm romper. "I'll go and get the gear ready while you change," I said. "The dress is on the bed."

"You mean this one?" Rachel said, holding up the maid's uniform again. I just rolled my eyes.

"No, this one," is all I said as I pulled the red dress out of the closet.

That more or less proved it to me. Rachel was deliberately messing with me. I didn't know why and I didn't really care. But I needed to get rid of her before she turned the session into a complete disaster. I would have to be very subtle about it; she was Amy's security blanket. If I openly suggested that she leave, for any reason, then I would lose Amy too, and the shoot would be over before it started.

I went to the sitting room to load my camera and get the gear I would need in the lobby. I put a film cartridge into the F4 and gently threaded the leader onto the take-up reel. I hit the shutter release and nothing happened. Nikon F4s have a built-in motor drive to advance the film, so I should have heard the internal servos taking up the blank leader and setting the counter to frame number one. But nothing happened,—at all.

Rule number one in photography, when something goes wrong, and it almost always did, check the simplest solutions first. I tried the battery test button on the bottom. I was expecting to see two green lights indicating the six brand new batteries I had put in not a half hour ago. Neither of the LEDs came on. My blood pressure began to return to normal. There was nothing wrong with the camera, I just had a bad battery in there. It happened once in a while, even with Duracells.

I opened the battery compartment in the grip to change the batteries and found that all three double As were in backwards. It was the same way for the other three double As in the bottom compartment. I could see me, maybe, putting one in wrong way round. But never all six. I am just not that careless, especially with my equipment.

I switched them around and I finished loading the camera. The film advanced properly, and to be on the safe side I checked all the camera settings to be sure no one had monkeyed around with any of them.

I didn't want to risk any more sabotage. I double checked the radio slaves to be sure they were all in order and put anything else I might need—extra batteries, sync cables, my 24-to-70, a light meter, some gaffer tape, and rolls and rolls of film—into the pockets of my work vest. I thought that if I had all this stuff in my pockets, Rachel wouldn't be able to mess with any of it. I had no idea when she had gotten to the camera to switch the batteries around, but I was not going to give her a second chance.

I put my 70-to-200 on my F4, hooked up the radio slave transmitter, and hung the entire thing around my neck like a tourist in Fantasyland. I hooked the receiver to a Photogenic 1250, plugged it in with a surge protector, and gave it a quick test pop. The entire chain was working. I pulled the plug on the monolight and looped the cords around a C-stand and checked that I had all the parts for my soft box. All I needed now was a flapper and I was ready to shoot.

And what a flapper I got. When she stepped out of that bedroom not even Clara Bow, Louise Brooks, or Greta Garbo could compare with Amy Dresden in that little red dress. Even Mary Pickford and Gloria Swanson would have been green with envy. The final effect was breathtaking.

"I want to start down in the main lobby on the grand stairs by the elevators," I said as I picked up the C-stand with the soft box and headed toward the door. "Rachel, could you be a sweetie and hang out here to keep an eye on my gear while we shoot? We won't be too long."

She gave me the hairy eyeball on that one but relented. "I guess that's okay, if it's okay with Amy."

"I'm fine with it. But don't you want some help carrying stuff?" Amy asked.

"No, I can manage," I said, even though I did want help, C-stands weigh a ton. "I don't exactly have a permit to shoot here. The fewer bodies I have around, the better." Not exactly untrue, but the main thing was I didn't want Rachel interfering with me while we were shooting.

***

We took the elevator down to the main floor. The lobby of the Harryhausen had a jewel of a design. The glass front doors opened onto a grand foyer, fully four stories high, leading back into the core of the building. At the far end of the lobby were two birdcage elevators. Wrapping around the cages, the elevators ascended and descended in elaborate wrought iron staircases leading to each of the four landings. Galleries ran all the way around the lobby space. The ceiling was made entirely of plate glass held in place with an intricate lacework of wrought iron.

We started on the ground floor of the lobby by the elevators. I set up the Photogenic head on a C-stand with a large soft box on relatively low power as a fill light. The idea was that it would soften the edge transfers and show surface texture in the intricate lace of shadows created by the wrought iron frames of the skylights.

I started to shoot and Amy was in the moment from the start. She nailed the mood I was trying for. But starting with my third shot the strobe began to go off almost at random. This can be a real problem when you need to wait for a head's capacitor to recharge for the next shot. Half a second is all the difference between a perfect expression and a blink.

The most common cause of strobes just going off on their own is someone else on your radio frequency. It could be almost anyone, another photographer using the same model of Radio Slaves, or someone using a walkie-talkie. It could even be a TV remote or a garage door opener. After all, no matter how cool they seem, radio slaves are really nothing but garage door openers.

So I switched the channels on my slaves and got back to shooting.

"Work with me now," I said in my worst British accent. "Give me that star glow." And she did. Few women could turn on the power like Amy Dresden. Five, six shots went by and the strobe began to pop on its own again. I switched the channel once more, and I was back on my knees before the altar of beauty.

I got about three or four more shots when the strobe just went nuts. It popped three times in rapid succession. No strobe works like that. Even on low power it takes about a second for the capacitor to recharge, so there is always a slight lag between shots. If you had some sort of supercharger that could fire that fast, the flash tube would overheat and burst.

I stopped shooting for a moment, much to Amy's annoyance, and checked over the head. It seemed to be all right, but I made a note to myself to have it looked at. But right now I didn't have time to waste. I had to get on with the shoot.

I clicked off a few more shots, not bad ones, but Amy appeared to be distracted.

"Is that guy supposed to be a part of the shoot?" she asked.

"What guy?" I said, standing up and looking around.

A funny thing about photo shoots. Even with the most ordinary girl as the subject, the instant you start to shoot, spectators come out of the woodwork. Some are harmless, they just stand and stare. Still others are a nuisance, they interrupt with a thousand stupid questions about the shoot, or the clothing, or my equipment, or the girl. One tries to be patient with them. Then there's the really troublesome ones, they try to hit on the model and when that fails they start up with cat calls. But the very worst are the "Uncle Henrys." They pull out their own cameras, get right behind you and start taking their own photos. Some even have the gall to shout directions at the model.

"There was a guy moving around right behind you," Amy said. "It was really distracting. Sometimes he's right behind you, or over by the light."

"I don't see anyone now," I said, looking around.

"I know I saw him."

"I don't doubt you at all," I said. "As lovely as you look right now, I am surprised we don't have a bigger audience. But if you see him again, shout out."

"Don't worry, I will," she said.

"What makes you think he was part of the shoot?" I asked.

"The way he was dressed," she said. "He was in an old-fashioned dark brown suit with a celluloid collar, a bow tie and a straw boater's hat. You don't see many of those."

"Maybe somebody else had the same idea I did about doing a period shoot here before they tear the place down. That would explain the strobe too. We're probably using the same Radio Slaves. Annnnnnyway. For the next shot I want you to go halfway up the stairs here and give me a quick twirl. Like you're leaving and someone called your name"

She reached the middle and gave a twirl. The light silk skirt floated on the air just enough to show the tops of her stockings, but none of the romper. Perfect on the first shot, but there is always safety in numbers. I told her to do it again, and she did.

On the third take though, when she turned her back to me, she waved me off.

"My heel is stuck," she called out. "Don't shoot." She bent over to free her shoe and my strobe fired on its own again. Amy stood up straight, her face purple with rage.

"There he is!" she screamed. "Stop right there, you little pervert!" Amy pointed down through the ironwork under the stairs. I didn't see anything but ran over anyway as she came charging down.

"That little shit is hiding under the stairs! He was taking pictures up my dress. I'm gonna kill him."

"I'll hold him down for you," I said. Nobody, I mean nobody, takes sneak shots of my models. That is even lower than being a *paparazzi*. I went around the stairway on the left, and Amy went right. There was no way he could have gotten away from the stairs without either of us seeing him. But when we met again, it was just Amy and me.

"He was right here!" she said.

"Are you sure you saw someone? It could have been a shadow from the flash," I suggested.

"I saw him. Not some fucking shadow. It was the same guy as before, in the old suit. My heel was stuck on the step, so I looked down and saw him standing right here. Pointing an old Speed Graphic straight up my skirt!"

"A Speed Graphic? You must be mistaken. They haven't made those things since the Sixties."

Her pale blue eyes drilled through me. "I work part time in an antique shop. I know what I am talking about. Antique cameras are popular collector's items. We get them in all the time."

"But there is nobody here, Amy."

She just stood there and glared at me. I think she would have stormed off if the elevator hadn't started rattling its way down the shaft. Under the stairs, at the base of the shaft, the old steel cage wheezed and rattled like an out-of-tune chainsaw. Rather than try and compete with the noise it was making, we came back around the front of the lift.

What we saw descending in the lift stunned us both into silence, but for entirely different reasons. Long supple legs clad in spiked heels and black fishnets were the first thing to come into view. Those legs seemed to go on for days, then the white ruffles of a short petticoat, followed by the French maid's uniform.

Rachel slid the lift's gate open and stepped out, putting the structural integrity of the uniform to stresses it had never been intended for.

"What are you doing?" Amy asked, in shock at her friend. It was clear Rachel just could not stand Amy being the center of attention. She was trying hard to upstage her. If those seams were just a tiny bit weaker, she might still pull that trick off, and black both of her eyes in the process.

"You know, Lewis, your assistant is a total creep," Rachel said without the slightest trace of humor.

"What are you talking about?" Amy said.

"That pervert just walked into the room like he owned the place," Rachel said. "He walked right into the bedroom without even knocking and grabs this—" she gestured to the dress she was almost wearing, "—and threw it at me. All he said to me was 'Here get dressed quick they need you downstairs ten minutes ago.' Not even a please or thank you."

"Then he just stood there staring at me like he expected me to change in front of him."

"Rachel, I don't have an assistant," I said.

"Bullshit, he walked right in bold as brass!" she snapped.

"How did this guy get into the suite? Did he have a key?"

"Yeah...I think...he must have."

My first thought was somebody was trying to steal my gear. I did have over twenty thousand dollars' worth of easily pawnable merchandise, all in one handy carrying case. This mystery assistant was trying to get her out of the room so he could steal my equipment.

We all squeezed back into the elevator and headed back up to the fourth floor. All the way I watched the other elevator shaft and the stairs for anyone trying to go down. I didn't see anyone.

"What did he look like?" Amy asked as we ascended.

"He was a mousey lookin' little guy. Short, about five-five or-six at the most." Rachel began. "He was wearin' the worst suit I have ever seen. It was so wrinkled it looked like he slept in it. He had a ridiculous bow tie on and he had a weird lookin' camera around his neck."

"Camera? What kind of camera?" I said thinking it might have been my backup F4.

"Oh I don't know, it was big, and boxy. Kind of old-timey looking. I didn't get a good look at it. He was holding his stupid yellow hat in the way."

We reached the top, I pushed open the gate and took off down the hall to room 458 as fast as my legs would carry me.

On the little writing table in the living room all of my camera gear was laid out like an exploded drawing of my case. It was all there, every last piece. But it had all been pulled out of the case and displayed with meticulous care. Again my suspicions began to drift to Rachel. She was playing some sort of very elaborate prank on Amy, and I was caught in the crossfire.

The girls came in a minute or two behind me. Just as I was making sure everything was still there. I realized I would have to test every last piece of gear when I got back to the studio. Who knew what sort of sabotage she had done? I was more than a little angry.

"Very funny," I said as they came in. "You know if any of this is broken—"

"Hey, what are you looking at me for?" Rachel cut me off. "I didn't touch any of that stuff. Come on Amy we're out of here!" She stormed past me into the bedroom.

"Is anything missing?" Amy said.

"No, it all appears to be here, but who knows if it's been tampered with."

Rachel screamed. Not the inarticulate scream of fear, but one of unbridled rage. Amy and I ran into the bedroom.

In the bedroom the sheets had been turned back and a black lace nightie that I had never seen before was neatly folded on the pillow. But the rest of the room had been tossed.

All of the drawers were pulled out and dumped on the floor, the furniture was all overturned and smashed. Anything that was not nailed down had been scattered and broken. Every last stitch of clothing I had brought for the shoot was torn to shreds and strewn around the room. The street clothing the girls had come in was no exception. But extra care was taken with those. Their own clothing looked almost as though it had been fed through a document shredder.

Rachel's makeup case was an odd exception. Every bottle, jar, tube, powder and cream had been removed and lined up on the vanity by size, like ornamental toy soldiers. So had the contents of their purses, including car keys, cash, credit cards, personal photos, packets of tissue, hairbrushes, two tampons and a diaphragm. All the strange and terribly personal items young women carry in their handbags.

"That's it, I'm done," Amy said with no tone in her voice at all. "Lewis, I don't know what you're trying to pull here but it's not funny."

"I'm just as confused as you are," I said. "I was downstairs with you when all this happened."

"So your buddy did it!" Rachel said. "That pervert with the bow tie." She unceremoniously scooped her belongings into the makeup case. "You're a really sick puppy, Lewis. You need to get some help." She stormed over to the door without bothering to change. Of course she had nothing to change into now. "Come on, Amy, let's get out of here before he pulls something else."

"Amy, I didn't—" but she was not listening.

"I don't understand what you were expecting us to do, Lewis, but it isn't funny. Don't ever call me again." With that she walked out, in my silk dress, and has never spoken to me again. Worse, I was out almost eight hundred bucks for the room and all the ruined clothing and had nothing to show for it.

But that was not the end of the story...

After the girls stormed out I called the desk and demanded hotel security send a man to my room right away. There was a pervert and a vandal running loose in the hotel and he had to be caught immediately.

Fifteen minutes went by before the hotel security officer managed to find the room. He barged in without knocking and held out his little tin badge, "I am Mister Wakelin" he said as if that should mean anything to me. "I'm the hotel detective. So what's the beef, Mack?" He looked like something straight out of central casting. He was dressed in an astonishingly cheap suit, with half a Chesterfield attached to his bottom lip. I was sure I had seen him chasing the Marx Brothers around the halls of the hotel in a vain attempt to catch them before they skipped out on their bill. He didn't exactly inspire confidence, I half expected to see Chaplin's footprint on his ass.

"'What's the beef, Mack?' Really? What are you, a Damon Runyon character?"

"Now let's not get personal, Pally. You called me," he said, blowing cigarette smoke in my face as he passed by me.

"Right. A pervert has been harassing my models. He broke in here and tried to trick one of the girls into undressing in front of him. When she refused, as soon as she was out of the room, he trashed the place."

Wakelin sort of looked around the room a bit then his eyes locked on my equipment laid out on the table.

"You some sort of shutterbug?" he said out of the corner of his mouth.

"I am a *professional commercial photographer*," I snapped back. "Not a *shutterbug*."

"All right, all right," he said. "You got some fancy stuff here. Bet it cost you a king's ransom. Any of it missing?"

"No," I said. "We aren't dealing with a thief, we're dealing with a pervert. He wasn't after my cameras he was trying to see the girls naked."

"But he didn't take nothin', and he ain't here now," Wakelin said.

"Right. But he did trash the bedroom while we were downstairs." I led Wakelin into the bedroom expecting the shambles. But the room was pristine. Even the torn clothing was mended and hanging in the closet.

"So lemme see if I got this all straight," Wakelin said in a patronizing tone. "You had yourself a couple of dames up here for some sort of photo party."

"You didn't really just say 'dames,' did you?"

"And this guy tried to crash your little soiree. Sounds to me like Windiz is up to his old tricks again."

"You mean you know who this guy is?"

"Yeah. Albert Windiz. He don't like people taken pictures in the hotel. Especially cheesecake."

"That's just too bad for him then. He can't just barge into a guest's room, or damage other people's property."

Wakelin sort of snickered. "I don't see nothing broke. Is anythin' missin'?"

"I want this Windiz arrested. You know who he is, arrest him."

"Now that's easier said than done, Mister Callahan. See... Albert Windiz has been dead since 1921."

"What are you talking about?"

"He got rubbed out by the mob right in this very room, sixty-eight years ago. So's there's nothing I can do about it now, is there?"

That's when the pressure valve in my head popped. I vaguely remember questioning Wakelin about his parentage and throwing him out of the room. Packing my case and storming out of the hotel, I only stopped long enough to tell off the manager about the treatment I had gotten. I was so irate at the time, and the manager was so apologetic that it didn't register until the next day that he said there was no hotel detective.

***

I dropped the two rolls of exposed film at the lab on my way back to the studio. I spent the rest of the afternoon testing the tampered-with equipment but found that nothing was amiss. But as I put my copy of Stardust Memories back on the shelf, the story about Albert Windiz danced through my overactive imagination. I leafed through the index, looking for the name, and found it. Boy, did I find it. He had about twenty photo credits in the book, images of most of the super-stars of the time. People like Anna May Wong, Lillian Gish, Regan Ryan- -Reilly, Theda Bara, Louise Brooks and even the 'It girl' herself, Clara Bow.

Albert Windiz's work was amazing. He was truly a master of light and shadow. It played on my mind. To think that someone with that much talent was murdered really got my curiosity going. I couldn't help myself, I had to know more. I grabbed my copy of *Notorious Unsolved Murders* by Wilbur Ardigo from the shelf and looked up the name. There it was, right before the murder of Thomas Ince on

Randolph Hearst's yacht in November of 1924 and the mysterious shooting of Desmond T. Williams in 1922.

But it was just enough to tease me. Albert Windiz was murdered in the Harryhausen Hotel in 1921. The murder remains unsolved to this day. The only details were that he lived in the hotel and was found dead in his room. The official story was that he woke up to find person or persons unknown in his room looking to steal expensive cameras. The would-be burglars panicked and killed him.

After a couple hours of fruitless reading I decided to call Dean. Dean O'Keefe and I had been buddies since Junior High school. In fact, we had both applied to the LAPD together. They accepted him but turned me down because of my dyslexia. But Deano and I had remained buds. So I gave him a call and asked if he could poke around a little in the old files. He said he would try but couldn't promise much. He'd get back with me in a day or two.

John Lennon once said, "life is what happens when you are making other plans." And so it is. The next three days I was busy with paying work and other mundane details of my profession. Over the next weekend I had to shoot a big wedding. So it was not until Monday morning that I had time to think about anything to do with the Harryhausen Hotel.

When I got to the office that Monday morning the usual pile of manila envelopes of proof sheets and negatives had been shoved into the letter box and the phone on my desk was ringing. I pushed through the door, snatched up the mail and ran to grab the phone.

"Callahan Photography, how can I help you today?"

"Let me talk to the Psychedelic Fur." It was Dean.

"You got him, oh Large and Smelly One. What's up?"

"I just got off a night shift. You got time to meet for breakfast?"

"Yeah, I don't see why not. Usual place?"

"See you there in twenty. Hey, I found some info on that Windiz guy for you." Dean went on. From the way he was chattering I could tell he was riding the tail end of a coffee buzz after a long shift, and it was best to let him ramble. As he talked I began to rifle through the proof sheets from the last week.

"Here's the deal. Back in the sixties the LAPD was running out of storage space for all the files downtown, so we purged a lot of old cases to make more room. Any files on closed cases before 1950 were destroyed. But the Windiz case was still unsolved. The files were lost but I did find the actual murder book.

"Windiz was big time. He was shooting for all the major studios from about 1909 right up until he got whacked. He shot all the big names of the time, men and women, even the studio executives. But he wasn't limited to just the Hollywood people. It was the in thing to have a portrait done by Windiz, so all the society people in LA came to him too.

What they didn't know was he had a sideline. According to the book, he'd slip them a Mickey to make them more cooperative, or if that didn't work, he had a bunch of hidden cameras in the dressing rooms. So, when the clients went in to change for the sitting, it was 'click, click, grin, grin, say no more.' Apparently he was making a killing selling naked photos of movie stars and other celebrities."

"What a scumbag," I said.

"So one day a cute, little, sixteen-year-old wannabe named Julliette Marino came in for some publicity shots, and he gave her the full treatment."

"That name sounds familiar, but I can't place it."

"Her daddy was Frankie 'the Blank' Marino."

"Oh shit."

"Yeah. A confidential informant told the detective working the case that when naked photos of his precious baby girl started circulating around the club scene, Frankie was not a happy psychopath. According to the C.I., Frankie sent a couple of out-of–town gorillas over to Windiz's place in the middle of the night and beat his head in with his own tripod."

"Holy Bob Crane, Batman! So how did Frankie get away with it?"

"In the usual way. There was no real evidence in the case. Just a rumor. And back then most of the cops were on the take anyway. The Mob ran L.A. in the Twenties and Thirties. Six weeks after this happened, Detective Wakelin was suddenly made lieutenant, and he declared it a cold case."

"Thanks a lot, bro," I said. That last sentence didn't sink in until much later. I was distracted by something else. "Hey, I gotta run, see you at Denny's. I've got something unbelievable to show you." I hung up the phone and took out my loupe for a closer look at the proofs in front of me.

On the two rolls of film I had shot of Amy at the Harryhausen, only about half were of her in the little red dress. Mixed together with my images were shots of her changing in the bedroom. Then came my shots on the stairs. Then images of Rachel undressing and putting on the maid's uniform.

I didn't take those shots. I couldn't have taken those shots. I wasn't even in the room. But there they were, in glorious Technicolor, for all the world to see. Any one of the men's magazines would have paid top dollar for the nudes even before she was in the headlines. But like I said I didn't take the nude shots of Amy Dresden, Albert Windiz did.

New On the Job

January-1990

Robert "Red Dog" Hinckley thought his head was about to explode when he opened his eyes. Even with the curtains drawn and a heavy blanket duct-taped over the window there was too much light in the cheap motel room. He crawled out of the stinking bed and groped around the floor until he found his jeans where he had dropped them the night before.

The pockets were inside out and his wallet was empty. That bitch had robbed him. She had taken his last seventeen bucks and his baggie of disco-biscuits. The Ludes pissed him off more than the money. He would get his welfare check in a day or two, but he had gone to great lengths to steal the pills from his grandmother's medicine cabinet.

The old broad had not allowed him into her house in two, or was it three, years. Not since the first time he had been charged as an adult. But the stupid old cow still left a house key hidden in a fake rock by her back door. So every Wednesday, when she went to bingo, Red Dog could slip in and raid her stash.

It pissed him off that the bitch he was partying with last night had stolen his Ludes. That was just disrespectful. He would have to do something about that. But first he needed to get well. He felt like bugs were wriggling around under his skin. He needed to get high.

He went to his wall safe. His running dog, Willy, had shown him this trick. Willy knew all the tricks. In motels and apartment buildings with central cooling there was a secret hiding place. All you had to do was open up the air intake vent to the AC and look behind the filter.

Red Dog opened the vent and breathed a sigh of relief. His stash was right where he left it. So was his gat.

He didn't like to tap into his reserve—it was his emergency stash—but he was desperate this morning. Once he got his tweak on he was ready to face the day. First he had to get some money so he could score again. He had smoked his last rock just getting well. He would need more soon. He would have to score some of the high octane shit this time, because that last batch didn't have any balls at all. He had to use almost twice as much to get half as high.

He dressed in dirty jeans, work boots and a wife beater. He liked slingshots because they showed off his sleeves. He had gotten them done on his last trip to Soledad, and they made him look hardcore. He shoved the gat down the front of his pants and covered it with his shirt.

He went around to the other side of the motel and banged on Willy's door. William Ross always knew were the action was. And if Willy didn't, at least he would know where to find that bitch that robbed him. She was a friend of Willy's girl, so Willy would know where she stays.

Willy was older than Red Dog, about thirty, and had been state-raised. He had been in and out of juvy from the age of fifteen. He was small and wiry, with bad teeth, a shaved head, and mean beady blue eyes that gave a rat-like visage.

"No way, man," Willy was saying. "We don't wanna go and fuck up Lilly's friends. We wanna go and fuck 'em. Lilly was tellin' me some shit last night that gave me an idea how we can make some real money. We play this right and we can have all the cooz we want for life, *and get paid for it.*"

"I don't get it. No bitch pays guys to do 'em. Not even if they're fugly," Red insisted.

"They aren't payin' us to do 'em, fuckwit. They need somebody to look out for 'em. The bonin' is just a perk."

"You mean like a pimp? I ain't no nigger pimp."

"Course not, man. Here's the deal; there's this witchy chick named Beatrix that hangs out in the old, abandoned church up in Chatsworth Park. She's got a string of girls that all turn tricks for her. She got 'em all convinced that they're all witches or vampires or some shit."

"You mean like drinking blood? I don't know, Willy, sounds pretty creepy to me."

"Didn't bug you last night when you fucked one of 'em," Willy said. "This Beatrix was making bank until one of her girls ran into a brother named Jazz. This nigger beat the dog shit out of her and made her tell Beatrix that he runs

71

all the hos in the valley, and if she don't start payin' him protection he's gonna start fuckin' up all her girls."

"Yeah, so what? What's it to us?"

"Beatrix would be *very grateful* to anybody who would straighten the toad out."

"How grateful?"

"An eight-ball to start with, and all the pussy we can eat," Willy said with a laugh. "All we gotta do is go grease this jig that fucked up her girl."

"Hell, I'd do that for free! Where do we find him?"

"Lilly said he hangs out in an arcade called the Wizard's Cave over on De Soto and Lassen."

"We'll need some wheels to get all the way out to the Valley," Red Dog said as he mulled over their plan.

Willy pulled a double-barreled, sawed-off shotgun from under the bed and snapped the chambers closed. "No problem. What kind do you want, Camaro or Mustang?"

***

Helen was determined not to let her training officer get under her skin. At first she had attributed his bad attitude to years on the street and the usual antagonism to newcomers in a fiercely fraternal social order. As time went on, it became clear that it was more than that. It was personal. There was nothing about Helen that O'Connor liked at all. He didn't like her lack of experience, the way she talked, her gender, her ethnicity, her diminutive stature, the color of her hair, her orientation, her choice of shoes, the way she took her coffee, her looks, or the fact that it was his responsibility to train her for the next year. O'Connor especially disliked that she had the highest marksmanship score in their precinct. He thought it made them all look bad if a rookie, a girl rookie at that, could outshoot them.

"This place seems pretty dead to me. What are we doing here?" Helen said.

"Weren't you paying attention at roll call, Wu? We are looking for vandals." O'Connor never called Helen anything except Wu. Not Officer Wu, not Miss Wu, not Helen, or Rookie, or even Dead Eye, the nickname that had followed her through the police academy.

At twenty-seven minutes after eight in the morning they were rolling through the Oakwood Cemetery in the middle class suburb of Chatsworth. The management of the cemetery had been complaining that juveniles had been stealing flowers from the graves.

Helen knew what he was really doing. He was deliberately wasting time. It was O'Connor's goal to take as much time as possible to do as little as possible, every day. He could take an entire shift measuring skid marks at a traffic accident and shooting the breeze with tow-truck drivers. Or making a detailed list of property on a burglary report. He had made an art form of procrastination.

The lush, green lawns of Oakwood Cemetery rolled gently downhill from the rock desert to the green suburban neighborhood on its east side, intersected by a spider-web of paved roads leading throughout the park. Old-growth trees provided shade for mourners and fostered a park-like atmosphere, undisturbed by standing tombstones. Toward the northeastern end, the trees were denser, creating the approximation of seclusion.

O'Connor parked the black-and-white on a side path in the shade of three old oaks and lit a cigarette. It was against policy for officers to smoke in the car, but Helen knew better than to say anything about it. Like it or not, O'Connor was her superior, at least for now. She knew that if she complained about the smoke he would just roll up his window and make it even worse.

O'Connor had chosen that particular spot because he could see all of the main roads through the cemetery and yet remain relatively unobserved by passersby. Not that there were many at 8:30 on a Friday morning. The spot was perfect for him, and he would be able to kill at least an hour there without having to do any real work.

O'Connor's perfect morning was disturbed when a light blue '77 Mustang came scurrying down the main path out of the cemetery past the cop car. Helen guessed its speed wasn't more than 15 or 20 mph. But the posted speed in the cemetery was 5 mph. In a low-slung car like that old Mustang, even that was a risk because of the speed bumps throughout the park's roads.

Helen knew O'Connor would have stopped the car even if it wasn't speeding. In the five short weeks since she had graduated from the Police Academy it had become obvious to her that O'Connor liked Mustangs. So he stopped them whenever he could, just as an excuse to check out the car. If he liked the driver, he would let them off with a warning. If the driver was rude or gave him attitude, or if O'Connor didn't think they deserved the car, he could always find something to write them up for. Worse than that, for at least a half hour after every Mustang stop, O'Connor would regale her with how and why his own Mustang was better than the specimen they had just examined. It was all very tedious, but it was the closest O'Connor would come to a conversation with her. She didn't dare tell him that American muscle cars were blunt instruments, with all the subtlety and grace of a sledgehammer. They lacked the style and sophistication of British cars. Her idea of a dream car was an Aston Martin DB5 or a Sunbeam Tiger.

O'Connor hit the disco lights and pulled out of his hiding place on the tail of the little Ford. He had closed the distance between him and the other car before they reached the front gates. The Mustang swerved from side to side for a moment as if the driver didn't know quite where to pull over. When it stopped, the cops could see a very nervous teenage boy hopping around in the car like a toad on a hotplate.

Helen picked up the mic for the radio and began to call in the license.

"Don't worry about that, Wu," O'Connor reassured her. "It's just a kid ditching class. That's all."

"But we're supposed to call in every stop and run the plates."

"We don't need a background check on every car we stop. All we got here is a teeny bopper smokin' a joint or two on his way to school."

"But, policy says—"

"Don't quote the rule book at me, Wu. This ain't my first rodeo," O'Connor said as he got out of the car.

Helen hated it when he did things like that. For one thing it meant that when she filed her end-of-shift reports, she either had to lie to cover his lazy, fat, white ass or be branded a snitch by the other cops. She had a hard enough time relating to the other cops as it was. And the other thing was all he was teaching her was his own slothful habits. She would never make the SWAT team that way.

It was the first time in her life that Barbara Brendlinger considered ditching school. But she just couldn't do it. It was not in her nature to miss class or break the rules. Even if she did want to curl up in a tiny little ball and disappear off the face of the earth. She still had just enough self-respect left to get up and go to school and face another day of abject humiliation. She had only thought it was bad when she was totally invisible to the rest of the kids. She had longed to be popular. To be known by everyone, to have people actually care about what she had to say. But not like this.

At the beginning of the semester her chemistry teacher had assigned Christy Butler, the Christy Butler, to be her lab partner. At first it wasn't too bad, as long as Barbara did all of the work, let Christy copy her notes, and didn't try to talk to her too much. To Christy, Barbara was such a non-person that she was not even worth being cruel to.

But that all changed when Mrs. Karkkainen caught Christy copying from Barbara's paper on a pop quiz. Mrs. Karkkainen did nothing to Barbara because she did not believe she was a party to the cheating. She did punish Christy. Not only did Miss Congeniality get a big red F on the quiz, she was suspended from school for three days. Worst of all, she could not cheer at three football games. That meant that copper crotch bitch, Ashley Richmond, would get Christy's rightful place on the cheerleading squad.

It didn't matter to Christy that Barbara didn't know she was copying. Christy believed that Barbara had told on her and that it was all Barbara's fault that she had gotten caught. So Barbara had to be punished.

It was easy for Christy to get the combination to Barbara's locker. Christy had planned to plant some pills and some weed in there and then have another student say Barbara had tried to sell it to them. But what she found was even more hurtful. Barbara's personal journal.

Barbara brought it to school with her every day so that her mother or her nosey little brother couldn't find it when she was out. It held her most secret, most personal thoughts. Things she could never even say out loud. It held the details of her deep unrequited love for Travis Smythe. Travis Smythe with the English pronunciation.

Worse than that was the fantasy story she had written about her and Travis. The story was forty percent *Gone With the Wind*, forty percent Disney Princess and twenty percent *Penthouse Forum*. It told all about how he would find her alone in a dark forest and take her precious virginity on a blanket of leaves in the wild woods. In livid detail.

She had written it only for herself. No one else was ever supposed to see it. By the end of a week, every person in her school had read the story. To the girls she was a laughingstock or a disgusting, wanton slut. To the guys, a licentious mutt, or an easy lay. All she wanted was to go back to being invisible.

Barbara wheeled her Schwinn out of the garage and halfway down the driveway before she looked up and saw the car parked in front of her house. She knew that car. It was Travis Smythe's legendary light blue '77 Mustang. Her face burned red as she fumbled to get on her bicycle. This was too much; she could never face him. All she wanted was to disappear.

Travis casually climbed out of the car and stood there for a moment, just sort of staring at her. He was beautiful:

77

tall, blond and perfect. He was wearing black Ray-Bans, a pearl gray Members Only jacket, cream-colored chinos and tan topsiders with no socks. *God he was gorgeous*. Barbara struggled to get her leg over the frame of her bike but she was too nervous, her hands were shaking.

"Hi there, *Barb*," he said, peeking over the top of his glasses and flashing the baby blues at her. "I think we need to talk. Can I give you a ride to school?"

Barbara dropped her bike. He had spoken to her. He had never done that before. Not going all the way back to the sixth grade when she first saw him. Not only had he spoken, he called her by name, well almost. That meant he did it on purpose. That was wonderful. He had asked her a question…that meant she had to say something back. That was not wonderful. Her tongue was tied in a Gordian knot in her dry mouth. *Oh god, think of something to say, think of something to say, quick before you die!*

Still speechless she bent down to pick up her old Schwinn, the heavy books in her backpack shifted and she lost her balance, stumbled and banged her knee on the concrete of the driveway.

Travis was suddenly at her side. He held out his hand to help her up with that mischievous, crooked, half-smile of his that made her knees go weak.

"Here, let me help you with that," he said, just as calmly as if he were a normal person and he spoke to people like her every day. He took her book bag and slung one strap over his wide shoulder. He righted the bike and picked it up in one hand by the frame. *He didn't push it, he carried it into the garage as if it was a feather. He's so strong! And oh that cologne!*

"You won't need the bike today. Today you're riding with me." He walked to the ultra-cool sports car and opened the passenger door. With a little bow and a hint of a British accent he said, "Come m'lady, your chariot awaits."

She shook her head mutely, still too spellbound to speak. When she was finally able to mumble something about Travis only wanting to tease her, he smiled that wicked grin of his and her heart melted.

"Now would I do something like that, Babs?"

How could anyone with a smile like that ever hurt her?

Barbara felt her feet slowly leave the ground and she floated a meter high across the driveway and into the classic Ford. She didn't see Travis turn and flash a thumbs-up to the red VW Rabbit parked halfway down the street after he shut the car door.

Travis dashed around to his side and climbed in. The old car was permeated with the scent of decaying vinyl and his cologne. Her heart was about to explode in her chest as he pulled away from the curb and down the street. Two minutes later, the red Rabbit followed.

***

Helen didn't bother with the radio. She could tell the big blond kid in the old Mustang was up to something by the way he kept peering over his shoulder out the back window at them. He had something to hide. Helen got out of the car and walked around to the rear right fender of the pony car where she could see in through both the back and side window with her hand on her Beretta.

O'Connor approached the car and stopped about a foot back. He stood there motionless for almost a full minute watching the young man fidget in the car.

Finally, when he felt the weight of O'Connor's stare, he settled down and tried to sound casual. "Is there a problem, officer?"

O'Connor waited a beat, playing the tough guy. "May I see your license, registration, and proof of insurance?" he said in a monotone.

"Of course, officer," the kid said, fumbling to get the wallet from his back pocket.

"Take them out of the wallet, please."

With trembling hands the boy pulled out the documents and handed them out the window to O'Connor.

"Is this your car?" O'Connor asked.

"Yes, sir."

O'Connor took his time examining the papers, almost as if there was some sort of discrepancy. Then he leaned over the car, resting one hand on the roof, and lowering his face to the window. "This is a nice car. Your parents buy it for you?"

"My—my dad went halves with me on the down payment. I worked construction all last summer to save up for it."

The answer seemed to satisfy O'Connor in some way. "You know you were speeding back there. The speed limit here is five miles per hour."

"I'm really sorry, sometimes this car gets a little away from me. You know how it is." He checked the rearview mirror than back to the cop.

"Yeah, I know how it is. I've got an '89 five-point-oh with a five speed, myself. You really got to stand on the brakes to rein them in."

"I heard that."

O'Connor stood up straight and looked all around him as if he was thinking something over. "So, Mister Smith—"

"Smythe. With a Y. It's the English pronunciation with the long I," the kid corrected him almost automatically. O'Connor did not like to be corrected. And he took his Irish heritage a little too seriously. He believed it was his duty as an Irishmen to harass the English wherever possible. He didn't really know why, but that wasn't the point. He leaned back in the window and put his face close to Smythe's.

"Okay, Mister *Smythe*, can you please tell me why a nice kid like you is toolin' around the cemetery at nine o'clock in the mornin' on a school day?"

Helen moved forward for a better field of fire. The way O'Connor was leaning into the car the kid could do almost anything before O'Connor even knew what hit him. If he had a gun, he could put it under one of O'Connor's chins and splatter what little brains he had all over the roof of the car before Helen could even break leather. For that matter, Smythe could bury a blade in O'Connor's throat or just hit the gas and break his fat, red neck in the window frame.

As she moved in, something caught her eye. The interior of the car was a mess. Dirty clothes, empty soda cans, papers and sports equipment littered the back seat and the passenger floor boards. All the typical signs of raging testosterone. On the passenger seat was a pile of neatly folded clothes. They stood out because their tidiness was so contrary to the disorder of the car. Faded blue jeans, a pale pink t-shirt with a kitten on it, and, partly hidden under the pink shirt, a white bra.

Smythe looked down at the steering wheel for a second, as he tried to come up with a good lie. "I was on my way to pick up Christy, my girlfriend. She lives over on

Andora at Cactus. I guess I was thinking about other things and I drove right by her place. So I pulled in here to turn around and got mixed up trying to find my way out. See, that's why I was speeding too. I'm sorta' late, and Christy doesn't like it when I'm late. You know how women are."

"Would you step out of the car, please," Helen said. She wanted to have a better look in the car. That pink shirt didn't belong to this boy. He was too jittery about being stopped, and he was clearly lying about something. Helen wanted to know what it was.

"What? Why? I didn't do anything wrong," Smythe said, a little too quickly.

"I don't think that will be necessary," O'Connor said and threw Helen a glare. Even though he was inclined to roust this punk and toss his car, he decided to let him go rather than agree with Helen on anything. "She's a little overzealous sometimes, you know how women are. Go on and get out of here. And watch the speed." O'Connor stepped back from the car and knocked on the roof a couple times as the boy drove away, shouting his thanks out the window.

After the Mustang had pulled away, Helen stood motionless, staring at O'Connor for a long time. She still had her hand on her pistol and the restraining strap off. Her face was an unreadable porcelain mask. Over the years, friends had told her that she would be a natural at poker because she could be so totally expressionless. She disagreed with that because she found it just as difficult to read other people's faces as they found it to read hers.

"You gonna shoot me, Wu?" O'Connor said, trying to sound sarcastic, but a little bit concerned that she just might. He was beginning to understand why they called her Dead

Eye behind her back. It had nothing to do with her shooting skill. Standing less than five feet high and not even one hundred pounds, she could still be one scary little bitch. Even without the gun.

Helen relaxed and buttoned her holster closed. "Why did you let him go? He was up to something."

"He was just playin' hooky."

"That kid was up to more than ditching class. He was way too nervous for that. Did you see the girl's clothing on the passenger seat? What if he was up here to dump a body, or a weapon?"

O'Connor walked back toward the car, shaking his head. "All you boots are the same. You all think everybody is Norman fuckin' Bates."

"Then why did that boy have girl's clothes in his car?"

"It could be his sister's, or his girlfriend's. Could be any one of a thousand reasons. Who knows, maybe he's a lumberjack."

Helen never would have taken O'Connor for a Monty Python fan.

They got back in the car, and O'Connor started the engine. Helen did not want to be remembered like Officer Don Fouke, who in October of 1969 had stopped and talked with the Zodiac killer, only moments after the murder of cab driver Paul Stine. Had Officer Fouke been more thorough in his questioning, he could have caught the infamous murderer with not only the murder weapon, but even a part of the victim's bloody clothing the killer had kept as a souvenir. Helen wanted to go back into the cemetery now to have a look around to see what Smythe had been trying to hide.

"Okay, *fine*. Let's just get out of here then. This place is giving me the creeps," she said. As Helen knew he would, O'Connor put the car in gear, and just to be contrary he drove deeper into the memorial park

.

***

StarCon was starting today. Clark Roberts had been looking forward to this all year. He had been working his fingers to the bone for it. His parents told him that if he got all As on his mid-term report cards they would let him get a weekend pass this year and stay in the hotel holding the con for the entire weekend. Even better, he had managed to get a pass for his buddy Kyle, too. *Two wild and crazy bachelors on the prowl with no curfew. Hide your daughters StarCon, Zaphod and Ford are out tonight!*

Getting straight As in his academic classes was no surprise to Clark; he usually got top marks in those without really having to try all that hard. But to his undying shame, he had failed P.E. last year. Most of the other kids in his class were done with P.E. after tenth grade, but Clark had had to repeat it. It had been humiliating. But he buckled down and did his best, running laps after school and doing pushups in his room at night. He had never had to work that hard to pass any class in his life. The irony of it being the most unnecessary class he had ever been forced to take was not wasted on Clark.

That morning Clark was ready for the con. He had five hundred dollars in cash he had saved up over the year from his part-time job at the video store, hidden in the secret compartment in his backpack, and another one hundred in his pocket. He had spent hours embroidering question marks on the lapels of his overcoat. It had taken him six months of combing through thrift shops to find the perfect, floppy, old hat. And the *piece de résistance*: after a year of wheedling, his Aunt Dru had finally given in and let him have "the scarf." In a sea of Captain Kirks and Han Solos, he was going to be *The Doctor*.

He filled his pockets with the sonic screwdriver he had made from an old socket wrench he had pilfered from his dad's tool chest, a bag of Jelly Babies—they were really gummy bears but they would have to do—his TARDIS key, and a packet of condoms. (One never knew, one might meet a companion at the con.) It paid to be prepared for anything.

When Clark came out of his room to have breakfast with his folks, his father's reaction was more or less what Clark had expected.

"Why in the hell are you wearing a trench coat and a scarf? It's eighty degrees today, for crying out loud," his father said, shaking his head at his son's strange attire.

"I am The Doctor. I'm not concerned with mundane details like local weather. Besides, I will be inside the hotel all weekend with the AC on. Everybody dresses up for the con," Clark said.

His father turned to his mother. "Are you sure *Doctor No* here passed his driving test?"

"Doctor Who! Or more properly, *The Doctor*," Clark whined.

"I guess I should just be grateful you're not dressed as Wonder Woman," his dad said.

"Yes, he did." Clark's mother pulled a yellow envelope from a pocket and held it out to Clark. "It's your driver's license, Sweetie," she said. Clark's heart was pounding in his chest as he pulled the card out. The photo looked like a mug shot, but that's the way it's supposed to be on driver's licenses.

Clark's father took a set of keys from his pocket and tossed them to him. Clark tried, but flubbed the catch, and the keys fell on the floor. His dad just rolled his eyes as Clark picked the keys up.

"What's that for?" he said.

"I know it's not exactly the Jupiter Six—"

"Jupiter *Two*, Dad."

"Whatever. Your mother and I decided that you can take my truck to your geek fest this weekend. You earned it."

Clark was speechless. His father just didn't grok fandom, and that made it hard for them to really connect. But this gesture was big. It was more than just letting him use the car. That truck meant the world to his dad. He had bought it new last year, and it was his pride and joy, or so Clark thought until now. It wasn't just a reward for struggling through another year of dodgeball. It was a sign of trust. The first sign of confidence his father had shown in him in years.

After Clark had dropped his father off at the office, he was on his way to StarCon in the candy-apple red, 4.7 liter, V-8, 1989 Chevrolet Silverado Step-side. *Kyle is going to blow his motherboard when he sees me pull up in front of his house in this. The con is going to be great this year!*

With the addition of the truck, Clark was beginning to think he was a real person. He was sorely tempted to forget all about his buddy, Kyle, and see if he could talk Barbara into going with him instead. She wasn't exactly Doctor Who companion Louise Jameson but she could pass for Elisabeth Sladen in a pinch. Barbara wasn't the hottest girl in school but Clark knew he wasn't one of the hottest guys either. But she was definitely hotter than Kyle. And she was one of the few girls he knew that grokked The Doctor.

***

O'Connor was taking his own sweet time about cruising through the cemetery. He had all day after all. For her part, Helen tried hard not to show the least bit of interest in her surroundings.

At last the squad car rolled into the back corner of the cemetery that the blue Mustang had emerged from. It made no sense at all to Helen that Smythe had gone this far into the park if he had just been looking for a place to turn around.

They made a right turn onto a narrow, tree-lined road that ran about one hundred feet from the back fence separating the green-forested park from the hard, dry, rock scrabble of the undeveloped land beyond. About one hundred yards from the turn was a picturesque, old, colonial church next to an outcropping of sandstone, all surrounded by shady trees.

In the small gap between the scenic rocks and the side of the church they caught a glimpse of someone rattling the blue shutters over one of the church's windows. At the sound of the approaching car, the figure looked in their direction and took off like a frightened deer around the sandstone boulders.

O'Connor hit the gas, and the cruiser closed the gap in seconds. When it screeched to a stop, he bailed out without so much as a word to Helen and dashed along the back wall of the church.

Helen jumped out with her gun in her hands and tried to follow. Years of beer and doughnuts had taken their toll on O'Connor's stamina, but over a short haul he still had the advantage of long legs. By the time Helen had reached the corner of the building, O'Connor and the burglar had both darted around the rock formation.

Running north to south, the little outcropping was about forty feet long, ten feet wide, and around ten feet high at its zenith. Helen could not see them running across the open lawn beyond the rocks, so she guessed they were coming back around.

She dashed southward, parallel to the mound, expecting to see the suspect come around the other side in their flight from the big Irishman. She was about three quarters of the way down when the girl came around the corner.

Helen stopped dead in her tracks and yelled, "Freeze!" with her Beretta raised and ready to fire. Stark naked, a teenage girl with frizzy, brown hair charged around the corner at a full sprint. When she saw Helen, she screamed and stumbled, trying to stop, total abject terror on her face. Gasping for breath, she desperately tried to cover up with her hands.

"Please don't shoot," she begged.

Helen pulled the muzzle of her 9mm. up, her eyes burned into the frightened girl's for a second. Then all two hundred and fifty pounds of O'Connor plowed into the girl. His momentum slammed them both to the ground.

The girl collapsed like a house of cards, with the big cop on her back. Driving his knee between her shoulder blades, he wrenched her wrists back and put handcuffs on her. Once sufficiently restrained, he jerked the crying girl to her feet.

Helen had not even blinked during the altercation. Once O'Connor had the diminutive suspect on her feet, Helen was no longer able to restrain herself.

"Nice tackle," she smirked.

"Fuck you, Wu," O'Connor said, still panting. "The bitch made me run." He put his face within inches of the restrained girl's. "You have any idea how much I hate to fucking run?"

The girl dropped to her knees at that, sobbing hysterically.

"Wow, she looks pretty dangerous," Helen said in a monotone. "Now that you have the suspect restrained, do you want me to call for backup? Or should I just get the taser?"

Helen holstered her weapon and knelt next to the frightened girl. Helen thought the girl might be under the influence of some sort of drugs, either voluntarily or not. "Do you know where you are?"

The girl nodded. Helen helped her to her feet and led her over to the car.

"If she ralphs in the car, you're cleaning it up, Wu," O'Connor called after her.

Once she was in the back seat, Helen went to get a blanket from the trunk. But by then, O'Connor was leaning over the open door, barking questions down at the girl.

"What are you on?"

"On?"

"What did you take?"

"I don't understand what you're talking about!" She was becoming hysterical and close to hyperventilating.

"You'd better stop playing dumb, or I'm gonna break an ammonia capsule under your nose. That'll sober you up right quick. Then, once you're done pukin' your guts out, maybe you'll give me some straight answers."

"I don't think she's high, O'Connor," Helen said sternly.

"You're already in a lot of trouble. I've got you for indecent exposure, lewd and lascivious conduct, trespassing, attempted breaking and entering, resisting arrest and assaulting an officer," O'Connor rattled on, ignoring Helen entirely.

"She's not stoned, she's in shock!" Helen shouted at him as she squeezed between him and the car. She covered the naked girl with the blanket.

"Of course, she's high. Why else would she be trying to break into a church stark naked? She's stoned out of her gourd."

Helen sprang up like a jack-in-the-box between O'Connor and the car and shoved him back. "Listen to me, you overgrown gorilla. That girl is not a fucking suspect. She's a fucking *victim*!"

"Bullshit!"

She shoved him back again, with surprising force for someone so small.

"Wu, I'm warnin' you, you push me once more, and I'll break your fucking neck, woman or not."

"You're real tough when it comes to people half your size, aren't you?" Helen's voice was so controlled that it sent a cold shiver down O'Connor's spine. "You try it, fat boy. You just try and put your meat hooks on me and see what happens to you." She stared unblinking up into his eyes. In the course of sixteen years on the job, O'Connor had faced down a lot of people. Some were just piss and vinegar, and some were genuine bad-asses. Others were raving lunatics, or out-of-control dope fiends with nothing to lose. But in all that time, he had never been more certain, now that he was looking directly into the black void of Helen Wu's eyes, that she could and would blow him away if he so much as blinked.

O'Connor stepped back one more pace and tried to save some face.

"All right then, if she's not high, you get a straight story out of her."

Helen went around to the other side of the car and climbed into the back seat with Barbara.

***

Willy's first idea was to go to one of the many used car lots that lined Sepulveda Boulevard. They would pick the car of their choice and ask to take it for a test drive. Once they were out on the road, Red Dog would pull his pistol, and they would toss the sales guy out on his ass somewhere.

But when they had settled on a sweet '83 Trans Am, the salesman asked to see their drivers' licenses and proof of insurance before he would let them test drive it. He was actually planning to make a photocopy of the documents. He said it was state law in California and he could not let anyone test drive a car without proof of insurance.

The only I.D. Red Dog had was his parole papers, and Willy couldn't even spell insurance, let alone afford any. So they were going to have to do this the hard way.

They caught a random bus down Sherman Way to Reseda Boulevard and picked the first gas station with two driveways and a mini-market. They went into the store and bought a couple of Mickey's Big Mouths and squatted out front in the shade of the canopy next to the ice machine to sip their beers while they waited for the perfect victim.

***

O'Connor sucked his teeth and stomped around the squad car like an expectant father. He stayed far enough back that his presence did not intimidate the girl but close enough to overhear bits and pieces of the story.

"First things first, let's get you out of those handcuffs," Helen said soothingly as she unlocked the restraints. "Now tell me what happened here, and I will see what I can do to help you." Once the cuffs were off, Helen covered Barbara with the blanket.

"He didn't just attack me, exactly, it wasn't like that," Barbara insisted. "He didn't force me to do anything. I was willing." She sobbed and looked down at her bare feet on the floorboards of the squad car. "I was more than willing. The other officer is right. It's all my fault, I'm a slut, and I deserve to be punished."

Gradually Helen got Barbara to tell her what had happened. Barbara explained all about her journal. How everyone at school learned about her secret crush on Travis. Then she told the part about how horrible it had been when everyone had read all about what she wanted Travis to do to her. And even worse, what she wanted to do to him.

Helen, for her part, was sympathetic to Barbara's plight. Helen too had had a secret crush in high school. It too had gone badly when it was made public. Helen knew how it felt to be used and tossed aside. And what it was to be an outcast because of it.

Barbara told how Travis had come to her house that morning and offered her a ride to school. She was in heaven. It was the first time in her life that any boy had paid any attention to her. And it wasn't just any boy, it was Travis Smythe!

Travis told her "I read her journal, and I was touched. To think that any girl could feel so deeply for me made me realize how shallow all the pretty girls I've dated are. None of them really liked me for myself. None cared about my feelings or his dreams. All they wanted was to gain social position by being seen with the captain of the football team. I'm tired of being treated like a trophy, like an object.

"Now, with you, I've found the real thing. You're different from all the others. You're real, you're love is real. I want to be with you and only you from now on. At last, I've found the real thing, true love."

He was just finishing his speech when Barbara realized they were not at school. He had brought her to the back of the cemetery and parked by the old church.

"What are we doing here, Travis?" she asked.

He looked deeply into her eyes without blinking. "You have made my dreams come true. Now I want to make yours come true, too," he said with those intense blue eyes burning into her soul. Barbara was just naive enough to believe him.

"What...what do you want me to do?" she said.

"Just like you said in your diary. That's why I brought you here. It's the only forest I know."

He leaned in and kissed her. It was her first kiss ever and left her head spinning and her toes curled. His fingers ran though her frizzy, brown hair. Her heart was pounding like a jackhammer. Then his arms were around her. She felt the clip on her bra unlock. She leaned into him, hungry for more.

Travis kissed his way down her neck to the color of her T-shit. His left hand slipped under her shirt. He was touching her! Her barest was actually in a real live boy's hand, on purpose, and not just any boy but Travis'. He started to lift her pink t-shirt over her head. She knew she should stop him but couldn't bring herself to do it. She wanted him to see, she wanted to be naked for him.

He leaned back and admired her breasts like only a teenage boy can.

"Go on, it's okay, you can do whatever you want. I want it too," she whispered.

"No!...Not like this. Not in the car. The first time has to be...special. Like your diary."

"I...I don't understand," Barbara said.

"Our first time together should be magical. Not just boning away in the car." He got out of the car and walked around to the passenger side to open her door.

"I want to make love to you under the blue sky, with the green grass for our bed. Get undressed, and I'll get us a blanket"

Barbara stepped out of the car and blinked in the bright daylight. He walked around to the back of the car and opened the trunk. Self-consciously Barbara took off all of her clothing, folded it neatly and laid it on the seat of the car. She had never been naked outdoors before, or let any boy see her body. She felt exposed and exhilarated at the same time.

When Travis slammed the trunk lid down he did not have a blanket in his hands. He had a video camera.

"Smile, Babs! You're on Candid Camera."

"What? What are you doing?"

Travis came around and slammed her door shut. Then she got it. Her face fell and she futilely tried to hide her body with her hands.

"Say hello to all the folks back home, Babs," he jeered at her. "You didn't really think that I'd ride a moped like you, did you? I thought nerds were supposed to be smart."

Barbara tried to hide behind the car but Travis followed her around, pointing the camera at her.

"What's the matter, Babs? I thought you 'longed to taste the salt of my manhood,'" he quoted her story. "Come on now, let's see you get those chubby knees muddy."

Barbara turned and ran toward the rock outcropping to try and hide herself.

"I thought you wanted to slurp my gherkin? It's your last chance to play the old skin-flute." He walked over to the rocks, laughing cruelly.

"Go away! I hate you! Leave me alone!" Barbara shouted from the other side of the rocks.

"You really want me to go?" he said with a cruel chuckle. "But I thought I was your 'one and only soulmate.' Didn't you write that you wanted us to 'make the beast with two backs?'"

"No! Never! You're horrible! Just leave me alone. I don't ever want to see you again. Just leave me alone!"

"Well okay, if that's what you really want, I'll go. But it's a long walk home, Babs," he said knowingly. He walked back to his car, chuckling. It wasn't really all that far back to her house from here, only about seven or eight blocks. But seven or eight blocks stark naked in broad daylight was a journey of epic proportions for a teenage girl.

After Barbara finished telling Helen her story, Helen got out of the car and walked quietly around to the grille where O'Connor was finishing a cigarette.

"Well, what sort of bullshit did she lay on you?"

"Enough that we could charge that Smythe punk in the blue 'Stang with sexual assault."

"He force her to do anything?"

"Well no, not exactly. He tricked her into getting undressed and then dumped her."

"But he never fucked her." It was a statement, not a question.

"No, but—"

"He ever touch her against her will?"

"No, but—"

"He ever hit her?"

"No, but—"

"Did he threaten her?"

"No, but—"

"But, but, but—you sound like a motorboat. At best, all we have is her word against his. There is no proof that an assault took place. There's not a mark on her."

"I saw her clothes in his car. We could—"

"That doesn't prove shit, Wu. If we bust Smythe, we'll end up draggin' that little girl through court and make her tell this story to roomful after roomful of strangers. Then a sleazy defense attorney rips her to shreds on the stand in front of God and everybody. They'll bring in the dirty diary and make her look like a total slut-puppy. Follow that up with Smythe saying it was all her idea. By the time it's all over, the D.A. will end up charging *her* with lewd conduct.

Hell that punk was only seventeen so we can't even charge him with statutory. Not to mention the mountain of paperwork we'll have to do on it.

"Look, Wu. This job is about making convictions for the D.A., and nothing else. Don't delude yourself into thinking that what we do has anything to do with justice or right or wrong. Thinking like that will drive you nuts. You'll either end up a drunk or eating your gun, or both."

Helen was shocked. She never expected O'Connor to be capable of this level of sensitivity to anyone. Granted, his main concern was avoiding all the paperwork involved. But still, he had actually thought of the girl as a human being.

"Then what do we do with her?" Helen said, trying not to show her surprise.

"We drive her home, and make sure she gets there in one piece." He flicked his butt out across the grass and headed for the car door.

***

Clark wondered how he would break the news to Kyle that he was taking a girl to the con instead of him. What if he told Kyle he had given away his ticket, then Barbara said no? Could he go back and get his buddy? Would Kyle be mad? Would his best friend understand about being stood up for a girl? This would require some thought. It would be a lot easier to figure out if he knew whether Barbara would go or not.

But first he had to see to duty. One of the many conditions for using the truck was that Clark had to fill the tank. That was a small price to pay for having his own set of wheels. So, the first stop on his way to pick up Barbara or

Kyle was the Chevron station on Sherman Way. Maybe he could get one more pass and all three could go. That way they could all see Rutger Hauer and Joan Chen live and in the flesh. They would both be hosting a panel about making *The Blood of Heroes* at the con. He might even get a chance to meet them. Clark was so lost in thought that he didn't even notice the two punks squatting by the ice machine drinking from paper sacks.

He got a forty-four ounce root beer from the soda fountain in lieu of ginger beer. He wondered what ginger beer tasted like. It must be good if The Doctor drank it, but root beer was the closest thing he had ever found on this side of the pond. He gave the clerk forty in cash and said, "Put the rest on pump five," and swaggered out to his cool truck.

Like jackals, Red Dog and Willy instinctively knew a weak link in the food chain when they saw one. The nerd in the long coat and goofy hat was totally oblivious to everything around him. He had even left the truck unlocked when he went inside the store.

They waited for him to finish pumping his gas. The dweeb had a hard time working the pump. It took him three tries to get the pump started, but he got it going eventually. Willy went around the passenger side of the truck and knelt down so the kid could not see him through the high windows.

Red Dog went around the driver's side and sort of loitered on the far side of the pumps behind Clark. Clark pulled out the pump nozzle and hung it back on the cradle.

Red Dog stepped out from between the pumps and pulled out the pistol he had stolen from his grandmother's house. With his free hand he grabbed the nerd's long scarf and yanked him around.

"Gimme the keys, or you're fuckin' dead," he hissed quietly.

"Hey, let go, What do you—" Clark began but stopped short as Red Dog pushed the small pistol under his nose. It smelled like old oil and gasoline.

"Don't play dumb with me, Poindexter! Gimme the fuckin' keys, or I'll blow your fuckin' brains out."

As Red spoke, Willy climbed into the truck on the other side and pulled his sawed-off from under his coat. "Get his wallet, too," Willy said.

"You heard 'em. Hand it over, bitch," Red Dog said.

For a brief instant Clark wondered what The Doctor would do. He thought about trying Venusian judo, it had been devastatingly effective at LARPs. But none of the LARPs guys had real guns. He slowly held out his father's car keys to Red. He felt Willie's hands slide under the long coat and pull out his wallet.

Willy took out Clark's driver's license and read his name and address out loud.

"Now we know who you are and where you live. If you call the cops, we'll come to your house and make you watch while I fucking kill your parents and fuck your slut sister in the ass and make her lick my dick clean after." Clark didn't have a sister but that didn't matter at the moment, "I'll even rape your fucking dog. And when the show is all over, I'll cut off your little limp dick and shove it down your throat and let you choke to death on it. Got it?"

Clark nodded dumbly.

"Good," Red Dog said as he slipped behind the wheel of the truck and started the engine. "Thanks for fillin' it up,

Poindexter." He put the car in gear and pulled away before he had even closed the door.

Clark stood there shaking for almost five full minutes. Not sure what to do next, he wondered what he was going to tell his father about the loss of his beloved truck. Then tears of shame began to flow, and he ran to the attendant to call the police. The two robbers had been terrifying enough but telling his dad that he didn't even put up a fight was going to be far more humiliating than losing the truck.

***

Sagebrush Ave. was a quiet cul-de-sac about one half of a mile to the southeast of Oakwood Cemetery. Drapes in busybodies' windows twitched at the sight of a patrol car in the quiet neighborhood.

Barbara told Helen that her parents both worked during the day, so no one would be home. But they kept a spare key hidden in a hanging planter by the front door. O'Connor pulled up the driveway so the girl, wrapped only in a blanket, would have the shortest distance to go. Helen let her out of the car and walked with her to the front door on the pretense of getting the blanket back. She really wanted to be sure that the key was there and the girl got in safely and to verify the story. A little C.Y.A. never hurt.

Helen got back in the car and said nothing. She knew if she mentioned his act of compassion O'Connor would make her regret it.

"Where to now?" she asked.

"We go and find ourselves a blue Mustang with a broken taillight and perform a spot safety check."

Helen did a double-take and tried to read O'Connor's face.

"But Smythe didn't have a busted taillight."

"He will."

A smile crept across Helen's face, and she checked her flashlight to see if it was in working order. "You don't suppose he might resist arrest a little?"

"I sincerely hope so."

***

Red Dog had a hard time controlling the truck. With its light rear end, it tended to fishtail unless he was careful on the gas. But caution was not a part of Red Dog's nature. He had never legally owned a car in his life, so he didn't understand—or didn't particularly care—about things like burning up his tires or scraping the paint off the fenders. The only times he had actually driven one was when he had stolen it. Those occasions usually ended in an accident of some kind or another, or jail, or both.

He stomped on the gas pedal. The back wheels of the truck spun madly, and it peeled out through the traffic, leaving a cloud of black smoke down the center of the street. He took Sherman Way all the way down to De Soto and hung a wide right, nearly sideswiping a pearl-white Corvette convertible in the process.

"So how will we know this guy? I mean they all look alike, and we can't just pop every nigger we see," Red said.

"Why not? Think of it as a public service. What's one less nig-nog in the world, more or less?"

"I'm all for shootin' cans but I only have eight bullets," Red said.

"Shootin' cans?" Willy asked.

"You know, Africa-*cans*, Mexi-*cans*, Jamai-*cans*, Puerto Ri-*cans*."

When Willy stopped laughing at Red's clever witticism, he asked, "Why don't we stop and get some more ammo at Big Five or something?"

"'Cuz this gun don't shoot regular 'merican bullets. My grandpa took it off a dead Jap back in the war, and it uses some sort of weird Jap bullets."

"Bro, that sucks," Willy said.

The gun had indeed belonged to Red Dog's grandfather. Red had stolen it from his grandfather's old footlocker in the attic the same day he had taken his grandmother's Valiums. But it was not Japanese as he had said, and his grandfather had not taken it from a dead enemy soldier.

Donald Räuber, Red Dog's maternal grandfather, had never been in combat a day in his life. His entire military service was in the quartermaster corps in Seoul, South Korea, during the Korean Conflict.

Räuber did a lot of horse-trading in his job. New movies from one unit, in exchange for ice cream from headquarters. A jeep from the motor pool for a shipment of chipped beef to a combat outfit. The trick to keeping all his balls in the air was to always have what somebody wanted to trade for. And war souvenirs were a hot trade item. Räuber earned the reputation of being able to get a hold of anything.

One stifling Wednesday afternoon a couple of Green Beret NCOs came to him in search of a bottle of high quality scotch to use for a tontine. All they had to offer in trade was a Chinese-made pistol and fifty bucks. Räuber gave them a bottle of ten-year-old Haig's Pinch in exchange for the money and the gun. It was a Chinese manufactured copy of the Tokarev TT-33 called the Type 51. A copy made under license from the Soviets. It was an eight round semi-automatic chambered for the 7.62×25mm Tokarev round. It was close to but not quite the same as a .32 ACP.

Due to Red Dog's limited education, he had assumed that the Chinese markings on the gun were Japanese, and that his grandfather had served in World War II. Red didn't understand that there had been a war in Korea, or that Korean people and Japanese people were not the same. After all a chink is a chink.

He had little understanding of anything beyond the borders of California. In fact the only times in his twenty-five-years he had ever ventured outside of Los Angeles County was on prison busses.

He did know there had once been a war in a place called Viet Nam, and that American POWs were still being held in tiger cages by sadistic V.C. in black pajamas waiting for Rambo and Chuck Norris to come and rescue them. He understood that the U.S. was in a new war somewhere in the desert with towel-heads because Iraq had invaded Kuwait, or was it Kuwait that had invaded Iraq? It didn't really matter to him, he had never heard of either place before they were in the news. In fact, he thought Kuwait was the frog from the Muppets. All that mattered was that Stormin' Norman was gonna kick some camel jockey ass.

"Lilly said that Jazz drives a two-tone blue pimped out Coupe De Ville," Willy said, bringing Red Dog back to the present. "So the first thing we do is drive by and see if his car's in the lot."

"What do we do if he isn't there?"

"Go play video games and check the place out. Then when he walks in the door we just start blastin'."

***

Latrivis Tenison was doing at least ten years up at Quentin for possession of dangerous weapons. The cops had got a tip from his baby momma that Latrivis had a stash of weapons hidden in the pipe chase of his apartment when she found out he was doing her sister behind her back. One morning at oh-dark-thirty the entire SWAT team kicked in his door and took Latrivis to jail. Just nineteen at the time, it was Latrivis' first felony conviction as an adult. The judge was not inclined to show any sympathy; in fact, he made an example of Latrivis. The prosecutor had demonstrated that Latrivis was not only a member of the Crips, but he was the armorer for his set. So Latrivis went down hard.

But he was a down homey, and he kept his mouth shut, even when his dump truck public defender worked out a deal. He could have gotten off with only one year in county for receiving stolen property if he snitched-off where he had gotten the stolen guns. But he kept his mouth shut and did his time like a man.

Some of the guns in Latrivis' pipe chase had been taken in a home invasion that had gone wrong. A crazy old white man tried to shoot Crawfish when he and Jazz had been cleaning out his gun safe. So Jazz had to bust a cap on him. It was his own fault. He shouldn't have tried to shoot at Jazz's homey. If Latrivis had told the cops that Jazz and Crawfish had given him the guns to hide they would both be looking at murder beefs.

Crawfish had been killed in a drive-by a year ago but Jazz was still covering his own ass. He knew that if Latrivis ever turned snitch that he would have that murder rap all to himself. So Jazz made sure that Latrivis was taken care of. Jazz put two hundred bucks in Latrivis' prison account each month for canteen and sent him care packages of cigarettes and candy bars every quarter. But the big thing that Jazz did for Latrivis was take care of his baby brother Fayard.

Fayard Tenison, aka Fleetwood, was all of seventeen in 1990, and had been a member of the gang for six years already. He worked for Jazz at the Wizard's Cave during the day.

The Wizard's Cave was the end shop in an L-shaped strip mall. Next to Joe's Mini-Market, a combination deli and grocery store run by an irascible Iranian immigrant.

Fleetwood liked the job because most of the white boys that came in were afraid of him and didn't give him any shit. Pushing the white boys around and making sure the punks didn't steal nothin' was fun. He liked watching for new talent for Jazz's string of hos even more. And, breakin' in the new bitches for Jazz's stable was even more fun.

Another part of his job was working the video games. Every morning when the place was slow he would open the money box on each machine and manually trip the coin chute. This would record a credit on the machine, and count as a sale. Every day he would run up five hundred credits on each of the twenty games in the arcade. Then he would restart each one to clear off the free games just in case a sucker came in. That accounted for 2,500 dollars a day in phony revenue. That added up to 17,500 dollars a week, for a total of 875,000 dollars a year. The difference in the sales total and actual cash would be made up by Jazz with cash he brought in from other, less legal endeavors. It was an effective way of explaining to the tax men where the money all came from.

It was about one thirty and all of the spoiled little rich kids had gone back to the high school after their lunch break when the two peckerwoods came in. Fleetwood knew they were trouble the second he laid eyes on them.

One was little with a shaved head and beady blue eyes. He was wearing tan Dockers and a camouflage army surplus jacket. The other one was a big youngster with a carrot-colored buzz cut and jail tats all up and down his bare arms. He had the classic prison yard weight pile build. Heavily muscled arms and chest, but no leg development. He was Schwarzenegger from the waist up, and Pee-wee Herman from the waist down. They stood just inside the doorway and looked all around like they were casing the place. If they were, they'd be sorry soon enough. The cops may have found Latrivis' guns in the pipe chase, but they didn't find *all* of Latrivis' guns. Fleetwood drifted over to the front counter and stood close to the cash box, and his Mac-10.

The Wizard's Cave was more or less one big room. To the right of the front doors, an L-shaped counter walled in a slightly raised platform. There were no other doors in or out besides the front. All the way around the room video games lined the walls.

Red Dog and Willy stood a little too long at the front door checking the place out. Willy felt Fleetwood mad-dogging them from the counter and gave Red a little shove to get him moving. They went over to the counter and Willy pulled out Clark's wallet.

"Let me have some tokens, my good man," he said.

106

"I ain't your man," Fleetwood grunted. "We don' have no tokens here. You want quarters?"

"Thanks, pal, that will do just fine."

"Who you calling pal, wood?"

Willy fought the urge to pull his gun then and there. But he wasn't gonna get paid for wasting this Punk Ass Lame. He had to wait for Jazz. But if this nigger got caught in the crossfire, that wouldn't break his heart.

"I didn't mean nothin' by it," he said with a smile. "We don't want any trouble, we just want some quarters."

Fleetwood looked at them sideways and thought it over. Better to have these two assholes were he could see 'em. Give him a little time to figure out what they're up to.

"How much you need?"

Willy pulled one of Clark's crisp twenties out of the wallet.

Fleetwood handed over the quarters and stashed the bill in the cash box. Willy split the coins with Red Dog and they headed over to the Hooligan's Alley machine in the back.

"What do we do now? He's not here."

"All we gotta do is wait till he shows up, then it's party time," Willy said. But the best laid plans of mice and speed freaks often go astray. It didn't take long for them to run through all eighty quarters. And they were growing bored with the games. They were also aware that Fleetwood was watching them. As the day wore on Red's high was beginning to wear thin, and so were his nerves. So when the last quarter was dropped into the slot Willy decided to make a play.

Willy ambled over to the counter and leaned against it facing the room. He pulled a Marlboro out of his pocket and went to light it.

"No smokin'" Fleetwood snarled.

"There's no sign," Willy said.

"Don't need no sign. No smokin'!"

"Right, right, no need to get all tense, bro," Willy said.

"You ain't my bro, wood." Fleetwood was losing his patience with these two losers. They were looking for something and playing Asteroids wasn't it. "Wha'ch you really want?"

Willy looked around as if he might be overheard. Then he turned to face Fleetwood.

"Want? What does anybody want?" Willy smiled showing his missing teeth. "A little fun, maybe a little feminine company, if you know what I mean."

"No, I don't know what you mean."

"Can I trust you?" Willy said. "See, me and my buddy heard that if we was lookin' for some action this was the place to go."

"You a cop?" Fleetwood said in an accusatory tone.

"No fucken' way man. Do I look like some rotten oinker?"

Fleetwood looked at Willy long and hard. He wasn't any cop, but he was up to somethin'. Fleetwood decided he was too high risk to trust.

"All we got here is video games. That's all."

"Come on man, you gotta know were a guy could hook up with some cooz."

"Only cooz' comes in here is underage valley girls, see-what-I'm-sayin', and ain't none of that for sale. If that be what you lookin' for, you best be gettin' the fuck up outta here fors I calls the po-po. Don't want no fucken' Chesters up 'round here, see-what-I'm-sayin'. Now yous both fuck off."

"Okay, all right," Willy said nodding at Fleetwood. "You be that way." He gestured to Red Dog and they walked out, real slow.

***

Jalal Shamlou left the army and joined SAVAK, Iran's version of the CIA, around 1974. It was a good career move for him at the time, and it put him and his family at the top of the food chain. But by 1976, Shamlou could read the writing on the wall. It would not be conducive to his health to still be in Iran after another power shift. After all, treason was just a word invented by the winners as an excuse to hang the losers.

With a little help from an American friend, Shamlou and his young wife immigrated to the United States in 1977, and settled in Southern California, getting out just two short years before the revolution of '79. With what was left of his savings he bought Joe's Mini-Market and Deli. The feared and respected Intelligence Officer Jalal Shamlou became Joe the sandwich man.

Here in America he didn't need to worry about the next coup. The Republicans didn't round up members of the Democratic Party after an election and exile them to Mexico. Democrats didn't send out secret police to torture and kill students that participated in pro-Christian demonstrations.

The only thing that Joe was worried about in America was the way street criminals were coddled by incompetent and effeminate police. If Joe slapped a punk for trying to steal from his store Joe would be charged with assault for violating the rights of the thief. But nonetheless, he would not be disrespected by spoiled American school children or stolen from by street trash.

He could tell at a glance that the big kid with the red hair had a pistol stuck down the front of his pants and the bald one in the dirty army coat had something tucked inside his sleeve. Maybe a large handgun or a piece of pipe. Either way Joe was not going to let this scum rob him. He took the Ruger Sp-101 from under the counter and slipped it into the pocket of his apron.

Red Dog and Willy were oblivious to Joe's .357. The only thing on their minds was beer and sandwiches, in that order. Willy got two forty-ounce Colt 45 Malt Liquors from the cooler at the back of the store while Red Dog ordered two foot-long sandwiches. Once Joe had finished making the food and Willy paid with Clark's money, they sat down at the little table in the middle of the store to eat.

Joe was still uncomfortable about the two hooligans. He picked up his cordless phone and called his brother-in-law, who lived in a nearby apartment and worked in the store. In Farsi, he told his brother-in-law to hurry to the store, just in case he needed backup. He also said to bring the van and some shovels, just in case. It would not be the first time would-be robbers had gone into Joe's with bad intent and were never heard from again.

Red was regaling Willy with the wild story of his first arrest. Red and a couple of his junior high school buddies had snuck out one night and drank a jelly jar full of red wine his buddy had pilfered from his parents' liquor cabinet. After that, to embellish the high, they wandered through an all-night supermarket, inhaling the propellant from cans of whipped cream. Then they got the bright idea to try and steal a bottle of scotch. They all assumed that the young woman working the cash register was the only person working in the store. One of his buddies went to the checkout line to buy a candy bar and distract her with his masculine charm while Red shoved a fifth of Johnny Walker down the front of his pants.

Unfortunately for their plan, the twenty-two-year-old college coed was singularly unimpressed with a thirteen-year-old boy, and she was not alone. Red was just about out of the liquor section when the store manager grabbed him by the collar. The other kids broke and ran, leaving Red Dog to take the rap alone.

The store manager took Red into the office and tried to reason with the boy. He would have called the boy's parents and let them sort it out at home rather than call the police into it and give the kid a record that would follow him the rest of his life. But Red went into his tough act, and he refused to rat on his friends. He wouldn't even tell the manager his own name. The night manager had no choice, he had to call the police and they charged Robert "Red Dog" Hinckley with shoplifting. His mother had to pay a three hundred dollar fine, and Red Dog was given one year probation and one-hundred hours community service. But he never ratted out his pals. Before Joe's brother-in-law arrived Red's story was interrupted by the racket of Jazz's arrival. They heard his approach before they ever saw him. There was the deep rumble of heavy bass with the distinctive syncopated beat of rap music. The rumble steadily grew louder before it was punctuated by the sound of steel scraping on asphalt as the lowered 1976 Coupe De

Ville's bottom grated on the driveway leading into the parking lot.

The car could never be anonymous even without the accompanying din of the overpowered woofers blaring obscenities at top volume. It was two-tone neon blue, with at least ten layers of metal flake clear coat. The landau top had been replaced with blue-on-blue leopard print vinyl. The original front grill had been supplanted with a "money grill" that looked like a gold plated model of a Roman temple. On top of that, the Cadillac badge that had originally adorned the hood had been substituted with an eight inch high golden statue of an overly endowed woman leaning into the wind and spreading her eighteen inch wide clear blue plastic wings. All of the car's original badges had been augmented with oversized gold-plated copies. Faux gold running boards adorned the sides. It rolled on tiny, twelve-inch, gold plated spoke deep dish rims with low profile racing tires, resulting in the car's almost nonexistent ground clearance. Highlighting the ridiculous size of the wheels there a full sized faux-continental wheel sat in the center of the trunk lid. And if that wasn't enough, a second, full sized, continental kit had been added to the oversized rear bumper.

The rolling juke box pulled into a space directly in front of the Wizard's Cave. The roar of the speakers stopped abruptly as the engine cut off and Jazz oozed out of the driver's side door. Treshaun Cochelle aka Jazz was an average-sized, extremely dark-skinned, black man. Twenty-seven years of street basketball had given him the hard slim build typical of inner city youth. He wore neon blue kicks and a light blue track suit with the pants pulled all the way down to show off his blue striped silk boxers. He wore more gold chains around his neck than he could swim with. He stood for a moment and looked around him then pulled a Swisher Sweet from his pocket and lit it with a gold-plated, diamond-studded Zippo lighter. Satisfied he had been seen and admired by one and all he pulled a dark blue gym bag from the passenger seat and glided into the Wizard's Cave. He was so secure in his position in the hood that he didn't bother to roll up the windows of his car. No one would dare fuck with his shit, not in this neighborhood of lames and mushrooms. Jazz was the king of all he surveyed.

Willy grabbed Red Dog by the strap of his wife beater and pulled him from the table.

"Come on Dog, that's our boy."

Red Dog dropped his pepperoni sandwich and grabbed his beer for one last slug to wash the food down. This was it, the turning point. He was stepping up to the big time now. Red had done his fair share of fighting in the past. He had won more times than he had lost. But this was going to be the first time he had ever actually killed anybody. It was cool though, after all, it was just a couple of niggers, not like they were real people.

Jazz was standing at the front counter just inside the Wizard's Cave's front door. Fleetwood was leaning over the counter telling him all about the peckerwoods that were casing the joint. Jazz had put the gym bag on the counter.

Red Dog and Willy didn't come to socialize. Red came through the door just ahead of Willy. Jazz turned toward them.

"That's them now—" Fleetwood started to say.

Red took two long steps with his left hand out as if to shake. Jazz didn't get to be twenty-seven in his line of work without knowing a trap when he saw it. His right hand went for the .25 Beretta in the pocket of his sweat jacket. Willy was already pulling out his .410 double-barreled, sawed-off, shotgun.

Red Dog grabbed Jazz by the right bicep and Jazz tried to pull the trigger on his Beretta Bobcat but the safety was set. Red pulled his Chinese pistol, jammed the muzzle into Jazz's hard stomach, and started shooting as fast as he could pull the trigger.

At the sound of the muffled shots Fleetwood tried to grab his brother's Mac-10 from under the counter. As he leaned down to grab the gun, Willy shoved the business end of his guage into Fleetwood's throat and gave him both barrels. Even though .410 is the smallest bore shotgun available it was enough to shred all of the soft tissue, perforate the fibrous material of the windpipe and sever the spinal cord. Fleetwood's head only remained attached to his body by a few shreds of soft flesh. His corpse dropped, clinging to the unfired submachine gun.

Jazz was another matter. Red Dog put all eight 7.62mm rounds into his lower chest. Tearing his lungs, liver, kidneys, stomach, and miscellaneous other organs to shreds. Jazz's bowels released and he collapsed against the counter, spitting up blood as he fell. He lay in a spreading pool of blood alternately gasping for breath and gurgling. In his agony he managed to get his Bobcat out of his pocket and fumble the safety catch before his arm dropped limp across his lap.

"Come on before the cops get here!" Red Dog turned to run but Willy grabbed his arm.

"Wait a second! Get the money out of the register," Willy insisted. It seemed like a good idea to Red at the time. Willy took a second to open the breech of his shotgun and

114

reloaded it. That reminded Red that he was out of bullets for good and all. Then he saw the gun in Jazz's hand.

He knelt down and discreetly took the .25 and put it in his pocket while Willy stood guard at the door. Then he went behind the counter. Fleetwood was a gory mess. Thick dark red blood was pooling around the shoulders of the dead man and bits of flesh and blood were splattered on the wall behind him.

Red saw the Mac-10 and it was love at first sight. His lust for the weapon overcame his revulsion of the gore and he pried the boxy gun from the dead man's hand with pride of accomplishment. He didn't notice at the time that he dropped his grandfather's war relic from his belt when he reached for the Mac-10.

On a shelf under the counter he saw the cash box and two spare magazines for the Mac. He shoved the two hundred dollars in small bills into his pocket and grabbed the ammo. This was proving to be the best day of his life.

"All right, there's nobody in the parking lot. Let's get the fuck outta here," Willy hissed. Almost as an afterthought, Red grabbed the gym bag off the counter as he and Willy ran back to Clark's truck and burned rubber out of the parking lot, turning right onto Lassen Street on two wheels and heading west toward the park.

Laughing and hooting over their victory, Willy noticed the gym bag for the first time.

"What the fuck is this?" he asked Red.

"It was on the counter. The Jigaboo brought it in from the car with him. I just grabbed it on the way out."

"What's in it?"

Willy opened the bag and fell silent in amazement.

"What the hell is it?" Red asked, straining to see.

115

"You won't fuckin' believe it...." Willy said weakly.

"Believe what, asshole? What's in the fuckin' bag?"

"Looks like a million fuckin' dollars!" Willy shouted at the top of his lungs in glee.

"No fuckin' way!"

"Totally! We're fuckin' rich!"

The bag contained three thousand, seven hundred and eighty-three dollars in small bills that Jazz had collected from the prostitutes and drug dealers in his employ. He had brought the money to the Wizard's Cave to launder it through the video games. It was far from a million, but it was the most money Red Dog or Willy had ever seen in one place in their entire lives. Both men began cheering and hooting in exhilaration. Willy began to pull handfuls of cash out of the bag and toss them in the air. Cash rained down like confetti inside the cab of the truck.

Red Dog skidded around the corner onto Farralone Avenue and put the pedal to the metal toward Chatsworth Park. Farralone Avenue was a through street that ran from Lassen all the way north to Devonshire. Nothing as mundane as speed limits or traffic signs was going to slow him down now. He and Willy were rich and they were on their way to the old church to meet with the mysterious Beatrix and get their party on.

***

Travis Smythe's home address had been on his driver's license when O'Connor checked it in the cemetery. In their search for the blue Mustang, O'Connor cruised down Romor Street past Smythe's house in hopes of finding him at home. But there was no sign of the car. So, O'Connor began to drive aimlessly around the subdivision.

When he saw a red pick-up truck tear down Farralone Avenue at twice the posted speed his reaction was more reflex than anything else. The Mustang could wait. He hit the lights and punched the accelerator.

When the blue lights flashed behind them Willy and Red's elation evaporated. Red stepped on the gas to try and run.

"No way, man, you can't outrun the fuckin' radio!" Willy said.

"Then what do we do? If they stop us, they'll run the plates and find out the truck is jacked. That's a third strike for me, man."

"Then we don't have nothin' to lose, do we? We just pull over like a couple of Square Johns and waste us a couple of pigs."

At the thought of shooting it out with the cops Red Dog's blood pulsed through his veins. He was a genuine outlaw. A legend in the making. He took his foot off the gas and coasted to the side of the road under the shade of a clump of old oaks. *This was gonna be fuckin' far out.*

O'Connor pulled up about ten feet behind the red truck and began to climb out of the cruiser.

"Wait a minute," Helen said. "We're still waiting for the make on the plates."

"We don't have time for that shit, Wu. This is just a couple of Junior Jammers playing Speed Racer in Daddy's new truck. It won't take a second."

"We are supposed to wait for the ID check before we approach a vehicle. That's official procedure," Helen said.

"I've been on the job for fourteen fucking years. Now don't you start quoting regulations at me, Wu. I know exactly what I'm fucking doing," O'Connor snapped at her and walked off toward the driver's side of the truck.

The monitor in the squad displayed the information on the Truck: STOLEN: SUSPECTS ARMED AND DANGEROUS, APPROACH WITH EXTREME CAUTION.

O'Connor approached the driver's side, when he got to the rear fender it was too late for Helen to warn him. But she did manage to slip out of the patrol car.

The driver's side door of the truck opened and a small man jumped out and fired both barrels of a sawed-off .410 shotgun into O'Connor's chest. Fortunately for O'Connor he was wearing body armor and Willy, like most self-proclaimed tough guys, did not understand the tactical application of a shotgun. He had seen a "bad-ass gauge" in a movie and thought it would blow away the cops. But with only eight-inch barrels, at almost twenty feet away from the target, most of the pellets sprayed harmlessly around O'Connor. None of the buckshot managed to penetrate his vest. But it did convey sufficient kinetic energy to throw the big cop to the ground and knock the wind out of him. O'Connor was down and Helen was on her own.

The other passenger of the Silverado tumbled out of the right side and opened fire on the police car with a fully automatic Ingram Mac-10. When Helen heard the shotgun and saw the boxy .45 caliber submachine gun she dropped and rolled under the cruiser.

Red Dog had only had the gun for about twenty minutes and never actually fired a submachine gun before. He was unprepared for the accumulative recoil of the .45

ACP. The relatively small gun got away from him as the first twenty slugs tore through the open squad car door, trailed across the grill, impaled the radiator, released a cloud of steam, shattered the windshield and smashed half of the light bar on the roof of the cruiser. The last five of the thirty round magazine flew harmlessly over the car and fell to earth three blocks away. He had failed miserably at his attempt to kill any police officers, but he had sent their car to that great parking lot in the sky.

When the submachine gun ran out of gas Helen sprang to her feet like a pop-up target in "Hooligan's Alley." Red Dog was briefly amazed to see her stand up. He had fired the submachine gun. He had even held it sideways, just like the cool dude in the movies. The little cop was supposed to be dead. He didn't understand. But he did reach into his pocket for another magazine.

Helen held her police issue Beretta 92F with both hands and fired a three-round burst. Two rounds hit Red Dog just above his right eyebrow, the third smashed his dilated eyeball. Even in his hyperactive state Red Dog never had time to miss the loss of his sight.

Willy snapped the breech of the shotgun closed on two fresh shells when he heard O'Connor groan. He couldn't believe the pig was still alive, and he didn't realize yet that Red Dog was not. He stood over O'Connor to finish the job, relishing how hardcore he was.

Helen emerged from the cloud of steam escaping from the mortally wounded police car's radiator like an avenging revenant. Her movements were quick and controlled. There was no panic, this was just business and Willy was a problem that needed to be resolved efficiently. She didn't give Willy any quarter. Three 9mm rounds tore through his left lung.

Gasping for air, he fell against the fender of the Silverado. Empowered by the amphetamines coursing through his rapidly diminishing blood supply, he tried to point the shotgun at the chink bitch that killed him. Helen fired three more rounds that pulverized his pockmarked face.

In the investigation that followed the shooting, no connection was ever made between Red Dog and Willy and the shooting at the Wizard's Cave. Because Red Dog had dropped his grandfather's pistol when he was recovering the Mac-10 the detectives assumed that Fleetwood and unknown accomplices had murdered Jazz over some internal gang dispute. Because the Chinese pistol was a war relic, there was no record of it ever existing in the United States, rendering it untraceable.

The Bobcat Red Dog had pried from the cold dead hands of Jazz was linked to the unsolved murder of a prostitute in Van Nuys six months earlier, and the death of a wealthy businessman in a home invasion eighteen months before that. Red Dog was given the credit for both crimes even though they had been the handiwork of Jazz.

It was further assumed that the bag of cash they were carrying was the result of drug traffic. As Red Dog and Willy were both facing third strikes, and sporting a stolen fully automatic submachine gun, it was taken for granted that they had decided not to be taken alive. The world would be a better place without them.

Helen Wu was a hero to her colleagues and a media darling to the brass of the LAPD. She was pleased that she saved O'Connor's life but didn't think she had done anything of note. She had felt nothing for Red Dog and Willy. She had no enmity or the slightest bit of remorse for either of them. They were nothing but small-time punks.

Two more just like them would take their place before the bodies were even cold. It was just a thing she had done. Like filing a report or making an arrest. It wasn't even a particularly good bit of shooting as far as she was concerned.

O'Connor milked his injury from the shooting for six months of paid sick leave before he was forced to return to duty as Helen's training officer. The incident did make a deep impression on him. While he would never be the sort of teacher Helen would have liked him to be, after that he did begin to follow procedures, mostly.

Travis Smythe vanished without a trace shortly before graduation. He was last seen leaving the school after football practice. His buddies on the team later told police that he was planning to run out and get a sandwich, then pick up Christy for a date. Christy was furious that he had stood her up.

Christy Butler died in 1992 as a result of massive hemorrhaging caused by a self-inflicted home abortion.

Clark Roberts was dumbfounded to learn that his father didn't care at all about the truck as long as Clark was unhurt. This revelation was not lost on Clark even after the truck was recovered with no real damage. As a result of Clark's connection with a real police shootout on the 6 o'clock news, he was an instant celebrity. Almost everyone at school lost interest in Barbara's boring diary. With all of the sudden notoriety Clark built up enough self-confidence to ask Barbara Brendlinger to the fall dance. They remained a couple all through college and eventually married.

Job Choices

April-1990

Lewis Callahan always wanted to be Arthur Fellig, aka Weegee, the famed photographer of life in the city, when he grew up. But because he never really grew up he never had the chance. Callahan was a wedding photographer. A job he did not entirely hate, but he dreamed of more exciting things. Weddings and business portraits paid the bills and more or less put food on the table, but there was no challenge, no thrill. He fought off the old *ennui* by doing the occasional "art" shoot whenever he could manage it. Tonight he had managed it. It had taken him years of nearly constant wheedling, whining, and outright begging his old school buddy, but Dean O'Keefe finally gave in—and against his better judgment—arranged a ride-along for Callahan. Tonight Lewis Callahan was going to "get his Weegee on."

Callahan showed up half an hour early dressed in khaki cargo pants, a black shirt, and what looked to O'Keefe like a khaki fishing vest, with its pockets stuffed full of camera accessories. On the excuse of kitting him out with a flak jacket O'Keefe pulled Callahan into the locker room.

As Callahan pulled his vest back on over the armor, O'Keefe discreetly peered up and down the aisles to be sure they were alone.

"Look, Furball, I had to pull a few strings and call in a favor or two to arrange this," he began.

"I know, Dean. I really do appreciate it."

"Shut up and listen to me for a minute, this is important. In order to get the pencil pushers to overlook the insurance liability issue of having a civilian in the squad car I had to make a deal with the P.R. department."

"Let me guess, I can only publish shots that make you look good? Right? Making you look good is gonna be hard, unless we use a paper bag."

"We got stuck with the Department's *little media mascot*." O'Keefe went on ignoring the friendly jape.

"Yeah? So what's the problem? Is the guy some kind of glory hound?"

"No. Not exactly. In fact she's not happy about having her picture taken at all. So, she's got some attitude about you being with us. But the main thing is…" O'Keefe paused for a moment, then blurted it out. "You can't be hitting on her all night. Okay? Just keep your dick in your pocket and try and act like a grown-up for once. Whatever you do, don't ask her if she's ever done any modeling, and for God's sake don't ask her to come to your studio for a free glamour shoot."

"Why would I do that? Is she hot?"

"Don't even go there."

"No problem broski. I'll behave myself, I promise. I was gonna tell you, I have a new girlfriend anyway."

"Yeah, did Cherry Blossoms finally deliver, or did you get a puncture repair kit?" O'Keefe said as he headed for the door.

"That mail order thing is all a racket. They never put any holes in the boxes. The damn things are already dead when the crates showed up."

"If she didn't come in the mail, and she's not inflatable, where did you meet her, at the Braille Institute?"

"I was doing some business portraits for the staff at Saint Joseph's. She works there."

"What is she, a nurse or something?"

"No, she's a doctor, an ophthalmologist. Her name's Chong. She's seriously cute."

"Chong? No way. Does she hang out with a *chola* named Cheech by any chance?"

"Why, do you want me to fix you up?"

O'Keefe and Callahan walked out to the parking lot behind the station and found Helen Wu loading a large black equipment bag into the trunk of the squad car. Before she saw them, Callahan snapped an image of her bending over the bumper into the trunk. At the sound of the shutter she spun around and glared at them. Just as quickly, Callahan adjusted the aim of his 200mm zoom to another squad car parked nearby.

"Helen, this is Lewis Callahan. Lewis, this is Patrol Officer Helen Wu," O'Keefe said as they approached.

Callahan slung his Nikon over his shoulder and held out his hand to the officer. "Nice to meet you, Helen."

Helen stared him straight in the eye, "*Officer* Wu." She turned abruptly on her heel and walked around to the passenger side of the car, leaving Callahan with his hand stuck out foolishly.

"Smooth. I think she likes you, Lewis," O'Keefe said. "For her that was friendly."

"You don't think she noticed that I was…"

"Taking pictures of her ass? No, that was real subtle, especially with the telephoto lens."

O'Keefe got behind the wheel and Callahan took his place in the back seat on O'Keefe's side so he could admire the left side of Helen's impassive face. What Callahan had told O'Keefe about having a new girlfriend was true. He was crazy about Doctor Chong Wong and would never even consider cheating on her. But he was an admitted Rice King and could not pass up the opportunity to appreciate Helen's faultless features.

"I thought we'd hit Hollywood Boulevard first," O'Keefe said to break the awkward silence in the car as he started the engine. Helen picked up the mic for the radio and called in a stream of code to clear them from the premises. Once they were outside in the clear California night, she stared out the window in obstinate silence.

"I figured Hollywood Boulevard would give you something a little more interesting to shoot than traffic violations. By this time on a Saturday night, all the freaks are out on the Boulevard."

"Most of them, anyway," Helen said under her breath.

"Yeah, they're probably wondering where you are tonight, Furball," O'Keefe said into the rearview mirror. He was shocked that Helen had made a joke, even if it was at Lewis's expense. Maybe she really did like the Fur; he just wished that Lewis would stop staring at her like he was waiting for the school bell to ring.

They rolled north up LaBrea at a leisurely pace taking in the sights. Dean O'Keefe, like most people of Irish descent, could not bear silence, so he launched into his monologue about the humorous things civilian drivers did when they saw a police car pull alongside of them. Soon he and Callahan were laughing and joking about the occupants of the cars around them. But Helen never joined in the revelry. Her face remained indifferent as she watched the street outside.

"Dean, where is Hopper today? Isn't he supposed to be your regular partner?" Callahan asked.

"He is on vacation for a couple of weeks. Helen's official training officer is on sick leave for the rest of the month, so I get Little Miss Sunshine until O'Conner's back on his feet. That reminds me, Helen, how *is* O'Conner doing?"

"He's still goldbricking," Helen said without looking away from the window.

"Goldbricking? He took both barrels of a sawed off shotgun to the chest. He's lucky to be alive."

"It was only a .410, and he had his vest on," Helen said.

"That's still like getting hit in the chest with a fuckin' sledgehammer. He had a couple of cracked ribs and—"

"It was his own fault. If he had followed procedure it would never have—"

"Are you lecturing a superior officer about procedure, Rookie?" O'Keefe snapped.

Helen turned her head slowly to face O'Keefe. *"Rookie?* If O'Conner had done his job properly, I wouldn't have had to save his ass from those two scumbags in the first place."

"Your partner got shot? What happened?" Callahan said, leaning forward to hear better. He had heard about the shooting on the T.V. news but didn't realize it was Wu until now.

"I shot the two assholes that shot him." Helen turned back to the window of the squad car making it clear that she was not going to say any more on the subject.

There was a long silence until O'Keefe turned right from LaBrea onto Hollywood Boulevard. Crowds of tourists searched for the names of their favorite stars in concrete and rubbed shoulders with dreamers and hustlers along both sides of the boulevard.

"Soooo, Helen, Dean said you're a rookie. How long have you been on the job?"

"*Officer Wu,*" Helen said, still staring out the window.

"You know I tried out for the LAPD a few years ago." Callahan went on doggedly trying to drag her into a conversation, whether she wanted to join it or not. "As a matter of fact, Dean and I applied together. They wouldn't take me because of my Dyslexia."

"They didn't take you because you washed out on the psych-exam," O'Keefe said with a grin.

"I wish you wouldn't go around telling people that. It makes me sound like some sort of a loony,"

"*You are* a loony," said O'Keefe matter-of-factly.

"I am not a loony, *I am not!*" Callahan insisted.

"Is that what the voices in your head tell you?" O'Keefe quipped.

"I never hear voices, just ask Harvey. He'll vouch for me." Callahan turned to the empty seat next to him. "Go on

Harvey old boy; tell him I'm not a loony." He paused a moment, as if someone spoke. "There, you see, and if you can't take Harvey's word for it, who's word can you take?"

"All right all right, as long as Harvey says so, I guess you're all right."

"Gentlemen," Helen said, pinching the bridge of her nose for an instant. "Could you please spare me the clever banter and witty repartee for just a few minutes and pay a little attention to the job? And just for the record, I am not Dorothy Lamour, and this is not *The Road to Santa Monica*. And so help me, if you two assholes break into a song and dance routine, I swear to John Browning, I will shoot you both on the spot."

"Looks like we have a little bit of a donnybrook going on," said O'Keefe, pointing to the left side of Hollywood. Helen picked up the mic and called in the situation. O'Keefe expertly tapped the switch on the siren, making the lights flash and two chirps as the car cut diagonally across the intersection of North Orange Drive and Hollywood.

In the public parking lot next to the famous Mann's Chinese Theatre a cat-calling audience had formed around two men. As the squad car pulled up the crowd parted to reveal the protagonists. O'Keefe and Wu climbed out of the car with their batons in hand, opened Callahan's door from the outside and approached the combatants.

"Holy Dynamic duel, Batman!" he shouted at the sight of the two arguing street performers.

One was a little older, in his late thirties or early forties and a bit bigger. It was clear he had spent a lot of time in the gym. He was dressed in the gray tights and deep midnight blue satin cape and cowl of the 1960s *Batman* TV show. The other guy was smaller, but not by much. He was in his late twenties and he wore the more elaborate dull black sculpted latex Bat-suit from the 1986 theatrical film.

"Get your runty ass off my patch," the older Batman shouted as he shoved the younger one.

"Back off, old man!" replied the young Batman. "This is a free country, and I can go anyplace I want to."

"No, you fucking can't. Everybody knows that I'm the only Batman from LaBrea to Highland. So, go peddle your papers out in front of the Egyptian."

"All right, guys, just step back and take it down a notch," O'Keefe said in an authoritative but not aggressive tone. "What's the trouble?"

Helen moved quietly to one side, allowing a free field of fire. Callahan followed her, shooting over her shoulder all the while. The older of the two Batmans seemed to recognize O'Keefe and turned to face him.

"Hey, just the guy to clear this up," he said in a friendly tone. "Come on, O'Keefe, tell this...*youngster* how it is on the Boulevard. LaBrea to Highland is mine."

"Come on officer, help me out here," said the other Batman. "He can't tell anyone they can't walk down a public street. This old has-been is just pissed off because I'm getting better tips than he is. You know as well as I do that this is where the big tippers are."

"I'd rather be a has-been that a never-was. I've been working this street for five years now," the old school Batman began. "This is my patch."

O'Keefe turned to the younger Batman. "I haven't seen you out here before. What's your name?"

"I'm Batman!" the youngster said, in a really poor Michael Keaton impression.

"Now don't get cute with me, boy, or you'll be spending the night in a psych ward. Now what's your name? And don't even think about saying Bruce Wayne."

"Doug Cable."

"See, now that didn't hurt too much, did it? Let's see if we can't talk this over like civilized people. Doug this is Bill Burke. He was one of the first characters out here. He's been doing this since '85 or '86 at least. But that doesn't give him the right to chase you off."

"Everybody knows that this is my patch. Everything from LaBrea to Highland is my territory. I built up the clientele here. It's me they're coming to see! It's my territory!" Burke shouted.

"Fuck that noise, the fans don't give a shit about you, it's Batman they want to see," Cable said.

"Nice language for the Caped Crusader. Look, I'm not out here for my health you know! *This is my job*." Burke suddenly bore down on Helen pointing a finger. "You! Yeah, you! You can't just go around takin' my picture any time you want either. I work for tips, you want to take my picture you gotta pay just like everybody else."

Burke was about six feet from Helen when she remembered that Callahan was standing behind her trying to get a shot of her with Burke.

"Actually, he can. This is a public street, and legally he can photograph anyone he likes. Any one of these people can take as many snapshots of you as they like. What *is illegal* is demanding money for posing with people. That's solicitation and pandering. Threatening people if they don't pay you is aggressive pandering. Technically, if I want to be a bitch about it, I could charge you with extortion for that, or verbal assault or even attempted strong-arm robbery.

131

"In fact, if you don't start acting a little more like a gentleman, I will haul your Bat-ass downtown and let the booking officer take your picture. Trust me, Mister Burke, you do not want to spend forty-eight hours in the drunk tank in purple satin and tights."

Burke froze in place with his finger still pointed at Callahan, looking more like Daffy Duck then the Dark Knight, flummoxed by the spooky little cop. Helen had not raised her voice. Perhaps that was what made her so threatening, but Burke just didn't want to tangle with her.

"What's the deal with the midget partner O'Keefe? Or is it bring your son to work day?"

Burke made an inarticulate sound, twitched for an instant then fell like a redwood. It took a couple of seconds for O'Keefe to realize that Helen had used her taser on Burke. The crowd made a combination of noises ranging from laughter to gasps.

"What in the Hell do you think you're doing?" O'Keefe shouted at Wu.

"Protecting our civilian observer," she replied with no trace of emotion in her voice.

Burke began to groan and got up on his hands and knees, shaking his head. O'Keefe rushed over and helped him to his feet. Cable watched open-mouthed and wide-eyed as the bigger Batman came back to his senses.

"Hey, you know what, guys? It's not that big a deal. It's not worth all that. I mean it's a big street, right?" Cable said, trying to keep his distance from Helen. "I...I can go work some other corner. Really. We don't need to get so...excited." Cable began to edge his way back away from the cops and the crowd of spectators.

"What about you?" O'Keefe said to Burke as he unhooked the two wires from the Bat-symbol on Burke's chest.

"I'm good with that. Just keep that psycho away from me."

"Come on now, Bill, is that any way to talk after he agreed to move to a different corner?"

"I wasn't talking about Cable. I was talking about him. Ya' know, that's why short guys shouldn't be allowed to be cops, they're always trying to prove they're big men," Burke said as O'Keefe helped him to his feet.

O'Keefe began laughing, "You keep it up with the short cracks and she'll zap you again."

Helen was now directly in front of them with her cuffs in her left hand. "I would never use the Taser twice," she said coldly. "You have the right to remain silent. I suggest you do."

"Hey, wait a minute, she's a girl!" Burke said when he got a closer look at Helen.

"Anything you say or do may be used against you in a court of law. You have the right to consult an attorney before speaking to the police and to have an attorney present during questioning now or in the future. If you cannot afford an attorney, one will be appointed for you before any questioning, if you wish," Helen went on doggedly.

"Wu, what are you charging him with?"

"Assault, disorderly conduct, and disturbing the peace. He may need to go to the psych ward for observation. He is clearly out of touch with reality."

"You can't put someone in the nuthatch just because he thought you were a short guy"

"Yeah, but you should at least make him get his eyes checked. Even Ray Charles could see she's *definitely* not a guy," Callahan said. Helen glared over her shoulder at Callahan and his glib tongue tied itself in a knot and tried to hide in his stomach.

"Lewis, don't fucking help me," O'Keefe said, shaking his head. "Go on, Bill, get the hell out of here and behave yourself."

"Thanks, O'Keefe. You're a standup guy, I owe you one," Burke said. Without ever turning his back on Helen he hustled off down Hollywood Boulevard. With the exit of the second Dark Knight the crowd of spectators began to disperse.

Helen gathered up the spent wires from her Taser and fitted a new cartridge into the weapon.

"Get in the car, Dead Eye," O'Keefe said, trying hard to keep his Irish temper in check. As they pulled away from the curb Helen cleared the call on the radio.

"Why did you let him go?" Helen asked.

"Why did I let him go? What the fuck were you thinking back there anyway?" O'Keefe demanded.

"The suspect was endangering our civilian passenger—" Helen started.

"Bullshit! He wasn't doing anything of the sort. You fucking tasered him because he pissed you off. You can't taser people for 361-P."

"The suspect was approaching our civilian passenger in an aggressive manner because our civilian passenger was taking the suspect's picture without the suspect's expressed permission."

"I was there, Wu. Don't talk to me like you're filling out a fucking report. You zapped him because he made a short joke. If we had busted that nut case, he'd have some ambulance chaser suing the department for everything from police brutality to violating his constitutional right of freedom of speech before we could finish the paperwork. The last thing we need is some shyster whining on the six o'clock news about how we tasered some poor, defenseless, homeless veteran with untreated mental illness. Thank God he was white, or we could've had a fucking race riot on our hands."

"What do you mean we, *round eye*."

O'Keefe did a double take at that, momentarily unable to respond. Callahan had known O'Keefe long enough to know that his head was about to explode, and it would not go well for Wu if it did. So, to change the subject he asked, "What makes you think he's a veteran, Dean?"

"Have you ever met a bum that wasn't a Viet Nam vet? All of the women are single mothers and all the men are disabled, Viet Nam vets, even the ones that were fourteen years old back in '69. I think it's a panhandler's union rule."

A radio call interrupted the argument. O'Keefe was still too angry to deal with Helen's implacable doll-like face, so he picked up the mic and responded himself.

"We have a 415 on Morgan Hill Drive. Neighbors are complaining about some loud music. It's probably just somebody having a party. Do you think we could please get through this call without you shooting anybody, Dead Eye?"

Helen just stared at him.

***

The squad car wound its way through the twisting maze of streets that made up the palatial subdivision. Morgan Hill Drive was a narrow side street that wound northeast from Foothill Drive and made a switchback up a steep hill before coming to a dead end.

The complainant's home was on the north side of Morgan Hill overlooking the end of the hairpin turn with the offending house on the tip of the property in the island formed by the road. To reach the complainant's residence, the cruiser had to drive by the entire length of the party house on the south side and then double back halfway along its north side. Even with the cruiser's windows closed they could hear loud music booming from the house. O'Keefe, Wu and Callahan parked in the driveway in front of the complainant's garage door and climbed a partly hidden flight of winding stairs that led up a rocky hillside to a deck on the roof of the garage overlooking the street and the other house.

Before they got across the deck, a glass door slid open. The complainant was a Hispanic man of about forty. He stood approximately five-eleven and weighed well over two hundred pounds, most of which was a spare tire. He was dressed in Bruno Magli slippers, bright red silk pajamas and a dark purple crushed velvet robe, left open to the waist to display a crop of graying chest hair. All topped off with an extravagant, but poorly applied toupee.

Just as he came through the door, Callahan whispered in Helen's ear, "Shhhh, don't say anything, but I think he has a trained squirrel on his head." She began to laugh out loud but caught herself and elbowed him in the stomach. O'Keefe glared back at them, and Callahan fell back a little to line up his shots.

Henry DeCesare was well known, but not well liked, by every member of the LAPD. From 1977 to 1983 he had been a teen heart-throb and the star of *Motor Patrol*. The program was mainly aimed at twelve-to-fifteen year old girls, featuring two beefcake motorcycle officers riding around LA solving crimes, and rescuing fashion models from wildly improbable situations by engaging in implausible high-speed car chases. All the while finding new excuses to tear off their own shirts and show off their freshly oiled pecs.

DeCesare stuck out one hand to O'Keefe as they approached, "Hi, guys, how's it going? What's with the *paparazzi?* Did you know you were going to meet a TV star tonight?" DeCesare flashed his unnaturally white, perfectly capped teeth for a photo.

"This is Lewis Callahan; he's working on a 'day in the life' photo essay. I'm Officer O'Keefe, this is my partner, Officer Wu," O'Keefe said, taking DeCesare's hand.

"Well *hello there*. Now I know what they really mean by LA's finest. Were you a fan of *Motor Patrol* when you were a kid? I'll bet you've always wanted to meet 'Cisco', haven't you?" he said, sticking a hand out to Helen. Helen just stared at his hand.

"No, not really. *Charlie's Angels* was more my speed."

He stood there still holding out his hand, trying hard to force his smile. "Well...er... Okay then."

"Mister DeCesare, can you tell us what the problem is?" O'Keefe said.

DeCesare turned his attention back to O'Keefe. "Can't you hear it?" He gestured toward the house across the street. "Old Mrs. Ryan-Reilly has always been a good neighbor until today. She has been in that house longer than anyone else in the entire neighborhood. In all that time, nobody has even noticed she's there. She's sort of a shut-in. Only time anybody ever sees her is when she comes out to work in her garden, and she hardly ever does that anymore. Not since the break-in."

"Break-in? When was that?" Helen said.

"Had to be eight or nine years ago now. It was all over the news for a while. Everybody was surprised to find out she was a big movie star back in the day. Her maid let her boyfriend into the house and they beat the old lady up pretty bad. They tried to steal everything in the house, antiques, china, jewelry. Anything they could lay their hands on. Can you imagine beating up a little old lady like that?

"Since then, she's been pretty paranoid about letting anyone in the house. She's always been pretty quiet until today. Then just out of the blue she cranks up the death metal at full volume."

"Did you say her name was Miss Ryan-Reilly? Not Regan Ryan-Reilly?" Callahan interrupted.

"Yeah, that's right. Why, have you heard of her?" DeCesare asked.

"Well yeah. Regan Ryan-Reilly was one of the biggest stars of her time. She was a major sex-symbol, bigger then Louise Brooks or even Clara Bow."

"Who?" Helen said.

"She was the biggest leading lady in Hollywood until her career was destroyed by the Desmond T. Williams murder scandal." Callahan looked from O'Keefe to Wu and back again. "What do they teach you guys in the academy? It's one of Hollywood's most famous unsolved mysteries. Williams was found dead in his bungalow....shot in the back...." Callahan trailed, off embarrassed.

O'Keefe, Wu, and Callahan left the car parked on DeCesare's driveway and crossed Morgan Hill on foot. As they reached the sidewalk O'Keefe turned back on Callahan and held up his hand.

"Hey, Lewis, can I get you to hang back a little on this one? If the homeowner is as reclusive as DeCesare says, she won't appreciate a camera in her face."

"But, it's *Regan Ryan-Reilly*, this is an opportunity of a lifetime..." Callahan began but trailed off. "Right, fine, I'll wait back here." As the cops walked up the front steps to the house Callahan found a spot on the sidewalk where he could get a shot at the front door.

The brass-plated door knocker was vibrating with the dulcet tones of Ozzy Osbourne screaming something about precious cups and deadly flower petals with strange powers, to a crudely played melody. Helen didn't get rock music at all, Dave Brubeck was more her speed. The music (if one could call it that) was so loud that she could feel the bass line pounding in her chest. After three tries with the ornate knocker O'Keefe tried the doorbell, twice.

On the third ring a shadow passed over the peep hole. There were voices inside, but what they said was drowned out by Ozzy shrieking something about bodies and corpses. Helen decided it must have been a love ballad.

O'Keefe's fingertip was about to touch the button a third time when the first of five heavy locks on the door began to turn. One by one they unfastened and the door slowly creaked ajar like the beginning of the *Inner Sanctum*.

The door only opened six inches, two thick gilt chains snapped taut and half of the face of a teenage girl peeked out at them. Her large sleepy-looking brown eyes were painted to look like a Pharaoh's, and black lipstick adorned the full mouth, all surrounded by freshly dyed, jet black hair. A low cut, black patent leather corset displayed her capacious cleavage.

"Can I help you, officers?" she said in a falsely husky voice, in an obvious attempt to sound sexy to O'Keefe. "Is there a problem?"

"Are you a resident of this house?" O'Keefe began in the polite but not quite friendly voice that all experienced cops used with the public. The girl paused for a second; her eyes darted up, then back to O'Keefe's, the first telltale sign that she was making up a lie on the spot.

"Sort of, yes. It's my Grandma's house. I'm just sorta' stayin' here for a little while."

"Can we talk with your grandmother, please?" O'Keefe went on.

"Err. No… She's….She's not here right now. And I'm not allowed to let anyone in when she's not here. Is there something I can help you with?"

"That would explain a lot," Helen said under her breath.

"The neighbors have been complaining that the music is disturbing them," O'Keefe went on. "You need to turn the volume down,"

"Way down," Helen cut in.

"…or we will have to issue you a citation," O'Keefe continued.

"You mean like a ticket?" the girl said with a sneer?

"That's right. And if you don't comply after that we can confiscate your stereo," Helen added.

"Right…fine. I'm sorry. I'll take care of it right now. The girl slammed the door in their faces. There was some discussion on the other side of the door, as the five locks were reset, followed by the sound of high-heels clicking on a marble floor. After a minute or two, Ozzy was silenced. O'Keefe and Helen looked at each other and shrugged.

When it became clear that the girl was not planning to return, Callahan walked up to the door.

"So what was Elvira's story?" he asked.

"She says she's the owner's granddaughter," O'Keefe said and relayed what the girl had told them.

"Bullshit," Callahan said.

"I know it's bullshit, but that's all we can do about it," O'Keefe said. "Without any proof, what can I do, kick the door in?"

"She's *not* Regan Ryan-Reilly's granddaughter."

"How can you *know* that?" Helen said, not entirely satisfied herself.

"Because Regan Ryan-Reilly was never married. She was madly in love with the director Desmond T. Williams. She was obsessed with the guy, wrote him love letters, claimed that they were engaged, hung around his sets when he was directing, drove the poor old guy insane. What we would call stalking today.

"In 1922, when he was found murdered in his living room, she was one of the prime suspects. But her mother gave her an alibi for the time of the shooting. She claimed that Williams had proposed to her and she was planning to run away with the guy against her mother's wishes. Her mother didn't approve because he was in his fifties and she was only seventeen. After the murder, she went into mourning for the rest of her life and never worked in Hollywood again. To make a long story short—"

"Too late," Helen interrupted.

"Regan never married. She cloistered herself in her house and never came out again."

"In that case, why don't we ask Vampirella for some I.D. and see what she has to say about that," O'Keefe said.

O'Keefe waved Callahan back to the curb and once he was a safe distance away he tried the bell again. With Mister Osborne subdued they could hear the distant clip-clop of the girl's patent leather witch boots returning. The locks rattled open one by one and the door swung open again. The same over made up face peered out.

"What now? I turned off my music," she said, rolling her eyes.

"We still need a little information from you for our report," O'Keefe said.

"Fine, right, *like whatever*. What do you need now?"

"Let's start with your name, and who else is in the house with you?" Helen asked.

She paused a long moment and stared at Helen blankly.

"Why do you need to know all that?" the girl asked.

"It's standard procedure. We need it for our reports," O'Keefe said, doing his best Joe Friday.

The girl just rolled her eyes again and seemed annoyed. "My name is Beatrix Bloodthorn, and I already told you that nobody else is here."

"Do you live here, Miss Bloodthorn?" Helen asked.

"No way! I live in the dorm over at USC. Like I said before, it's my grandma's house. I'm house-sitting for her." Beatrix said.

"Where is your grandmother now?" O'Keefe went on.

"She's visiting my aunt in Miami. Aunt Emma just had a new baby and Gramma went down to help out. I'm just staying here until she gets back, you know, to feed her cat and make this old mausoleum look lived in."

"Can we see some identification please?" O'Keefe asked.

"*Identification?* What do I need that for?"

"It's just routine," Helen said letting a little of her impatience show in her voice. Beatrix gave her a second glance and a flicker of nervousness flashed in her cognac-colored eyes. Helen pressed her attack before Beatrix could come up with another lie. "Any picture I.D. will do, a driver's license, state I.D. card, a school I.D. or even a bus pass. Anything that has your name and your picture on it."

Beatrix stared into Helen's eyes for a second before turning back to O'Keefe with a feigned smile.

"Sure thing, officer, anything you want. My driver's license is in my purse, all the way upstairs in my bedroom. Give me just a minute or two to go get it." Before O'Keefe could say anything else she slammed the door in his face and was resetting the locks.

"Move back away from the door a little, and be ready to move fast," O'Keefe said to Helen softly. "She's up to something."

"Really?...Whatever gave you that idea?" Helen said with no attempt to hide the sarcasm in her voice. Casually she popped the button on the restraining strap on her Beretta.

"You aren't going to need that," O'Keefe said sternly.

"You just said to be ready for anything."

"Yeah, but not too ready. Let's try not to shoot any minors tonight."

They both moved back from the door a few steps and strained to hear any murmurs from inside the house, but nothing stirred. Helen was sure she could hear the house itself creak and settle.

"Dean, Helen!" Callahan shouted from the sidewalk. "Quick, the garage!"

The house ran along the ridge of a hill, with its sprawling rooms spread out over several levels. The front doors opened to the central level a full story above the garage, which was at the lowest level right in the crook of the switchback.

O'Keefe and Wu vaulted over the ornamental railing around the porch and dropped directly onto the roof of the garage. They ran to the edge and dropped down to the curving driveway.

Helen was a bit lighter on her feet than O'Keefe, so she was a few seconds ahead of him, but because it was a longer drop to the ground for her it took her more time to recover.

Inside the garage was an immense, gloss black, 1972 Cadillac Fleetwood. Inside the Fleetwood was a young man of about twenty-two. His dingy blond hair was cut in a curly mullet, and he was wearing a faded AC/DC T-shirt with the sleeves cut off and leather bands with chrome spikes on both wrists. He was desperately trying to start the old car, but the battery had shuffled off this mortal coil sometime during the Nixon administration.

The battery was so flat that it didn't even have enough power left to work the door locks. This left a sultry blonde girl of about seventeen struggling with the door handle on the passenger side. She was dressed in a black wife beater and skintight black leggings decorated with red pentagrams.

Beatrix herself was coming out of the interior door to the house carrying a beautifully lacquered walnut box about

144

twice the size of a bread-box. When she saw Helen hit the ground she hurled the heavy wooden box at her and turned back into the house. Beatrix threw like a girl, and the box only made it about five feet then hit the concrete and burst open. Gold and jewelry was strewn across the dusty floor.

The Blonde looked up in time to see Helen go for her Beretta as she stood up. Before Helen could break leather the blonde turned and ran back into the house on Beatrix's stiletto heels. The boy rolled out of the car and half ran half crawled toward the house. Keeping the car between him and Helen the whole time.

O'Keefe landed with a thud and came up with his old Model 19 in hand just as the boy reached the threshold. The boy turned back and fumbled at his waist for an instant.

O'Keefe yelled "Drop the gun!"

Helen didn't wait. But she had a bad angle and the car was still partly blocking the shot. Two slugs tore into the door jam and one sailed on into the room beyond. Splinters spewed into the boy's shoulder and caused him to lose his grip on the weapon snagged in the waistband of his black jeans. The Luger pulled free and spun out of his grasp, over the old car and clattered across its roof top, down the windshield and across the sprawling hood. After Helen's shots the boy was not even remotely interested in recovering the gun. He disappeared into the house.

O'Keefe and Wu charged into the garage. They took up positions against the wall on each side of the door with weapons drawn.

Because Callahan had caught the gunfire on film, Helen would be continually teased by other cops for years to come about shooting the gun out of the kid's hand, even though she hadn't. Callahan dashed into the garage and squatted by the front fender of the big car with his camera up ready to shoot.

"Stay in the garage, Lewis," O'Keefe said in a stage whisper. He counted down from three and led Helen through the door into the dark house.

While Callahan was waiting in the garage he took a moment and photographed the Luger, careful to get the hood ornament in the composition. He took a couple close-ups of the bullet holes in the door frame then something caught his eye. It took him a moment to understand what he was looking at. But his overdeveloped sense of aesthetics could not pass it over.

The garage was as neat as a pin. It was likely that no one had been in there since the last time the Cadillac was driven. Tools were hung by size on pegs over a work bench and everything was in its place. Except a pile of half-thawed frozen food packages and freezer-burned cuts of meat still in their cellophane packages, all sprawled out across the work bench surrounded by a gradually expanding puddle of pink water.

Next to the work bench a deep freezer hummed softly in the semi-darkness. Then the last detail hit home. A scrap of gauzy pink silk dangled out of the freezer. Callahan knew better, but the silk beckoned him.

He stood slowly and crossed the floor almost in a trance. He paused when he touched the cool metal top of the casket-like freezer. He lightly stroked the silk with his fingertips then took a deep breath. With both hands he opened the lid and gasped.

"Holy Norma Desmond, Batman!"

Regan Ryan-Reilly had played her last scene.

It was difficult to say whether Beatrix Bloodthorn was a runaway or an escapee. She had come from a loving, middle-class family of good Catholics and had never been abused or mistreated in any way. Then, she had been called Grace Mathers. At the age of ten she began to develop a fixation with horror movies. Grace became obsessed with the works of Joan Barley, Stephen King, and H.P. Lovecraft. By the time she was thirteen she had started dressing "goth." Her parents hoped it was just a phase she was going through, and she would grow out of it in time.

Then there was the pregnancy scare. At the tender age of fourteen she demanded that her Catholic parents arrange an abortion for her because she was "knocked up," as she so delicately put it. The main thing she learned from the incident was that performing fellatio on a middle-aged man while he drove her home from a babysitting job did not cause pregnancy, even if she did swallow.

The Mathers loved their daughter unconditionally, no matter how troubled or rebellious she became. They tried everything in their power to help her. The first thing they tried was to arrange counseling with the family's priest. That was a catastrophic failure. Grace was by then so engrossed in her fantasy world of vampires and Satanic rituals that she imagined she would gain magical powers from seducing a priest. She routinely exposed herself to Father Windsor in each therapy session in a crude attempt to entice him. Father Windsor had no interest in having sex with a teenage girl, a failing Grace always attributed to her not being a pre-teenage boy. But because of her crude attempts to seduce him, the priest refused to continue. Father Windsor felt a female, secular psychiatrist would be better suited to helping Grace than he would. That didn't work out much better.

After only two sessions, Doctor Nancy Bradley diagnosed Grace as being bipolar. Doctor Bradley prescribed the mood-stabilizing medication lithium to control Grace's manic episodes. It seemed to be working. But after a few weeks Grace secretly quit taking the pills.

What Doctor Bradley failed to take into account in her zeal to earn her commission on prescription sales was that Grace liked her manic episodes. When she was up, she was really up. It was the ultimate high, far more powerful than any drug. The world around Grace became more real to her. She felt like "Look Ma, top of the world," A-number-one head bitch in charge of everything. The most mundane things became hyper-intense. Colors were more vibrant, sounds more penetrating, emotions more tangible. And when she was down she was really down, in the depths of despair, at the bottom of a dark well, end of life on Earth down. But, at least the despair was real, not a drug-induced haze.

To Grace it was a fair trade-off. A far better way to live than the unreal void the lithium left her in. Even at rock bottom the intensity of her depression was far more valid than the dull gray artificial state the pills left her in. So, she quit taking them and tried hard to hide her symptoms.

Just after Grace turned fifteen came the final crisis for the Mathers. They were faced with an almost impossible choice. Their younger daughter, thirteen-year-old Hope, staggered into the neighbor's house, covered in blood and collapsed on the kitchen floor. They called 911 and she was rushed to the hospital. After her stomach was pumped and a broken arm was set, the details of what had happened came to light.

When the Mathers were out, Grace had ground up some of the lithium she had hoarded and put it in Hope's lunch. As Hope began to lose consciousness, Grace told her that she needed her to perform a virgin sacrifice in order to awaken her master, sleeping Cthulhu. Sometime later, Hope awoke lying on a plastic tarp in the attic of their home. A butcher's knife was lying on a makeshift altar at her feet. Hope tried to get out but the door was locked and there was no key. Even in her drugged state Hope knew that this was not some cruel teenage prank to frighten her. Her crazy sister was actually going to slit her throat and drink her blood. Hope lacerated her hands badly when she smashed out the attic window and broke her arm jumping from the roof to the back yard below.

Grace's illness had led to serious criminal acts. The state of California wanted to put Grace in juvenile hall for assault and attempted murder. Worst of all, she was putting Hope in danger. The Mathers had to face every parent's cruelest nightmare; they had to choose between Grace and Hope. After facing some extraordinarily hard facts and spending almost all of the family's savings on lawyers, they got Grace placed in a "rehabilitation center for troubled teens" in the Santa Monica hills.

But Grace was not even remotely interested in rehabilitation. The way she saw it, she did not need to be rehabilitated; she was not a drug user. In fact, she was incarcerated because she refused to use drugs. She was a victim of her parent's repressive religion. They were oppressing her for her spiritual beliefs, just like the Wiccan of Salem were unjustly persecuted. And like the Wiccan of

Salem she too would be crucified if she did not escape from their Christian totalitarianism.

Beatrix Bloodthorn's cellmate was an eighteen-year-old hooker and junkie named Janet Gordon. Janet went by the street name Lilly Carlo. At first, Lilly didn't want to hear anything Beatrix had to say. Lilly had troubles of her own. But after a couple of weeks together Lilly began to open up.

Lilly knew all the ins and outs of the street. She had learned them all the hard way. Just after her eleventh birthday her mother's boyfriend *du jour*, with the assurance that she was the best French kisser in the whole trailer park, traded her to his pusher for some heroin. It didn't take Crawfish very long to get her completely strung out on heroin too and turning tricks to feed her habit.

She was fourteen the first time she was busted. But because it was an election year, the judge was inclined to demonstrate how tough he was on street crime. He gave her the maximum sentence under the law, six months in Juvenile Hall.

Once Lilly was securely locked up in Central Juvenile Hall it became apparent to the staff that she was a junkie. She was forced into detox and then rehab programs whether she wanted them or not.

Like most girls in her position, as soon as she was out, she went straight back to Crawfish and heroin and the life. The first day she was out she was turning tricks and fixing.

This story would repeat itself again and again with no change for the next three years. Lilly had lost count of how many times she had gone around on the carousel until everything changed. Some Bloods decided they were going to take Crawfish's territory. As luck would have it, that night she was working the corner of Sepulveda and Plummer in front of the junior high school, when Crawfish came by to make collections. She had had a slow night and Crawfish thought she was trying to hold out on him. He started to slap her around a little and she panicked. She tried to run, but it was hard to run on five-inch heels when you're high. Lilly tripped and fell behind the bench of the bus stop just as the neon red Lincoln Continental Mark III screeched up to the curb and two teenage Bloods opened fire with an AK-47 and a Calico M950. Crawfish was shot 26 times before his dead body hit the pavement.

One of the other girls from Crawfish's stable heard Jazz, Crawfish's homie, was convinced the only reason Lilly wasn't killed too was that she had set Crawfish up. Jazz didn't care that she had only survived the shooting by pure bullshit luck. Or that she didn't know shit about what was going down that night. All Jazz knew was the code of the street, and that said Lilly had to die for setting Crawfish up.

With nowhere else to go in the world, Lilly found Detective Bell, one of the most obvious undercover cops in the vice squad. She let Bell pick her up and explicitly offered to fuck him for fifty bucks. It was an open and shut case and she was back in Central Juvenile Hall in forty-eight hours flat.

Janet "Lilly" Gordon turned eighteen in Central Juvenile Hall. Her only birthday present was a choice from the state of California: she could go on to CIW Frontera, or she could go into rehab. Fearing that Jazz might have home girls in Frontera she chose rehab. And that was where she met Beatrix.

Even though Lilly thought Beatrix was a straight J-cat from the first day, she was smart, and she could talk people into almost anything. So, when Beatrix came up with an escape plan Lilly was down with it.

Again, Beatrix saved up her pills, this time she put them in some pruno she made with the oranges she got in her sack lunches. Once the homemade hooch was fermented she let one particular night orderly catch her and Lilly drinking when he came to do the nightly bed checks. All the girls knew that Lee Winchell was a total pervert, and that they could get anything they wanted from him as long as they were willing to....cooperate.

Beatrix and Lilly let Winchell think all they were up to was getting drunk. But drinking in rehab was against the rules. So, Beatrix offered to share with Winchell if he promised not to tell on them. They didn't have to share much, the drugged pruno kicked in before Winchell could do much more then get Beatrix's t-shirt off. Once he was zonked out on the floor he was at Beatrix's mercy, not the other way around. They used their bed sheets to tie Winchell to their racks. The next shift found him in the morning, hung over, dehydrated, sick-as-a-dog and stripped naked. By that afternoon, Winchell considered himself lucky to just be looking for a new career, and not facing criminal charges himself.

Using his keys the girls were out of the "hospital" with no real troubles at all. The most difficult part of their escape came in the employee parking lot. It took them some trial and error to locate Winchell's burgundy 1977 Oldsmobile Cutlass. They abandoned the Cutlass in the parking lot of a taco stand in Chatsworth and made their way up into the park.

Carl Walsh had been the caretaker for Chatsworth Park North since 1968. He had acquired so much seniority that he would have had to burn the park to the ground and salt the ashes in order to be fired. So as long as he managed to keep the park relatively tidy, his superiors overlooked a little on-the-job drinking or an occasional overnight guest. Lilly said that Old Carl, the park's caretaker, would let them crash at his place for a while. All they had to do was keep his buzz going and maybe a little hand job now and then. He was perpetually too loaded and too old to be able to do much more than that. Besides, after they had been there a day or two, he would begin to believe that they actually lived there.

As long as Beatrix and Lilly kept Carl comfortably numb, they had a place to stay, and they had their run of the park. It didn't take Beatrix long to find the abandoned church in the foothills. It was the perfect place to hold her Black Mass. As soon as word began to spread around the neighborhood about Beatrix the teenage witch, heshers and lodies with dark daydreams about being vampires and warlocks made their way to the "Church of Darkness." As more and more disenfranchised teens began to drift in, Beatrix's devotions to sleeping Cthulhu evolved into full-scale, drug-fueled orgies, with her as high priestess.

Most of the park locals knew that Mark Coleman could lay his hands on copious amounts of weed and it didn't take long for Beatrix and Lilly to learn this too. Rumors about the mysterious source of his weed varied. Some said he was part of Solderin' Rod's gang of bad-asses. Some said he was with a certain motorcycle club, even though he drove an old battered Datsun mini-truck, not a Harley. After all, who else would be brazen enough to try and sell weed on Rod's turf. Others thought he was with the Colombians, even though he was as white as homogenized milk, and never had any coke, only grass. Either way, most of the guys gave him a wide berth just to be safe.

The truth was much more mundane. Mark Coleman was a nineteen-year-old community college dropout who worked for his father's pool maintenance business cleaning other people's pools. He was as meek as milquetoast. But Mark had a taste for getting high and partying with the cute stoner chicks in the park. He knew that not one of them was really into him at all, but he didn't care. He understood the basic fact of life that they only fucked him because he got them high. That was cool with him, he didn't give a shit about them either. All that mattered to him was that he got laid.

The mysterious source of his weed was it was all home-grown. Not his home, mind you, but the homes of his father's clients. It was a simple scam he had worked out. The straights that paid his dad to clean their pools never even looked at the pumps and other equipment that kept their pools clear and blue. So, in each house he put one or two pot plants behind the heaters and pumps.

As long as he kept his harvest small, he would have more than enough weed for his purposes. He wasn't trying to get rich or anything. He just wanted to get his party on with the slutty stoner chicks in the park. Until he met Beatrix.

With her it was lust at first sight. Mark couldn't get enough of her. When she began to demand more than just weed, the pressure was all on him. At first, he was able to lay his hands on a little acid, but only tiny amounts and the only guy he knew that had any blow wouldn't part with it on credit. He would trade a little coke for a shitload of grass, but Al wanted almost half his stash in exchange for just an

154

eight ball stepped on so many times that it gave him the runs.

Mark thought of Beatrix as his girlfriend, in spite of the fact she was fucking anyone and everyone that came to her ceremonies in the old church. Alone or in groups, boys or girls, she made no distinction. Mark needed to be important to her, he needed to be special to her, he needed to show her he was more of a man that any of the others. Mark needed cash to buy drugs to give to his girlfriend in order to keep her being his girlfriend.

He realized that the only way to get the money he needed was to turn to crime. He couldn't try robbery because he didn't have a gun, or the balls to use one, so he decided to try burglary. That seemed like a good idea at the time. He had a perfectly safe way of doing it too. He was in and out of the back yards of the rich and famous all over Beverly Hills and Santa Monica every day cleaning their pools. He was part of the scenery, just like the postman, nobody ever saw him. But he saw them, and he knew what houses would be the best targets.

One of Mark's pools belonged to the aging silent film star Regan Ryan-Reilly.

***

The garage door led into a finished basement guarded by the stench of mold and decay. Sometime in the Hoover administration, this room had been built to be a screening room but judging from the smell and deterioration no Hoover had been in the room since Lyndon Johnson occupied the Oval Office. The plush chairs were tattered and threadbare. Dusty old boxes were stacked as high as

Helen, and piles of old newspapers were bundled all around the room. It was a cop's nightmare, dark with a million places so set up an ambush.

To Helen's right was a flight of stairs that led up to the main level and they could hear the high heels cantering across the floor above like two coconuts being banged together. Rather than risk crossing the dark basement with its possible traps, they gave each other cover as they climbed the stairs.

Above was a large kitchen. Moonlight filtered in through a dingy window. The smell assaulted Wu's and O'Keefe's olfactory senses like a pit bull on the neighbor's toddler. Every counter space and tabletop was piled high with dirty dishes and rotten food. The droppings of rats trailed across the floor and counters. Paper bags full of long-spoiled groceries piled in heaps where delivery men had left them twitched when their occupants were disturbed by O'Keefe and Wu daring to enter their domain.

Helen was by nature compulsively clean, so the stench hit her harder than O'Keefe. It was so pungent that for a moment Helen gagged and was unable to keep up. O'Keefe hustled through to the next room, heedless of Wu's temporary incapacitation.

Unwilling to be left behind, Wu pressed on. The door led to a formal dining room that was no more tidy than the kitchen. Piles of old newspapers and magazines mixed with the ghosts of meals past rolled off the table and spread across the floor forming the habitat for brazen rodents. An open set of double doors led out into a massive great room beyond. Helen was anxious to get into a larger space to escape the stench.

Helen was reminded of the *Munster's* living room. It was huge with high ceilings and had at one time been sumptuously furnished. But time and vermin had taken their tolls. Light from the street dimly filtered through tattered drapes. An elaborate grand staircase led up to the floors above. Opposite that was the entry hall with its marble floors and a grime-caked chandelier over the heavy front door.

At the front door, the saucy blonde girl in the skintight black pants was desperately struggling with the five locks and numerous sliding bolts. The idiot boy with the mullet that had dropped his Luger was beside her trying to help. But in his panic, all he managed to do was refasten the locks as fast as she opened them.

Helen held her place in the doorway. *Where the hell is that witchy chick? And where is O'Keefe?*

"Good of you to join us, *sow*," Beatrix said from the darkness off to Helen's right. "Lilly, Mark, leave the fucking door alone and come over here." O'Keefe emerged from the shadows with his revolver held over his head. Beatrix's slim body was half hidden behind his girth, but Helen could see she had an old-fashioned Smith and Wesson Lemon Squeezer pressed into the small of his back. The little .32 break-top revolver was so outdated that Helen had never actually seen one in person before.

"All right, piggy, drop the gun and kick it over there," she said. O'Keefe slowly lowered his right hand to his waist and dropped his .357 on the floor with a soft thud. He put his hands back up and kicked the gun. It looked like a bad kick because the gun spun around on its side and only traveled about three feet from him, well within his reach if he made a sudden dive. Helen also knew he had a little .38

157

in an ankle holster and a .32 ACP Derringer in his shirt pocket as a holdout.

"That's the Poppa Pig. Now for the little baby piggy. Drop it, slope," Beatrix said.

Visions of onion fields danced through Helen's head. Even though she had her Model 36 in her back pocket she was unwilling to give up her primary weapon. She brought her Beretta up and pointed it between Beatrix's irresistible, cognac-colored eyes.

"No," Helen said bluntly.

Helen didn't blink. She had a clear shot. She could put three rounds through that pretty face before Vampirella knew what hit her. The first time Helen had pointed a gun at another living person was at the tender age of fourteen. She had mistaken her sister's boyfriend for a burglar. The feeling of immense power she got from having total control over another human being was intoxicating. But actually shooting someone was entirely different. In fact, it had been something of a letdown. When she shot Hinckley and Ross, she felt *nothing*. It was no more than swatting a fly. No thrill, no high, no feeling of god-like power. But no guilt either. No sense of loss or regret, or the tiniest bit of remorse. She felt nothing at all. Not even the satisfaction of making a particularly difficult shot. Her only reward was a tedious pile of paperwork, endless review hearings and the constant badgering of the press.

It would be as easy as pie to take out Beatrix with one shot. Pop, all over. Beatrix had the little .32 pressed into the small of O'Keefe's back, it was right into the center of his vest. In the unlikely event that taking a 9mm right between those bedroom eyes caused her to clench her fist and fire the gun, the relatively weak round didn't stand the slightest chance of penetrating O'Keefe's armor. Judging from the way the nickel plating was flaking off the frame of the antique it was just as likely to blow up in her hand, if it even fired at all. Just a twitch of Helen's finger and it would all be over.

The 5150, cop-talk for nutcase, did have a gun in O'Keefe's back, and it was one of the unwritten laws of street cops that they could not let anyone get away with that. It had to be understood by everyone on the street that if a punk pulled a gun on a cop there would be consequences. It was more than respect, it was self-preservation. If they let just one punk get away with it, then it would be open season on cops all over LA. And because the teeny-bopper had pulled a gun Helen could justify the shooting. Legally she was free to take the shot. But it wasn't as black and white as all that. Did this twist deserve to die today?

Helen stared into Beatrix's eyes. This decision was not just whether to end the life of one messed-up kid. It was also about the direction her own life would take from this point on. If the brass upstairs had assigned her to the SWAT team where she belonged, she would never have to make a decision like this. In SWAT she would be facing enemies that were her equal, not desperate, teenage girls backed into a corner with nothing but an antiquated pea-shooter between her and oblivion.

It would be easy to blow this kid's pretty little brains out—real easy. Helen began to understand if she did shoot this youngster, it would be even easier to shoot the next one, and the one after that, and the one after that. It would get far too easy to just blow their drug-addled brains out and go for coffee and maybe one of those nice cinnamon buns she liked so much.

Helen also knew that with Callahan sniffing around at her heels, the press would be all over this. What a news story that would be, *Female, Asian-American, LAPD officer Helen Wu has been involved in her third fatal shooting in just six short weeks. This time the victim was a sixteen-year-old honor student at Bela Lugosi high school, who was innocently holding a Bible study group in her Grandmother's home when officers forced their way in and began indiscriminately shooting.*

There was no way around it; there would be no taking the easy way out this time. Helen had to find some way to take this kid alive.

"I fucking mean it, Noodle Nigger, drop the fucking gun or I'll drill him."

"Go ahead, I never liked him anyway," Helen said.

"Wu, this is no time to play cute. Do what she says," O'Keefe said.

"I'm not playing. Drop your gun, or I will kill this pig where he stands."

"Go right ahead, and you'll be dead before his body hits the floor. The only reason you don't already have a sucking chest wound is he is in my way. He's always in my way."

"Wu, have you completely lost your mind?" O'Keefe said.

"Here's how it is. If you shoot him, then I get to kill you, and both of them. Which is kind of a shame because your friend there has a nice ass. But you know how it is, I can't leave any witnesses around."

"What are you talking about?" Beatrix said, completely baffled by Helen's attitude.

"My promotion, silly girl. You shoot him, then I shoot you, and her, and him, and anybody else handy, and I'm a

160

hero. But it only works if I'm the sole survivor. That way there's no one to contradict my story."

"Story? What story?"

"Oh, big, brave O'Keefe threw himself in front of a bullet meant for me. He gave his life in the line of duty to save mine. He'll get a posthumous commendation and maybe even a medal they can pin on his coffin. In the wake of his epic sacrifice, I had to kill every last motherfucker in this room. You die, he dies, she dies, they die, everybody dies! Except me. So, hurry up and shoot him so I can get on with the fun," Helen said like a child talking about a trip to her favorite playground.

"You'll never get away with it, Wu," O'Keefe said through gritted teeth. He thought he was catching on, or at least he hoped he was. She was trying to do the old good cop, bad cop routine (well good cop, raving homicidal psychotic cop routine). He tried to play along.

"Well, are you going to shoot him for me or not? We don't have all night, you know," Helen said. "The way I see it, you don't have any choice now. And just between you and me, Sweetie, I kinda' like shooting people, and I don't care too much who I get to shoot one way or the other. As long as I get to shoot somebody."

"You still have a choice. But there's only one way for you to get out of this alive," O'Keefe said, his voice fatherly and reassuring. "If you give me the gun, right now, she can't get away with shooting you, or anybody else. Just give me the gun and that crazy little bitch can't hurt you or your friends."

"Don't listen to him Bea, their tryin' to trick us. She hasn't got the guts to shoot," Lilly said.

"It's a good thing blondes are cute, because they're really stupid. You just try me and see if I don't pop your pretty little airhead," Helen said without looking back.

"She means it! She'll do it! Just look into her eyes, she's crazier than a shit house rat. You can see it in her face. Give him the gun Beatrix, it's the only way we're getting out of this alive," Mark said.

"I will remember you said that, Bleach Boy," Helen said.

Beatrix's big brown eyes seemed to grow even bigger, and her pale skin got even paler. Her eyes darted from Helen to Lilly and back. She swallowed hard and began to tremble. For the first time since Lilly and Colman had known Beatrix, Grace came to the surface.

Lilly knew that after what she and Beatrix had done to Winchell, neither one of them was going back to a country club rehab. They were both going directly upstate. That may have been okay for Beatrix; as nuts as she was, they'd put her in a rubber room anyway, but the pen meant Jazz's home-girls would be waiting to put a shank in her back the first chance they got. Lilly was not going down without a fight. Beatrix let the little revolver roll backward in her hand, the butt came up in front and she let O'Keefe take the weapon.

O'Keefe took the grips of the Lemon Squeezer with his left hand and seized Beatrix's wrist with his right. With the finesse of a dancer he twisted her arm around behind her back until she thought it would snap off.

Coleman broke and ran for the grand stairs. Seeing her only chance to get away, Lilly dove for O'Keefe's model 19 like a ball player coming in for home plate on a tie-breaking score in the final game of the series. Helen knew that gun was well maintained and would fire its .38 special jacketed hollow points quite proficiently if Lilly got ahold of it.

Helen pulled up her Beretta in her right hand, took one long stride toward the blonde and brought the steel toe of her right boot up into Lilly's rib cage as her body, already halfway to the weapon, stretched out horizontally above the floor. As Helen followed through with the kick, she could hear ribs cracking through the girl's abundant frontal padding. All of the breath was evacuated from Lilly's lungs as she was lifted off the floor. She dropped on her side, with a wet thud, unable to even gasp.

Helen had not been in a physical fight since she was in high school, and she lost that one. So, she was not inclined to let her opponent recover. A second blow with her left foot to Lilly's jaw sent three teeth skittering across the floor and left her unconscious.

O'Keefe unceremoniously smashed Beatrix face down on the grimy floor, breaking her delicate nose in the process, and added a lovely set of chrome bracelets to her wrists.

Helen took a step backward from Lilly's unconscious form and resisted the temptation to kick the bitch again.

Helen snapped the Beretta back on target. "Halt! Or I will shoot!" It was the first time she had raised her voice since they had entered the house. Even though she was shouting her voice was still a monotone. Colman stopped halfway up the stairs with his hands up. He sank to his knees without even being told and began to moan incoherently.

"Nooo! Don't shoot me, man. We didn't do it. I swear she was dead before we even got here."

"Hands on your head. Come down the stairs and lay face down right there." Helen said, all business now.

O'Keefe hurried over and recovered his revolver. Then he cuffed and searched Coleman.

O'Keeffe was angry and embarrassed. He let a teenage girl get the drop on him, and to add insult to injury it happened in front of Wu. More damaging to his ego, she saved him. He was furious with Wu, but he didn't dare take it out on her because even though he thought that the whole "shoot everybody in the room" thing was an act, he was not completely sure. This made him want to vent his rage all the more, preferably on someone's face. Wu knocked out the blonde with the nice ass, he already busted Beatrix's nose, so that left the sniveling punk that tried to draw down on him in the garage. But a good old-fashioned ass whooping wasn't possible with Callahan's camera snapping away. A little flashlight therapy would make O'Keefe feel a lot better, but it would have to wait for some other time.

While Wu cuffed and patted down the blonde, O'Keefe grabbed Coleman by the back of his mullet and shoved him across the room. The punk stumbled and fell face down. O'Keefe jammed his knee into the center of his back and yanked his arms back to put on the handcuffs.

"Is there anybody else in the house?" he demanded. The kid shook his head and whimpered something about "We didn't do it. She was already dead when we got here."

"Who? Who is dead?"

"The old lady, man."

"What old lady?"

"The one that lives here. Like I thought she was on vacation or something and we could, ya know, sorta party here for a day or two. We weren't hurtin' anybody."

O'Keefe looked around him again. Wu seemed to be under control and the suspects were contained. He didn't think that there was anybody else in the house, but you never could tell. The place was such a labyrinth he didn't want to risk a search. There would be a million places to hide, and he had already been caught flat-footed once tonight, he wasn't going to push his luck.

"Wu, can the blonde stand?" he said as he shined his flashlight into the dark shadows around them. The room was filled with stacks of old newspapers, books and fashion magazines dating back to the sixties.

"An ammonia capsule should be able to motivate her," Wu said as she fished one out of her Sam Brown.

"Good. Let's get them outside. I'm not taking another step into this death trap without backup."

Helen nodded and said nothing. She knelt down in front of Lilly and broke the glass capsule under her nose. Lilly gagged, choked, and spit up one more broken tooth, but she came around all right. With just a little "coaxing" from the officers the handcuffed teens were led out of the house through the garage.

Callahan was beside himself when they came out.

"Dean, you gotta see this!' he said, sounding like a small child wanting to show his father he learned to tie his shoelaces.

"Not now, Lewis. Did you see where the gun fell?" O'Keefe said, sloughing him off.

"Yeah, it's on the hood of the Caddy here. But forget about that, this is more important."

"You didn't touch it did you?" Helen asked as she guided the blonde away from the Luger on the car.

"No, of course not, but look at this over here." Callahan was almost jumping up and down with excitement.

The cops led the three teens across the driveway and down to the curb at the bottom.

"Dean you've got to see this," Callahan persisted.

"Lewis, shut the fuck up. I'm busy now. Just give me a minute, all right."

Helen stood at the end of the driveway watching the suspects as O'Keefe began talking into the radio microphone on his shoulder in a stream of code. He requested back up officers to help them secure the area and an ambulance to take the injured suspects to the hospital for treatment.

"You'll need the coroner too," Callahan said abruptly when O'Keefe finished.

"What?" O'Keefe said, doing a double take.

"Regan Ryan-Reilly is in the fridge in the garage."

***

After O'Keefe had a look in the deep freeze, he called in a potential homicide, and within an hour the place was swarming with cops and the press. Because O'Keefe and Wu thought the suspects were all underage, Dick Valley from the Juvenile division was the first detective to show up. Valley worked hand in glove with the D.A's office and had made a reputation for never letting the truth interfere with a conviction. But even in this one, he was disappointed.

Valley saw himself as the next Vincent Bugliosi and this case had everything a publicity–seeking bootlicker like Valley needed to make his career. It had guns, sexy teenage rehab escapees, a satanic sex cult, and even a dead movie star in a freezer. But his hopes were dashed when the coroner revealed Regan Ryan-Reilly died of natural causes.

166

In his first interrogation, Mark Coleman refused to say anything that could implicate his beloved Beatrix Bloodthorn in any crime. She was his one true love, and he would give his life and liberty to protect her honor. In response to that, Valley showed Colman, age nineteen, one Grace Mathers' birth certificate.

"Ask your cell mates what happens to guys that molest seventeen-year-old girls," Valley said, as he stood up to walk out.

Colman spilled his guts. He told all about his pot business and how he met the girls. How the bewitching Beatrix Bloodthorn cast a spell on him with her mystical powers to make him break into the homes on his pool-cleaning route to steal for her.

Coleman picked the Ryan-Reilly house because he saw the newspapers and mail were piling up and assumed that she had gone on a vacation. Sure no one was on the premises, he broke in and lifted some jewelry. When Beatrix and Lilly saw it, they had to know where it came from. Beatrix wouldn't let up until he finally took them out to the house on Morgan Hill Drive.

But once they were in the place, Beatrix wanted it all. Everything. She started going through room after room searching for valuables. That's how they found the old guns. They were hidden in a false bottom of a desk drawer.

The only problem was the smell. The whole place reeked. Coleman just assumed the stench came from the filthy kitchen. But Lilly said it was from upstairs, and she was right. They found the mortal remains of Regan Ryan-Reilly in her bed, stinking like a dead cat.

Beatrix was delighted by the find. She thought that with the old lady dead they didn't need to rob the house, they could just move in. It was certainly nicer than the abandoned church, and they wouldn't have to blow Old Uncle Carl any more just to keep a roof over their heads. All they had to do was take the stiff down to that freezer in the garage so it wouldn't keep stinking up the place, and maybe open some windows to air it out. And that's when the cops showed up and ruined everything.

Regan Ryan-Reilly was interred three days later at Forest Lawn in the plot next to her mother and her sister. Mark Coleman was too stupid to have worked out a deal for testifying against the girls so he was convicted of burglary, grand theft, possession of a stolen firearm, and assaulting a police officer. After six years in CDC Soledad, he graduated to real crime.

The girls were sent to separate facilities. While in Sybil Brand, waiting for trial, Lilly learned that Jazz had been killed in a gang dispute and no one was waiting to jump her in the shower at CIW Frontera. She became a model prisoner, found Jesus and was back on the streets in three years.

Because of her psychological issues, Grace Mathers was incarcerated at the Menlo Park Veterans Hospital for further treatment. She escaped again years later and found her way to Arizona, where she took up residence on an Indian reservation. Under the assumed name of Dark Moon Rising, she made costume jewelry and sold it to tourists.

Lewis Callahan continued to eke out a living shooting weddings and portraits.

Wu and O'Keefe were none the better for the experience, but none the worse either. Even though O'Keefe would never be entirely convinced that Wu was putting on an act. It was just another night on the job for them.

The Lost Job

1990

Friday, August 10, 1990

That olive green wagon was on a mission. It clearly knew where it was going, and it was in a hurry to get there. It was going way too fast and made too many turns to be lost.

Lieutenant Colonel Steve "Hannibal" Utley of the sixty-ninth Special Operations Unit watched the civilian vehicle turn off the access road onto the hidden driveway that led up to the armory through his field glasses. Undercover cars were always the same; they were either Crown Vics or station wagons, and they were always brown, dark tan, or pea green. The real give away was the lack of wheel covers. Even when they were smart enough to take off radio antennas and the spotlights they never put a cover over the black pressed steel rims. The dark green station wagon was obviously an unmarked government vehicle. it might as well have had said "POLICE" on the side and had a light bar on top. That car had to be the FBI, or CIA, or maybe even NSA. The feds were on to them.

With only days left to zero hour, he hated to abandon the operation now and go back on the run with Lieutenant Colonel Crouch. He and Tom had worked so hard to prepare Operation White Dragon that he just couldn't walk away without knowing how their security had been breached. That meant interrogating the traitor driving that car.

***

Amy Dresden slammed the door of her baby-shit-green '72 Vista Cruiser so hard that the sun visor fell open. The jolt was too much for the brittle old rubber band holding all the business cards, receipts, snapshots and other miscellaneous junk. They fluttered down on her like confetti. She pounded her fists against the steering wheel and made a sound not unlike a cat stuck in a washing machine. How could she have been so stupid?

It was a good part, that's how, and it would have led to other parts too. It wasn't exactly Blanche DuBois but it was a speaking part. Okay, her only lines were asking the sheriff if he wanted to come inside the saloon, have a drink and maybe take her upstairs before he shot it out with the outlaw. But it was screen time opposite the star of the picture. She would even have had a close up, and a real screen credit.

But the sleazeball director decided at the last minute that all the women in the saloon had to be topless. He didn't even have the courtesy to say it to her face. After sitting around all day waiting for her scene in full costume, the director's cowardly assistant came into the makeup trailer and whispered to the wardrobe woman.

The next thing Amy knew was the wardrobe mistress was telling all the girls in the bar seen to strip down to corsets, stockings and bare breasts. When Amy refused to grin and bear, it she was fired on the spot.

Amy over-cranked the ignition and the starter motor made a noise much like the one she had just made. It wasn't good to drive angry. The last thing she wanted was to hit a rock on the dirt road and take off her oil pan or get stuck in a ditch. It was well over thirty miles back to LA. She tightened her fingers around the steering wheel, took a deep breath, and let it out slowly.

She should have known better. It was always like that in this business, especially with independent films like this one. If the producer didn't expect her to put out at the auditions, the director would eventually want her to put out in front of the camera. Talent didn't enter into it, casting always came down to just two things and whether or not she was willing to put them on display.

She put the car in gear and glanced in the rearview mirror before backing up. On the opposite side parking lot, glittering bright red even through the thick layer of dust from the dirt road that led to the shooting location was the director's shiny new Mercedes-Benz SL convertible. Ever so slowly she eased her foot off the brake pedal. The 455-cubic-inch Oldsmobile engine was notorious for jumping off the line if she wasn't careful. The crunch of crumpling fender and tinkle of breaking glass from the Nazi war machine was at least a small consolation for refusing to deploy her own airbags.

"Whoopsie."

She didn't even bother to get out and look at the damage. She knew good and well that the huge steel bumper of her early 70s land yacht gave better than it got. That's what bumpers were for after all. Only the lack of a paved surface prevented her from burning rubber as she launched out of the parking area. She turned the wheel straight and punched it, kicking up rooster tails of dust behind her and showering the little roadster with dirt and gravel.

That will take some time to buff out.

She knew she was going too fast for the dirt road, but she didn't care. The dust cloud she was raising would hang in the air for at least an hour and cause the director of photography to rush his precious Panaflex Platinum cameras into the trailer to protect them from the grit. That would set the shooting schedule back at least two hours. It was mean and evil, but so was suddenly forcing her and the other extras to go topless or be fired.

The dust and her rage had another consequence she hadn't even counted on. Because of the loss of visibility, she became confused on the maze of back roads leading in and around Vasquez Rocks Natural Area. After an hour of driving aimlessly in circles, she found herself on a dirt path that was more like a horse trail than a road. It seemed to be heading in the opposite direction to where she wanted to go.

She slowed down a little; after all, it wouldn't do to get stuck. Especially way the hell out here in the back of beyond. There was no way a tow truck would come all the way out here to get her even if she could find a phone to call one. And how would she tell the driver where to go if she didn't have any idea where she was.

She passed through a cattle gate and took that as a good sign. That meant she was getting close to something

174

at least. She slowed to ten miles per hour. About a mile past the gate there was an old, sun-bleached, wooden barn.

At first glance the building looked abandoned, but the scrub grass had been beaten down into tire tracks leading up to the door. It didn't take Davy Crocket to see someone in a car was coming and going pretty regularly.

As much as she hated admitting she needed help to find her way back to the main road, she had to find someone, anyone, to tell her the way. At least as a woman she could admit she was lost and stop to ask for directions. A man would have driven halfway across Arizona before he stopped.

She parked about twenty feet from the big door. Mostly out of habit she slung her oversized bag over her shoulder and locked her car door before she approached. The main door to the barn was open just wide enough for a person to squeeze through without too much difficulty. Still, she tried knocking first. There was no answer. She stuck her head through the door and called out. Nothing.

After the glaring desert sun, the interior of the barn was almost pitch black. She slipped through the opening and stood there motionless while her eyes adjusted to the darkness. Gradually, shapes began to emerge from the shadows. First, sharp-edged white stripes where the sun forced its way between the boards of the walls made an abstraction of shapes in a herringbone pattern. Finally the shapes began to take familiar forms. There were empty stables along the walls, and rusty farm tools scattered all around, making the place seem abandoned.

Except. Thinking at first it was a mirage she blinked and rubbed her big blue eyes. It didn't make any sense at all. It was so out of place in this rustic setting that Amy had to

175

stare at it almost a full minute before she believed it wasn't a trick of the light. But one of those stripes of daylight cut through the gold and brown shield and illuminated the logo, u.p.s. all lower case.

What in the name of *Schweinepriester* was a UPS truck doing out here in the middle of nowhere? The back doors of the brown truck were open. Amy cautiously peered inside. She didn't know what she expected to find. But instead of piles of boxes to be delivered, the entire twenty-four-foot cargo space was filled with steel fifty-five-gallon drums.

Maybe it was some kind of special food for the livestock, she was after all in a barn, and the driver was off looking for the farmer to take delivery. But there weren't any animals in the barn. Maybe it was fertilizer, but she hadn't seen any crops either.

"Find any clues, Daphne? Drop the bag and turn around nice and slow."

There was no way she was going to drop her bag on the dirt floor. It was a genuine Coach bag, and even though she had bought it from an outlet store for a considerable discount, she still had to shell out two hundred and fifty dollars for it. She turned around very slowly and smiled.

"I'm so glad I finally found someone, I must have turned..." She fell silent when she saw the gun. The guy behind the gun was close to her age, give or take a year. He was dressed in an odd combination of civilian hunting gear and army surplus desert camouflage and some sort of khaki bullet proof vest with silver oak leaves on the collar. His skin was baked a dark brown from months under the desert sun. Amy dropped her expensive bag in the dirt.

"Kick it over here," he said without moving. As much as she liked her bag, she understood it wasn't worth her life.

"I didn't mean to trespass, I—"

"Don't try and bullshit me about trespassing. You know goddamn-good-and-well you can't set foot on private property without a warrant."

"A warrant? What are you—"

"Cute, *Them* sending in a pretty woman. Probably figured we wouldn't shoot a chick, huh? Who sent you? The FBI, ATF?"

"Nobody sent me, I'm just lost."

"Lost my ass. Who do you work for?"

"I don't work for anybody; as a matter of fact, I just got fired. I must have made a wrong turn in all the dust. I was just looking for someone to give me directions back to the road."

"Right. How dumb do you think we are? Hot babes like you don't go randomly wondering around in the desert poking into old barns. Steve and me'll get the truth out of you as soon as he gets here. In the meantime, hands against the van, feet apart." He gestured with the gun. She moved around to the side of the van turned her back and put her hands on the hot steel.

How could this be happening? Five minutes ago, her only problem was finding her way back to the road. Now this mouth breather was going to feel her up. Why did every man she meet think he could do anything he wanted to her just because she was pretty? She couldn't let him get away with it any more than she could let the director force her into getting naked.

Not satisfied, he came up close behind her and hooked his foot around one of her ankles, forcing her to lean her entire weight against the truck. After he kicked her other foot out far enough to get her off balance, he stood close behind.

Amy glanced to her right so she could see what he was doing in the oversized side mirror of the delivery van. He stood between her outstretched feet with his left arm extended all the way holding onto the back of her neck. With his right hand he awkwardly worked the gun into a tan nylon holster strapped to his right thigh.

Once he had secured the pistol, he slid both hands around her torso and squashed her breasts like he was milking a cow. He lowered them and worked his way around her abdomen. Then back up across her chest again, double checking that she didn't have a .357 wedged in her bra. He obviously liked searching her chest. But there was little she could do as long as he kept her off balance and leaning against the truck.

His hands went south, across the Mason-Dixon Line, and did a quick once over of all six pockets of her cargo shorts. Finding nothing he did a little more exploring. His right hand found its way to her crotch and lingered there.

It was clear where this was going if she didn't do something about it. Amy gritted her teeth and forced herself to endure the groping. As much as his touch appalled her, she had to go along with it.

"I bet you like that, don't you?" he grunted. "If you like this, just wait till Steve-reamer gets here." He pressed his groin against her butt and started to dry hump her. With his left hand he began to unbutton her shorts.

"Are all feds this slutty, or is it just you?"

Amy exhaled sharply and doubled over. Years of aerobics had made her so limber that reaching between her legs and grabbing his ankles was no problem for her. With a quick flex of her knees for added lift, she yanked his feet out from under him.

He fell backward like Buster Keaton in a tornado. She turned counterclockwise and crushed his tiny teepee with her left heel. The crippling pain made him curl up into a ball on his left side gasping for breath. She had the advantage for now but it wouldn't last long. If he was able to get back on his feet he was not going to be in a forgiving mood.

As he writhed in agony, Amy ripped the handgun from his holster, took three steps back, and pointed it at her attacker with both hands. She just stood there.

"I should blow your head off, you fucking pervert." But the gun did not fire. She clenched her teeth and tightened her grip on the gun so much that her knuckles turned white. The gun began to tremble in her hands, and sweat was making the black plastic stocks slippery. She adjusted her grip on the weapon and shifted her weight from one foot to the other. If she didn't shoot soon, he would be back on his feet.

"Or—I could shoot you in the leg, blow your knee cap off." She nodded. "That wouldn't kill you, but you would just have to lay there and suffer until the cops came and got you."

The gun was getting heavy, and hot. But she just could not make herself do it.

"Maybe not the knee though. I could shoot you in the leg, so you can't get away until the cops can come and get you." *I could do that, just wound him. That way the police could take him to jail and make sure he never tries to rape anybody ever again.* She pointed the gun at his calf. *What if I hit an artery and he bleeds to death before they get here? I still don't know where the hell I am...*

Her attacker's groans began to subside. She lowered the muzzle of the gun a little and looked around her.

"I suppose I could tie you up."

Still gasping for breath, he rolled over on to his stomach and started to get up to his elbows and knees.

"Oh no, you don't." Without any hesitation she made a running start and kicked him so hard in the ribs that his body was lifted off the floor. She was convinced she felt ribs crack before he collapsed face first into the dirt, wheezing for breath.

He had attacked her and was obviously planning to rape her, at least. If she didn't do something, he would eventually realize that she couldn't bring herself to kill him, and he would attack her again. She had been able to take him by surprise before because he was preoccupied with groping her, but he wouldn't fall for that again, and if she couldn't bring herself to use the gun, he had the advantage. She was tall and lean and remarkably strong for a woman, he had at least sixty pounds on her. She would be able to put up a good fight, but like the instructor in her self-defense class back home always said, "the only good fight is a fight you win."

I should at least tie him up. She looked around at the rusting tools and old farm implements decaying in the barn. There had to be some tack or bits of harness left she could use.

But she didn't dare turn her back on him to look for any, and the gun was gaining weight faster than Kirstie Alley at an all-you-can-eat buffet. Even with both hands, she could hardly hold it up anymore. She couldn't stand here all day kicking him every time he caught his breath until someone else showed up.

Until someone else showed up. Who exactly did she expect to show up out here in the middle of nowhere anyway, the U.S. Cavalry, or maybe Lassie? It wasn't as if anyone was out there looking for her. The police weren't exactly patrolling the neighborhood either. She was on her own in the middle of nowhere. Then it hit her. *Steve.* "Steve and me'll get the truth out of you as soon as he gets here," he had said. The groper was not alone.

It was time to go. Amy crab walked over to her good but somewhat dusty bag keeping the stainless steel anvil pointed in the groper's direction. Giving him a wide berth she made her way to the door.

Pressing her back to the door and pointing the gun at him, she listened just to be sure Steve, whoever he was, wasn't waiting out there for her. The only sound was the wind. She took a quick peek, then with the gun pointed ahead of her she squirmed through the gap and made a break for her Vista Cruiser.

As she ran, she kept her head up, eyes darting all around for any sign of Steve. When she got to the car she squatted down with her back to the front left tire and dug around in her purse for her elusive car keys with her right hand, still holding the gun in her left.

Phone book, wallet, compact, box of Kleenex, empty Tic-Tac dispenser, half a dozen of Ted's chipped guitar picks, a broken strand of fake pearls, one of the jade hoop earrings she had been looking for all last week, a packet of band-aids, old wadded up receipts, dried out ballpoint pens, and finally the car keys. Why was the thing she needed always at the very bottom under everything else?

Keys in hand, she took a deep breath, stood up and made one last scan of her surroundings. So far, no sign of the fabled Steve. Just as she jammed the key in the lock, it dawned on her. She had seen it as she ran to the car but hadn't realized it. All four tires were flat. She was desperate enough to try driving on four flats on a paved road but even with its monstrous 455-cubic-inch engine the Vista Cruiser wouldn't get ten feet on this rutted dirt road.

She looked back at the barn. He was still in there, and Steve, whoever he was, was coming. She was stuck here with both of them. She looked at the weapon in her hand. The deep blue finish made her reflection seem dark and sinister. Without being able to bring herself to use the gun, it was like an albatross around her neck. She considered throwing it away but didn't want to risk him getting it back. Even though she couldn't bring herself to use it, at least as long as she had it, he couldn't use it against her.

If she didn't want to end up with a starring role on *Unsolved Mysteries*, she was going to have to use it. She sank back down on her hunches with her back to the car door, holding the gun in both hands. Could she really do that? It was them or her, but could she actually bring herself to take a human life? Even if they were planning to rape and do god only knows what else to her.

How could this be happening? All she did was take one wrong turn off the road and she was in the middle of a life-and-death struggle for survival. All she had to do was take her shirt off and she would have been in the movie with her name, along with a couple of other things on screen and a paycheck big enough to make three month's rent. Would it really have been that bad? But what would she have told Ted or her father?

Was this the universe trying to tell her something? If she wasn't willing to sell her body and her self-respect, it would take them by force. For refusing to take money to exploit herself she was now stranded in a wasteland in a running gun battle with two loonies. Was letting someone see her boobs really worth all that? Was not flashing her tits for thirty seconds in a movie worth letting a couple of militia nut jobs rape and kill her?

A couple of militia nut jobs. A couple? She hadn't seen any proof that Steve existed. Maybe Romeo in the barn was alone and bluffing about the other guy to intimidate her. Or maybe there were more than just two? How many bullets were in this gun anyway? Six? No, that was for old-fashioned cowboy guns. This was an automatic. It could be as many as fifteen or twenty for all she knew.

She knew that there was a clip in the handle that held all the bullets, but it didn't budge when she pulled on it. There had to be some sort of release or something, but before she could figure it out, she heard the distant sound of a car engine.

Jumping to her feet she saw the dust rising up over the road she had come in on. Her first thought was to go running to her rescuer. But was it a rescuer? Could this be Steve? Would he be armed too?

She crouched back down against the driver's side door and held the gun in both hands. Better to know for sure than be caught by yet another psycho. She glanced back toward the barn; did she see someone move in the shadows? She pointed the gun at the door. If the pervert was up again, she didn't want him coming out after her. Nothing moved.

She heard the car pull up; it stopped abruptly with her car between it and the barn. She heard the door open; its hinge could use a little WD-40. Boots crunched on the dry ground. Footsteps.

She looked to the barn door, something tan moved in it. Definitely. He was up again. The black plastic grips of the gun were getting slippery in her hands. The footsteps were closer.

"Slashing the tires, good job, Tom," a male voice said from the far side of the car. It had to be Steve; who else would think that was a good idea? Half a face peeked over a window frame in the barn. She pointed the gun at it and it disappeared like a threatened prairie dog. But he had found enough wind to shout. "Look out, Steve, she's got my nine!"

Amy stood straight up and faced Steve over the hood of the car. He was right there just six feet away staring at her over the hood in full combat gear with a handgun in one hand pointed up at the sky like Don Johnson in the late night reruns Ted liked so much.

She didn't think about it, there was no time, she just did it. She pulled the trigger. Steve's eyes widened, his jaw dropped and he screamed like a twelve-year-old girl at a New Kids on the Block concert. His eyes rolled back in his head and he dropped as if all of the bones in his body had turned to jelly.

For that instant, Amy thought she really had shot him. But there was no bang, weren't guns supposed to kick or something? She still had the trigger pulled all the way back. But the gun hadn't fired. No smoke no recoil no noise, her ears weren't even ringing. And yet, she had killed him.

"Steve!" the one still in the barn shouted. Amy turned back to him and tried to shoot. Still nothing. She released the trigger and pulled it all the way again, but it didn't do anything, not even a click. What the fuck?

She remembered seeing people cock guns like this one in the movies. Maybe that was the problem. She tried pulling back hard on the top part of the gun. The entire upper half slid easily back. An unfired bullet burst out of a hole in the side and bounced off her stomach. She jumped and almost dropped the gun.

She ran around the front of the car and found Steve sprawled out like a broken doll. As inert as Ted the morning after a gig or when the word "work" was mentioned. That was it, Steve wasn't dead, he was just passed out. The big bad tough guy that was coming to help his buddy rape and murder her, had fainted dead away at the sight of the gun.

It was so ridiculous she actually laughed out loud. All dressed up in his paramilitary best he had fainted like a southern belle with the vapors. She moved around him to get the car between her and the barn then squatted down on the balls of her feet to retrieve the gun from his hand.

With her left foot on his limp wrist and the useless gun still pointed at his head, she crouched down. His gun was a little different, instead of being a deep blue color it was a chrome silver and had part of an old bicycle inner tube wrapped around the walnut panels on the handle. She grabbed the middle part over the trigger guard and yanked. As she pulled it up out of his hand his pudgy finger got caught on the trigger and the weapon discharged in her hand.

A burning shell case ejected out of the side, just like the unfired shell from the other gun, but this time burning powder and lead fragments stung her fingers. The top part snapped back and closed itself, recocking the gun as it flew out of her hand.

Amy screamed and jumped back counting her digits. Once she was sure they were all still there, she gingerly picked up the gun with two stinging fingers of her right hand. Well, at least she knew this one worked.

"Steve, did you get her?" the other attacker shouted as he wiggled halfway through the barn door. He stopped short and his face went pale when he saw her stand up, now with a gun in each hand. She leveled them both on him. His lip trembled and a dark stain appeared on the front of his pants. He made a whimpering noise and disappeared back into the barn like a Whack-a-Mole.

Amy switched hands and fired the silver gun in the general direction of the barn. To her surprise she was able to hit the broad side of it, but only just. After five shots the slide locked open and gun was empty.

Satisfied now that her friend in the barn would stay put at least for a few minutes, she shoved the muzzle of the empty gun in her back pocket and crouched over Steve again. She retrieved the keys for their Toyota Land Cruiser from a chain attached to his belt and jumped into the car.

Her dad had insisted that all of his daughters learn to drive a standard transmission, but Amy had not done it since she was sixteen. After stalling the car twice she finally got it into gear and got it moving. It was a hard jerky ride at first but it did not take her long to get the hang of shifting gears.

Close to sunset she stumbled across the information center for the wilderness area. One of the park officials was explaining to a group of tourists how Little Joe Cartwright had overcome his fear of heights on this very peak and Captain James T. Kirk had overcome the infamous Gorn not far from where they were standing.

She only had to tell her story to the park workers three times before they called the police. After repeating it to them six times, they finally did something about it. Privates Tom Crouch and Steve Utley were caught in the stolen UPS van stuck in a ditch two miles south of the barn. The body of the UPS driver was found sealed in one of the drums in the van. The other drums were all filled with a combination of ammonium nitrate fertilizer and fuel oil.

As they were both AWOL from the army post in San Diego, Utley and Crouch were turned over to the military police. With charges ranging from desertion to grand theft, illegal possession of stolen weapons, possession of explosive devices, assault, attempted sexual assault, and murder, they were sent to Fort Leavenworth for a total of 173 years each.

Recovering the Vista Cruiser only wound up costing Amy three hundred dollars in fines and repairs. But being able to sleep through the night took some time. For almost a year, she would wake up in a cold sweat after seeing Steve's gaping eyes as she pulled the trigger.

She had tried to kill him. She would have killed him if the gun had worked. She had actually tried to kill a human being. The fact that he was an aspiring mass murderer was little comfort in the small hours of the morning. Just knowing she would have killed him left her stomach tied in a Gordian Knot of regret. She had to live with the fact that all it would take was one wrong turn, and she could be a killer. All it would take was the right set of circumstances, and she would be back in the jungle willing to take a stranger's life to save her own.

The After School Job

November 1990

While Helen Wu's training officer, O'Connor, was still out on convalescence from the shooting, Helen was detailed to plain clothes on a special assignment. She was thrilled. She was told she would be out of uniform and working with detectives in an undercover sting operation. She was sure it would involve getting evidence to put some mafia chief in prison for life. It was unheard of for a rookie to get an opportunity like that. She was convinced if she pulled this off, she would be on the fast track to a promotion. Helen didn't exactly want to be in plain clothes or a detective, but she knew an opportunity when she saw one. All she had to do was ace a couple of jobs like this and she could have any permanent assignment she wanted in the department. Helen Wu was determined to be the youngest female officer ever posted to the LAPD SWAT team.

But her optimism was short-lived. It didn't even survive her first briefing with Detective Bradley Reid, the officer in charge of the detail. Helen had assumed that she had been chosen for the job because of her abilities, or for the recognition she had earned by saving her partner's life, or that weirdness in Hollywood with the teenage runaways. But she was wrong on all counts. She had been chosen by Reid based entirely on her looks. It would not have been so humiliating had he chosen her because she was attractive. She would have at least had some dubious consolation in that. But he had chosen her only because she could pass as a teenager.

A flasher had been cruising Johnny Carson Park for the last six weeks, exposing himself to the female students of Providence High School when they went through the park on their way home from school. Parents and the school administration had demanded action.

Helen's assignment was superficially simple; she was to pose as one of the students and blend in with the crowd at dismissal. So, at three o'clock that afternoon, Helen found herself dressed in a Catholic high school uniform, complete with little plaid skirt and blue blazer. Reid and another detective named Gene Bell were listening in over a mic hidden under her white oxford blouse. They were supposed to be watching her the entire time through high powered cameras to document the assault. All she had to do was wait until the suspect exposed himself, then they would capture his crime on film for posterity and converge on the pervert to make the arrest.

Even undercover, Helen Wu was not going unarmed. Her Beretta was too big to effectively conceal under the blue blazer, so Helen stuck her off-duty gun, a little Smith and

Wesson Model 36 revolver, in her blazer's outside pocket and resigned herself to the job at hand.

Providence High School was located at the intersection of South Buena Vista Street and Riverside Drive. An onramp to the Ventura Freeway ran parallel to the south side of the campus, and Johnny Carson Park butted up against the west side of the school. A massive, four-level parking structure for the Providence Saint Joseph Medical Center stood on its northern border.

Bell dropped Helen off on South Buena Vista Street on the east side of Providence High School at precisely two fifty-five in the afternoon. It was unseasonably damp for Los Angeles that late November morning. The sky was gray and cloudy. Fine, cold rain drizzled down off and on all day. Helen loitered near the school's main entrance, waiting for the students to be released for the day. But it wasn't the cold that that made her shiver. It was being in a school uniform again.

The bell rang and kids began to pour out of the main gate, surrounding Helen with a flood of sound. She let herself drift along with the flow, just another girl in the crowd. None of the regular students seemed to take any notice of the strange little woman walking along with them. Helen tagged along through the school's parking lot and into Johnny Carson Park. The crowd began to disperse in different directions. Some climbed into cars alone or in groups, others were picked up by family members or friends. But a rugged few trudged into the park for the shortcut to the bus stops along Alameda three blocks to the north.

A hard-packed dirt path ran to the northwest, roughly parallel to Johnny Carson Park Creek. About one hundred feet into the park one of two bridges turned off the main trail and crossed the creek. It led more or less due west past the park bathrooms and children's playground and ultimately out of the park onto Bob Hope Drive.

Several rowdy boys were roughhousing with one another and trying hard to impress the girls with their masculine exploits when they reached the bridge. The boys headed straight on so Helen, two girls and one boy broke off from the group and crossed the bridge.

The flasher had not yet approached any groups, only girls on their own, so Helen lagged back letting the other kids put some distance between her and them. Most of the reported attacks had happened on this trail, but some had been on the other. The pervert would come out of the trees dressed in jogging clothing. When he was sure the poor girl had an unobstructed view of him, he would pull down his pants and expose himself.

All of the young girls that had seen him screamed and ran the instant he appeared. The descriptions were all rather vague. It wasn't his face that most of the girls got a good look at. A white guy, maybe Hispanic, anywhere between twenty and fifty, Hair color unknown, he always had the hood up on his sweat jacket. He usually had on gray sweatpants, sometimes dark blue, and a gray or blue hooded sweat jacket.

Even with increased police presence the flasher was growing bolder and more aggressive in his attacks. At first, he had kept his distance, but with each incident, he was getting closer to the girls and more deviant in his behavior. Initially, he just displayed his genitals, but as his confidence grew so did his excitement. He had worked his way up to masturbating during the assaults. He had not touched any of his teenage victims, yet, but it was only a matter of time.

Helen walked along the path within sight of the other students until she passed the baseball diamond on the west side of the thicket of trees. She tapped on the radio hidden in the small of her back to get Bell's and Reid's attention.

"It's too open out here and too crowded. I'm going to turn back and head east to the bridge again." She didn't wait for a response because the radio was one-way. A receiver for her was not in the operational budget for this case, and a full-sized two-way was too big for her to conceal. She was pushing the guidelines by carrying her .38. She had no way of telling whether or not Bell and Reid had received her message. But they were supposed to have her in sight the whole time, so she wasn't too worried.

Reid was sitting in his warm and dry personal vehicle in the northwest corner of the high school parking lot. Helen could see the car and couldn't help but wonder why anyone would use a juvenile POS like that on a stake-out. Only in a high school parking lot would a black '88 Trans Am, complete with the screaming chicken on the hood, not stand out. What was it about male cops that made them all drive macho muscle cars or 4x4s? Bell was in an unmarked blue Crown Victoria over on Bob Hope Drive. *Nothing conspicuous about a black man in a cheap suit with a clip-on tie parked in a Crown Vic with half a dozen antennas on the trunk.*

The cold rain was becoming more steady. Helen's wool jacket was beginning to soak through. She could feel the icy water running down her spine. She had considered bringing an umbrella but had decided against it because she didn't want her hands encumbered with more crap. Now she was beginning to regret that decision. When she reached the bridge, she tapped the alert button on her radio and tried again.

"Reid, it's getting pretty wet out here, and so far, no sign of the suspect. Blink your headlights if you want to try again."

The headlights of the Trans Am flashed. Without another word Helen turned her back on the bridge and headed back into the trees. She was about halfway through when she heard thunder and lightning flashed. Albert Hammond was proved right when he said, "It never rains in California, but girl don't they warn ya. It pours, man it pours." The sky opened up, and she was drenched to the skin before she could take two steps.

Helen was sure that the flasher was at home, warm and dry, with a copy of *Barely Legal* and his Brooke Shields hand puppet. But because it was Helen's first undercover assignment, she didn't want to be the one who pulled the plug. She'd stay out here even if it started to snow. But still, there was no point in standing in the rain like Gene Kelly. She hit the alert button again. "I have to go 10-100," she said, and dashed for the ladies' room.

At the time, she didn't know that Bell and Reid weren't the only people watching her. She splashed through the mud over to the north side of the little recreation building that overlooked the playground.

Every day, Herman Rubenfeld watched those stuck up little cock teases walk through *his* park in their slutty little skirts. He knew good and Goddamned well that not one of them had anything on under there. And they were just waiting for the chance to catch a guy in their bitchy little trap. First, they flash little gash, then they run crying to the cops when they catch you looking.

194

He knew the type. They come on to you, all friendly like, get you to blow a week's pay to take them out and show them a good time. But when you try to collect on your investment, they start screaming. *"Oh, he just grabbed me for no reason. I'm just an innocent little fourteen-year-old virgin. I don't know anything about boys."* Rubenfeld knew only too well that less than an hour ago she was performing superlative fellatio on her English teacher for an A on her report card or dyking out with the other sluts in the locker room after cheerleading practice.

This one was no exception. The little dink slut had paraded by here three times now. Back and forth, back and forth. Oh, she is asking for it all right. All of those Jap bitches are the same. They play all meek and innocent until you give them five bucks and a couple of Hershey bars, then it's me-lay-you-long-time. Only problem was afterward they stab you in the back and rob you blind.

Rubenfeld slipped out of the janitor's storage room and crept around the side of the building to the ladies' room. *Ladies' room my ass, the sign on the door here should say "whores' room."* He got a good look at her when she ran around the corner and into the bathroom. She was young, maybe fourteen or fifteen, but it was hard to tell with slopes. She didn't have much in the titty department, and she wore her hair short. In fact, if she didn't have on a skirt, he might have thought she was a boy. Until he got a look at that ass.

Inside the bathroom Helen shook her head and ran her fingers through her soaked hair. She hated public restrooms. They were never clean enough to suit her, and she always felt exposed. Like she was on display with an audience watching her pee.

She reported her location into the radio, then went into a stall. She didn't really need to go when she came in, but now she felt obligated. If she didn't go, she would have been lying. Inside the stall she peeled off her sodden blazer and hung it on the hook on the stall door. All of her clothing was soaked through, her shoes squished with each step and her white oxford clung to her skin. She was wet and cold and pissed off. But there was nothing she could do about any of that now.

After she had finished the paperwork, a puddle had formed on the floor under her sodden wool blazer, and it smelled like a wet sheep. She left it to hang a bit longer. She considered removing her shoes too, but just could not bring herself to walk on this grimy floor even if she kept her drenched socks on. She emerged from the stall and crossed to the sinks to wash her hands. Of course, the sink had those stupid push button valves. Designed to save water, they always turned off halfway through, when your hands were still covered with soap.

With the water running, Helen didn't hear the door.

"*You speekie Engrish?*" a man said in a mocking voice.

Helen spun around to face the intruder. He pulled the hood of his sweat jacket off his head to reveal a harsh hatchet face with a weak, pointed chin, beady blue eyes, and thinning greasy brown hair. He was about five-ten, or maybe a little taller. He was lanky, but not emaciated like a speed freak. He was hard and wiry. Helen's wet soapy hand jumped to her hip where she usually had her weapon, but she had left the .38, as well as her badge, in the wet blazer.

"This is the women's room, men aren't allowed in here!" she admonished as she gave the alert button on her radio three quick taps, the emergency signal.

"Are you sure I'm a man?" Rubenfeld said with a depraved smile. "Let's see." He stepped closer to her. With one hand he pulled down the elastic band of his gray jogging pants, and with the other, he began to stroke his growing erection. "You like what you see? Pretty big compared to those little yellow ones you're used to, huh?"

"Get away from me," Helen warned.

"Oh, your mouth says no, but those big, hard nipples say yes, yes, yes."

Helen's hands instinctively covered her chest. She found bras to be uncomfortable, and with such diminutive breasts they were usually unnecessary. Her nipples were swollen from the cold, and they showed clearly through her sodden cotton blouse. This deviant was taking that as a sign of arousal, and consent.

"You want to touch it? I know you do, don't you?" he said taking a step closer to her. Helen could not believe this was actually happening to her. Had he pulled a gun or a knife she would have reacted instantly. But this situation was so outside of Helen's experience that she was almost hypnotized by Rubenfeld's audacity. *Where the hell are Reid and Bell anyway?*

"I bet a little China doll like you has never seen one this big before." He was only two steps away now. He held his pants up at the top of his thighs with one hand and slowly stroked himself with the other.

"What's the matter, sweetie, *no speekie Engrish*? That's okay, you don't have to talk. I have other plans for your mouth anyway. *Sucky fucky? You rove me rong time?*"

Where in the name of John Moses Browning are Reid and Bell? Helen snapped out of her shock as the pervert started to get between her and the stall and her .38. Helen lunged forward toward the stall but he had fast reflexes. He brought up an overwhelming backhand across Helen's face that sent her sprawling back against the sink counter and left her dazed. He pounced on her, grabbing her around the neck with both hands.

Helen Wu was tough, and remarkably strong for someone so small, but even so, she was still only eighty-seven pounds and fighting an opponent nearly twice her size, with the added adrenalin rush of the insane. He picked her up from the floor by her throat and shook her like a dog's chew toy. As her airway was cut off darkness began to close in around her peripheral vision.

She began to go slack. He sat her on the sink counter with her shoulders leaning against the polished steel that served as a mirror.

"Let's have a look at those bee stings." He tore open her oxford, sending buttons flying, and peeled the wet cloth open.

He roughly pushed her skirt up around her waist and tried to rip her panties off. But the garment wouldn't tear. Frustrated, he tried to yank them aside. She tried to shake the cobwebs from her head and forced open her dark eyes. For an instant, they looked into each other's eyes. He grabbed her by the throat with his left hand.

"You're gonna like this, little girl." He fumbled with his erection, but her panties were still in the way.

Where the fuck are those slapdicks, Reid and Bell?

Palm open, she lashed out with her left hand, and buried her thumb into his right eye socket all the way to her second knuckle. Her thumbnail was not quite sharp enough to puncture his eyeball, but it left a livid slash across the cornea and the pupil.

He screamed in agony, staggered backward, and tried to run. But with his sweatpants now around his knees, he tripped and fell against the stall doors. The unlocked door swung in and he fell, face first, into the stall she had just used. He landed over the toilet like an Irishman on the morning of March 18th.

She jumped to her feet and charged after him. With the full weight of her body, she rammed her right knee between his shoulder blades. There was a loud crack as his head smashed into the bottom of the bowl. For the first time in her life, Helen regretted flushing.

His arms and legs began to flail uncontrollably when he realized that he was drowning. Helen pulled his head out of the toilet just long enough for him to get a breath, then she slammed it back down into the dirty water. She held him there until he began to twitch and struggle. She yanked his head back out again.

"Me drown you rong time," Helen said with an exaggerated accent. Then she jammed his head back into the dirty water.

A pair of large black hands wrapped around Helen's shoulders, locking her into a full Nelson. She screamed with rage as she was pulled backwards out of the stall, kicking and screaming like a wild animal. Someone else was in the stall and pulled the suspect's head out of the toilet. He couldn't do that, she wasn't finished drowning him yet.

Someone was calling her name. She struggled against her new assailant. There was a white guy in front of her. He was saying something. He slapped her across the face. Then he went pale and took an involuntary step backward.

Gene Bell pulled Wu off the guy and tried to hold her back while Brad Reid pulled the perp's head out of the toilet. The scumbag started to cough and choke, and blood was gushing out of his eye socket, but he was breathing. Reid cuffed him and turned around to face the out-of-control rookie. She was thrashing like a wildcat on meth. He called out her name a couple of times, but she was out of her mind with fury. Reid slapped her to get her attention. The complete and total calm that came over her made his testicles contract. Now Brad Reid knew why the other uniforms all called this rookie "Dead Eye".

Helen went completely slack in Bell's arms. All of the rage and madness was just gone. Not suppressed, gone. Totally gone, like Jimmy Hoffa gone. Helen Wu was absolutely calm and controlled.

"Wu, are you...are you all right, now?" Bell said when she quit fighting. Then he released her unsurely. He half expected her to go off again. He would have felt better if she had.

"I'm fine, you can let me go." She turned her cold, black eyes on Reid. Her voice was hoarse and raspy but composed. "Where were you two? You were supposed to be watching my back."

Reid felt a chill go down his spine and the small hairs on the back of his neck stood up.

"You went out of radio contact. The rain must have shorted out your transmitter. Then you ran off..." he started to say. "What er... happened?"

Helen pulled her shirt closed and looked around her. "The suspect entered the restroom while I was...indisposed," she began, in a detached monotone as if she was testifying in court or reading a grocery list. As if it had all happened to someone else. Someone she didn't even know. Reid told Rubenfeld he was under arrest and read him his rights. Then he sent Bell out to the car to call for an

200

ambulance for him. Helen refused to see a doctor herself. The extent of her injuries from the ordeal turned out to be bruises around her throat, and she found it difficult to speak for a few days.

Rubenfeld was rushed to Providence Saint Joseph Medical Center where Doctor Chong Wong was able to save his eye in spite of Helen's best efforts to remove it. During his three-week convalescence, Rubenfeld met with his attorney in the hospital and decided to file a brutality charge against the LAPD.

Because of the failure of the radios, it all came down to his word against Helen's, who already had a history of violence. Rubenfeld claimed that Helen had come on to him and enticed him into the restroom with the offer of a sexual tryst, only to attack him once they were inside. There was enough gray area that with all the bad press the LAPD had been getting about the use of violence, the District Attorney was considering dropping the charges against Rubenfeld in exchange for him forgetting the brutality charge against the department. But of course, if they did that, Rubenfeld could sue Helen in a civil action for great bodily harm and his pain and anguish.

It all became a moot point when Rubenfeld was released from the hospital and transferred to Men's Central Jail in Downtown L.A. While he was being processed in, he was left alone in a holding cell with several white supremacist inmates. Skinheads do not like Jews to begin with, and when a deputy "accidentally" let it slip that Rubenfeld was charged with exposing himself to high school girls and attempted rape of what he thought was a teenager, they reacted badly. It only took them two minutes to beat Rubenfeld into a coma. A coma from which he never woke.

The idea that she could have lost everything she owned, ever worked for, festered in the back of Helen's mind. Granted the only things of value she had were a halfway restored '69 MG-B with a dodgy carburetor and a dozen handguns and rifles. It didn't improve her outlook much when the brass denied yet another transfer request to the Special Response Team. Were her superiors really too stupid to see she was obviously of more value to the department on the SWAT team than staked out like a Judas Goat trying to entice the first pervert that happened by to rape her while Reid jerked off safe and warm in the parking lot lost in his juvenile schoolgirl fantasy.

It was clear the politicians and bureaucrats that ran the LAPD valued her more for her gender and ethnicity to show off their diversity hiring policies than for her skills as a police officer. To them she was nothing but a shill. They were only interested in her as long as she looked good "live at five" on the "eyewitness action news." They were perfectly willing to throw her under the bus if her Nielsen Ratings started to slip.

Bad Day On the Job

1992

Craig Dworaczyk had never missed a day of work in his life. So the first time he ever called in sick he was surprised at how simple it was. He was no good at lying either, so he was not entirely convinced that the office believed he had the flu that Monday morning. But that was far less humiliating than the truth. How could he tell the other accountants at Morrissey, Jackson, and Jordan that he had to go downtown to pick up his good-for-nothing brother-in-law from the County Jail?

Bob Duryea had not always been a total loser. He had been an all right kid, for a jock, back when Dworaczyk was dating his older sister. The Duryeas didn't have a lot of money, so when Big Bob's football scholarship didn't materialize after high school, his only shot at going to college was a hitch in the military. That's where things started to go bad.

As an aspiring athlete, Bob Duryea was a bit of a health nut. He watched his diet, never ate junk food, and never ever used drugs or alcohol. Until the Marines. In the Corps he learned that beer was a part of military culture. In fact, drinking beer was a competitive sport, and Bobby was extremely competitive.

It started as recreational drinking at first, but after the Invasion of Grenada in '83 something in Duryea changed. Dworaczyk never saw Bob sober again.

Things got worse after Duryea got out of the service in '88. Bobby learned quickly that there were not a lot of job openings in the civilian world for professional machine gunners. He had a string of manual labor jobs, but could not hold even those, because they interfered with his drinking. Then he met Heather Rae Hobbs. She was waiting tables on the night shift at Denny's and studying to be a dental hygienist during the day. The family all thought that Heather would be a calming influence on Bob. That he would settle down, get a job, maybe go back to school and grow up a little. That didn't happen.

Bob and Heather Rae had a passionate romance for six months, at the end of which they were sharing a one bedroom apartment in North Hollywood. Then Bob's savings began to run out. When Heather Rae started to suggest that he get a job, Bobby did try. But every time he found one, he would either end up in a fist fight with a co-worker or show up to work drunk, or both.

That was when the fighting started. He'd lose a job, or get into a bar fight, and Heather Rae would tell him off. Or she would get tired of working overtime to pay all the bills, while he just slobbed around the apartment all day watching cartoons and drinking beer she could not afford. She would not have minded it so much if he would at least enroll in school or something. Take some sort of interest in their future.

When the arguments got to be too much for Bob he responded in the only way he knew how. Heather Rae's response to being hit was a complete surprise to Bob. She didn't cry or even hit back, she just went into the bedroom and locked the door. It didn't occur to Bob that she had called the police until Officers O'Conner and Wu knocked at his front door and took him to jail for the first time. Or the second time. Or the third.

So the cycle began: he would drink, she would nag, he would beat her up, she would call the police, and he would go to jail. Then she would pay his bail, and they would reconcile. He would come home and in about a month it would all begin again. Over and over for two years.

But not this time. This time something had changed. This time Heather Rae did not come down and pay Bobby's bail. When he tried to call her from jail there was no answer to any of his collect calls. She had not refused to accept the calls, she just had not answered. After a weekend in the gladiator dorm Bob had had enough. He called his sister and had her bail him out and send Craig Dworaczyk to pick him up.

Stacy Dworaczyk had a pretty good idea why Heather Rae had not answered the phone when her brother had called, and Stacy didn't blame her. So She insisted that Craig wait around until Bobby got into his apartment, just in case Heather Rae had changed the locks. She didn't want to see Bobby going straight back to jail just hours after getting out.

Craig was a little afraid of Bobby, so he didn't want to seem like he was being nosy. Instead of asking to come up to see if Heather Rae had locked Bobby out, Craig asked to use Bobby's bathroom before he went back to the office.

The locks to the third floor walk-up had not been changed. Bobby let Craig in and then shouted, "I've been robbed!"

The apartment was a mess. Things were scattered all over the living room. But even Craig could see that the television and the stereo were gone. So were several other things that Craig could not quite place. But a lot of valuables were still there.

"My guns," Bobby gasped as he ran into the bedroom. Craig heard the closet door slide open and Bobby called out in relief.

"Thank God! They're all still here!" Craig looked into the kitchen and saw that all the cupboards were open, and empty. What sort of a burglar steals dishes and cooking utensils?

"This don't make any sense," Bobby said, coming out of the bedroom with his Ruger Redhawk in his hand. "They took some clothes and all Heather Rae's CDs but they didn't touch any of my guns?"

"Not they," Craig said. "*She.*"

"What? I don't get it, what makes you think it was a girl?"

"Use your head, Bobby. All of *your* stuff is still here. The only things that are gone belong to Heather Rae. You haven't been robbed, you've been dumped."

"What?"

"Heather Rae left you. She moved out. She probably went home to her parents."

"No way, she wouldn't dare."

"Look around you, Bob. She did. It's probably all for the best, anyway."

Bobby grabbed the phone and started to make calls. First Heather Rae's mom. She told Bobby that Heather Rae had in fact moved out. No, she would not tell him where Heather Rae had gone, and no, he could not talk to her. In fact, Heather Rae didn't ever want to hear from him again. She had a new boyfriend now, one that has a real job and won't slap her around. So, don't call her or bother her. She is starting a new life, and he should do the same thing.

Bobby slammed the phone down and screamed like Brando in *Streetcar*. He went to the fridge and grabbed a beer, then picked up the phone and called Audrey Frigo, Heather Rae's best friend. No, Heather Rae was not at Audrey's place and don't ever call here again, you creep.

Craig Dworaczyk slipped out of the apartment quietly while Bob was calling some other friend of Heather Rae's. He didn't want to be around when Bobby was angry and drinking. It was a volatile combination. Dworaczyk secretly hoped this would be rock bottom for Bobby. That this would be the catalyst that would get him into a program and off the sauce. But he thought it just as likely that Bobby would tie one on and decide to end it all. Craig felt guilty for thinking it, but in the long run that would be better for Stacy. And cheaper. A funeral would cost him less than years of rehab that most likely would never work, or the ever-mounting legal bills from getting his loser brother-in-law out of jail.

***

Helen got in the patrol car and slammed the door. She was not happy. It was humiliating enough that O'Conner never let her drive, in direct violation of LAPD policy that partners split driving the squad car equally. It was not because she was a woman, or because of the stereotype of Asian drivers. She was, in fact, an excellent driver. O'Conner never let her drive because the patrol car had a bench seat.

Standing one inch under five feet tall, Helen had to move the seat all the way up in order to reach the pedals. Which meant that O'Conner, who was a little over six feet tall, could not even fit in the patrol car. To make room for him they had to move the seat all the way back. So he always drove.

"I wanted to smack that idiot," Helen sneered as she stowed her posse box and nightstick.

"We can't slap citizens around for being stupid," O'Conner said, grinning like the Cheshire Cat. "You're just pissed off because he asked if you're an Explorer Scout."

They had spent the last hour taking a statement from the owner of a small liquor store. A crowd of teenagers had come into his store and grabbed everything they could lay their hands on and ran.

"I mean, it's not his fault that your uniform and vest make you look like a fifteen-year-old boy." O'Conner went on, "Maybe you should try letting your hair down, or wearing some makeup."

"When I let my hair down it gets in my eyes and drives me nuts," Helen fumed. "And I've tried wearing make-up. It just makes me look like a *queer* fifteen-year-old boy."

O'Conner burst out laughing. Helen just glared at him. He picked up the mic for the radio and cleared the call. He put the car in gear and began backing out of the parking space.

"All right, Dead Eye, it's almost the end of watch," he said, using the nickname that had followed Helen from the academy. "Feel like a cup?"

"Always."

"So, are you going to Jones' bachelor party next week?" O'Conner asked as he pulled out into traffic and headed toward the doughnut shop.

"Oh boy," Helen said, with mock enthusiasm. "Binge drinking, strippers, and getting hit on by married assholes because they're too cheap to pay the hookers to blow them. What fun. Maybe after that I can go to the all-night dentist and have a root canal."

"You know, Helen, it wouldn't hurt you to socialize with some of the other guys more," O'Conner said, suddenly turning serious. "Developing relationships with other cops will help you throughout your career. Besides, you may need to count on one of them someday."

"The only relationship any of them want to develop with me involves a cheerleader's uniform and a handlebar helmet. No thanks. Speaking of relationships; what's the new girlfriend going to say about you going to a bachelor party with strippers a week after she moved in?"

"Heather Rae's cool with it," O'Conner said. "She knows the party was planned long before she moved in."

"You don't think you're moving a little fast with her?" Helen said.

"What do you mean? We've been together for almost two years."

"She's been seeing you on the side for two years," Helen said. "All that time she was still shacked up with that whack-job drunk. Then suddenly she just moves in?"

"It's not like that, Helen. We have been planning this for a while. She just…had a hard time leaving the guy because she felt sorry for him."

"She felt sorry for a jackass that beat her up all the time? I just don't get that. If anybody pulled that crap on me, that would be it. Why would she keep going back to him? There's got to be something wrong with both of them. Maybe she likes getting her ass beat."

"Maybe," O'Conner said. "I know she does like a good spanking now and then."

"That is something I just did not have to know."

The black and white pulled into the parking lot of Big O's Doughnuts alongside six other squad cars.

"Looks like a full house," O'Conner said. "It's close to end of watch."

"Too crowded. Maybe we should come back later," Helen said.

"Come on, I'm buying," O'Conner prodded her as he got out of the car.

"Since when have you ever paid for a doughnut in your life?" Helen said.

Helen did not like crowds. Worse still, most of this crowd didn't like her much either. Because of the LAPD's Affirmative Action policies, Helen had received opportunities and advancement that other, more experienced or better qualified officers deserved more. She had not received the offers because she was better at her job than most of them, but because she was the department's token "double ethnic."

210

This made the other cops jealous and hostile. It made Helen insecure and unsure of herself. She was never sure that she was getting praise because she had done a good job or if it was just because she was a Chinese woman. Ironically, the brass's desire to make her a media star and keep her in the public eye prevented her from getting the job she was best suited for. The LAPD shied away from giving any form of publicity to the SWAT Team, and that was what she wanted to do most.

Big O's Doughnut Shop was the end store in a busy strip mall and had two walls facing out that were made almost entirely of plate glass. Inside the shop, the sales floor was L-shaped with tables running all along the windows and the central counter filling the center of the L.

When they entered there was a boisterous greeting for O'Conner from the ten other cops crowded around the corner table. Some were standing, some sitting at the table drinking free coffee and eating free doughnuts and gossiping. None of them acknowledged or even seemed to notice Helen. They were all too interested in taking the Mickey out of O'Conner over his new roommate. Gossip moved fast among cops. And the story of Heather Rae moving in with O'Conner was just too juicy to keep. Helen had already heard more details about Heather Rae than she wanted to.

The owner of Big O's had tried to turn the place topless six years before, but OSHA had just too many safety regulations to let that happen. He still based his hiring policies on two rather obvious criteria, and while he did not require the young ladies to wear uniforms in the shop, he did not require them to wear much else. The girl that waited on Helen that morning was no exception.

Helen went to the far end of the counter to avoid the noise of the other cops and waved to get Sandy's attention. Sandy wore her pale, blonde hair in a short pixie style that made her large green eyes look even bigger. Today, she was wearing hot pink shorts and a tight, white, lacy top with spaghetti straps. She had a heart-shaped pendant around her neck that fell into the valley of her cleavage. When she saw Helen, she flashed a warm smile and poured a large black coffee without being asked.

Sandy hurried to the end of the counter and handed the cup over to Helen with a wink and a smile.

"Hi, Officer Wu, the usual?" she said. As she handed Helen the coffee, Sandy stroked Helen's hand. Helen noticed the silver band on Sandy's thumb for the first time. "You're always so quiet in here. Can I ask you a personal question?"

"Okay…I guess," was the best comeback Helen could muster.

"What's your first name?" Sandy said. She leaned over the counter on her elbows and the little golden heart fell free, dangling in the space in front of that golden valley. Helen's throat went dry and everything else went out of her mind at the sight.

"Er…Helen," she stammered, utterly embarrassed that she couldn't speak or remember her own name. She felt her face burning red. She turned her back on Sandy and looked out the window to try and hide her awkwardness.

"Why on earth would someone wear full camouflage in the city? It just makes people look like loonies," Helen heard herself say to Sandy. Helen's mind snapped back to earth just as Bobby Duryea stopped in the center of the parking lot and shouldered his FN FAL rifle.

"GUN!" Helen yelled at the top of her lungs. She dropped to the floor and rolled under a table by one of the windows. Some of the other cops looked over at her, still smiling and laughing. Others looked around mildly concerned.

Bobby Duryea took a second to aim before he let loose. The first volley of armor-piercing 7.62mm slugs brought down the plate glass window between him and the cops in a waterfall of splintered glass. The first rounds found their primary target easily and tore through O'Conner's body armor as if it wasn't there. Officer O'Conner never knew what hit him.

When he saw O'Conner fall to the ground, Duryea began to spread his fire. That initial burst killed four others and wounded six. The officers that were not dead or dying all dropped to the floor and tried to take cover.

The shooting seemed to go on forever, but when the first wave was over Duryea had only expended one thirty-round magazine. He put a fresh magazine into the gun and pulled a little surprise from his pocket.

When Helen heard the gun run dry she popped up from her hiding place and looked around her to survey the damage.

Sandy had not been hit in that first blast. She dropped down behind the service counter and was screaming hysterically but remained unhurt. The cops at the corner table weren't as lucky. The crowd of LA's Finest had been reduced to a groaning pile of bloody limbs and bodies. None were sure who was hit, and who wasn't, or how bad. Helen couldn't count on any of them for help.

She looked up at the convex security mirror in the corner of the shop and saw Duryea run up on the shattered

213

window. He was carrying his rifle by the pistol grip in one hand, and he had something round and green in his other hand. Helen threw herself back into her hiding place, covering her head with both hands. She heard the grenade bounce onto the floor and clatter on the tiles. The concussion in the confined space was devastating. It blew out all of the remaining windows and turned the glass cases on the countertops into a wave of shrapnel.

The smoke began to clear, Sandy had stopped screaming, and only three of the other cops were still able to moan. Helen climbed out from under the broken tabletop and crouched down in the debris to look around her.

Duryea walked into the shop through one of the blown-out windows with his FN at the ready. He looked around at the carnage and chuckled.

"I'm disappointed. I was hopin' you pigs would put up a better fight then that," he said. "Guess you're not so tough after all, are you?" He walked to the counter and kicked the body of O'Conner onto his back. He slung his rifle over his shoulder and pulled a Ka-Bar fighting knife from his belt. "Okay, O'Conner, how 'bout I cut those big brass balls off you and take 'em back to that whore, Heather Rae, and see how she likes 'em now?"

Helen was not sure until then that he was alone. At first, she had not recognized Duryea and thought it was some sort of organized militant terrorist attack. But now she saw her chance. She stood up and aimed with both hands. Helen hated her Beretta 92F. Mostly for not being a .45 ACP, but also because the double-stack magazine made the grips too large for her small hands, and the lightweight 9mm round just didn't have enough stopping power to take down an angry squirrel.

Only thirty other cops in the entire department could empty all fifteen rounds in less than three seconds on the firing range, only ten could keep all fifteen shots in the black. Only Helen could do it and keep all fifteen in the ten ring. She didn't dare risk anything fancy like a head shot at this point, so she dumped the entire magazine right between Duryea's shoulder blades. Small bits of lead and brass careened back, deflected by the trauma plate in Duryea's body armor. Even though the soft hollow points favored by cops didn't have the penetration to go through Duryea's armor, the light 9mm still had enough kinetic energy to make her point.

Duryea staggered forward, fell over O'Conner's body and sprawled onto the bullet-riddled counter. He coughed loudly and twisted around toward Helen. Their eyes met.

For a long moment they just stared, frozen.

"I 'member you now," Duryea said. "You're this prick's little partner. You're the bitch that kept tellin' Heather Rae to press charges an' dump me," His hand jerked to a holster on his belt.

Time slowed down to a nightmare pace. Helen ejected the empty magazine from her Beretta with her right hand, while her left reached for a fresh one. Duryea's hand was on the rubberized grips of his Redhawk. Helen could see the empty magazine falling, her left arm felt like lead as she pulled the fresh one out of her Sam Brown. The cylinder of Duryea's Redhawk cleared the black nylon of his holster. Helen had the magazine halfway to the empty weapon. She could see the barrel of the Redhawk sliding out of the holster. The magazine was into the frame. The front sights of Duryea's Redhawk cleared the holster. Helen's thumb was on the custom oversized slide release of her Beretta. The yawning black mouth of the Redhawk .44 Magnum's muzzle was coming up. The open slide of the Beretta slammed home and Helen fired.

Bobby got off one last shot as the first of nine slugs began smashing into his face. His round was far to Helen's left, but she felt the shockwave from the massive blast. She didn't stop shooting until there was nothing left above Bobby Duryea's chin.

***

After all the dust cleared, the final score was eight cops killed outright by Duryea and three badly wounded. Of the four that survived, Officer Mayberry spent the rest of his life in a wheelchair, paralyzed from the waist down. Bannon and Rodgers went back to active duty but after a year, Rodgers developed a drinking problem and was put on disability for life.

Sandy suffered minor lacerations from flying glass and sued the LAPD for ten million dollars. She settled out of court for an undisclosed amount and moved to Oregon.

Helen Wu had had enough of the whole scene, and so she quit the police department and got herself a steady job.

The Paint Job

1994

Tuesday, April 5, 1994

Genuinely platinum blonde, remarkably tall and authentically curvy, Amy Dresden looked more like she belonged on a catwalk than in the grimy waiting room of a Sepulveda Auto repair shop. Aware of her effect on other people, she tried to downplay her looks with conservative clothing. But loose slacks and bulky sweaters could scarcely hide her figure. Only a *hijab* could hide her striking features, and even that would have done nothing about her startlingly aqua blue eyes.

She felt like she had been stuck here for days. In reality, it had only been two hours since the tow truck had dragged her POS '88 Econoline off the side of the road where it had belched smoke and clanged to a dead stop. She kept hearing Ted's voice in her head saying, "You know what Ford stands for, 'Found On Road Dead.'" He had at least been useful for looking after the old Vista Cruiser they bought for the move from Chicago to LA. But just as she had outgrown Ted when he degenerated from musician to drug dealer, she had outgrown the Oldsmobile when she had bought out the inventory of the antique store where she worked part time to make ends meet in order to open her own antique business.

She needed a van because she was always moving fragile antique furniture either to her shop from wherever she bought it or to the home of a customer after she had sold it. In either case the old wagon just wasn't big enough.

The van however seemed to be spending more time in Lyle's shop than on the road and burning through every dime she had. She was two months behind on the rent of her apartment and one month in arrears on the shop. All she had in the pantry at home was a bag of wheat germ, some wilted celery and half a bag of dry cat food for Jane Austen.

She had managed to save the last seventy-three dollars she had in the entire world by playing the dumb blonde with the tow truck driver and convincing him she had simply forgot to pay her AAA dues, not that she had let them run out because she was broke.

Lyle, the mechanic, finally came out of the garage wiping his hands on a rag so oily that it only smeared the smudges around. He pulled a clipboard from under his arm and made a show of flipping through the papers on it. What he was really doing was looking her over.

"Miss Amy, I got some bad news for you." He didn't look too distraught over it. "Remember last month when I told you that you needed to fix that leaky radiator, and you said you'd get around to it later?"

"Yes, and I remember you saying it was going to cost me at least three hundred bucks I didn't have."

"Yeah." He grinned slyly and let his eyes wander. Even in tailored gray slacks and a teal cable-knit sweater, men ogled her like she was a Playboy bunny. "Well now its gonna cost you even more. 'Cause you kept lettin' that motor overheat, you went and blew out one of your head gaskets."

"Oh, a gasket can't be too bad. Can you fix it?"

"Well the gasket itself ain't too bad, parts are three, three-fifty. But I gotta tear the whole damn engine down to the block to even get at 'em. Then re-grind the heads so they'll fit right and rebuild the whole thing. God only knows what else I'll have to fix along the way. All told, you're looking at about fifteen hundred bucks. And that still leaves the radiator. If you don't fix that, it'll just blow the head again. You're lucky you didn't throw a rod."

Amy said a rather unladylike word that rhymed with firetruck. "I didn't have three hundred last month, where am I going to come up with five times that much this month?"

Lyle didn't answer; he just tried to see through her sweater as she considered how desperate she was.

"Do you think I could at least get it to Sepulveda and Vanowen before it overheats on me?"

"Like it is now, you're not gonna get two blocks before it pops it's top. And I'd be afraid it'd do even more damage if you tried. Odds are you'll crack the block at least. And if that happens, you'd be better off junkin' her. Don't suppose you could put it on a card?"

"No, my ex maxed 'em all out and pulled a Houdini on me." That was mostly true. She had not seen or spoken to Ted since she had walked in on him with a teenage groupie.

But she had done most of the maxing to keep her antique business afloat. But a little of Lyle's sympathy couldn't hurt.

Amy could not help notice the way he stared at her. Most men stared at her, but he clearly had something specific in mind. She had gotten to the point that if all they did was stare and kept their greasy mitts off her, she counted herself lucky.

"Sorry to hear that. Guy must be some kind of idiot to walk out on a pretty gal like you. You're probably better off in the long run though. Girl like you could do a whole lot better than that little runt." Lyle was not exactly making eye contact as he spoke. His mind was clearly on her head lights, not her head gasket.

"I need that van. Is there any way you could work with me a little?"

He looked at her like she was a used car at a suspiciously low price being sold by a man named Honest John. He was definitely considering the trade in value, or at least a test drive. Why was it that all men assumed she was a slut or a whore just because she was blonde? Men salivating over her like that made her seriously consider dyeing her hair brown and eating junk food until she was as big as Shelley Winters. Of course, men would still think she didn't know a valve job from a blow job, but at least they would only try to take advantage of her bank account.

"I can't do any sort of credit work on the parts. I'd need at least three hundred up front. But I think, seein' as you're a regular customer and all, maybe we could do a little somethin' on the labor."

"How much of a discount did you have in mind?" On guard now, she was careful not to use the phrase "how much can you take off?" because she was sure it would involve articles of her clothing.

"Why don't we work out some sort of payments. I can't do anything for you on the price, but if you can come up with three hundred for the parts by, say, Friday, I can get started on it. Then, say, maybe a hundred a week till it's paid all off."

"I just don't have anywhere near three hundred dollars. How about a trade? I have a lot of nice things in the shop. How would your wife like a solid oak grandfather clock? They go for about three grand," Amy said. Lyle broke eye contact and blushed. Here it comes, the proposition.

"I wouldn't know what to do with anything like that. But there is one thing you could do for me…"

Amy didn't have to give up a valuable antique grandfather clock; all she would have to do is clean his clock in the back room.

"You're a model, right?" One hand came up to the back of his head as he worked his way through the next couple of sentences.

"I'm trying to be a model, but I'm not having much luck at it. I run an antique shop." Her blue eyes drilled into his.

"Yeah…well. Your boyfriend Ted—"

"*Ex*-boyfriend Ted."

"Right, ex-boyfriend Ted. He used to like to show around some pictures of you in a biki-er–bathing suit, you know, washing his Corvette."

"What about them?" Amy folded her arms over her chest, narrowed her pale blue eyes and gave him what her dad called "the Eastwood glare."

"Er...well I was plannin' to take out an ad in the *Recycler*, for the shop, and I was thinking, maybe, if you still have one layin' around. I could use one of those pictures."

"For an advertisement?" Amy was stunned; usually they wanted services not goods. He didn't even want nude pictures.

"Yeah. For an ad. Nothin'—you know, over the top. Just a pretty face and a fancy car to bring in some customers."

"Those shots were of more than just my face." Lyle looked down at the floor and smiled sheepishly. "Sure, why not. It's not like I'm under contract or anything. You have a deal." They shook hands. "Tell you what; I'll even bring you some 8x10s to pick from. Some real professional photos, not just Ted's snapshots."

"Well, in that case, that 302 Ford engine is pretty common. I could maybe scrounge the parts from somewhere. We could just trade out the parts for the pictures and start out at a hundred a week for just the labor. That'd make it, twelve hundred, but seein' as you'll be representing the place, I could throw in an employee discount. Call it a grand even. But I need to have those photos before I can start any work. Friday at the latest."

"You're a lifesaver, Lyle." Not wanting to push her luck any further, and not altogether sure where she was going to come up with the hundred bucks, she promised him to be back by Friday. She didn't dare ask for a ride back to her shop.

Even though her apartment was only three blocks from Lyle's garage, she still had to go to the shop. She had already missed half the day but she wasn't going to sell anything if she didn't get the place open. And if she didn't sell anything, she wouldn't have the hundred bucks to pay Lyle. Besides, if she went back to her apartment, she would have Connie Lopez, the building manager's tween daughter, knocking on her door for her "momma's rent money."

So she walked to the first bus stop in front of Lyle's Repair Shop. Although the corner of Sepulveda and Plummer at eleven-thirty on a weekday morning was not exactly Hollywood and Vine, Amy still had an unwanted effect on traffic. Car horns blared and would-be suitors shouted their offers in English, Spanish and Ebonics.

Amy never understood cat-calling. Did men really think yelling "shake those titties, Blondie" from the window of a moving Toyota Corolla with only three hubcaps would make her fall in love with them? But the cat-calls weren't nearly as bad as the business offers.

Once at the bus stop, she tried hard not to stand out. But tall, blue-eyed blondes were few and far between in this predominantly Hispanic and black neighborhood. The proximity of flea bag motels running up and down Sepulveda didn't help the situation.

Her gray slacks had hardly touched the damp particle board bench when a late-model silver Impala made an abrupt U-turn across three lanes of traffic and jerked to a stop directly in front of her. The power window slid down to reveal a middle-aged white man in a wrinkled white dress shirt and badly knotted tie.

Amy feigned disinterest in the car and driver but kept them both in her peripheral vision just in case. He sat there staring at her for a full minute. To a woman, a minute of being stared at by a stranger at a bus stop felt like a lifetime.

Finally, he moved. It was almost a relief. He leaned over the passenger seat and called out to her.

223

"Hey there, Honey, you looking for a ride?" Amy didn't answer. He flashed some bills, dangling them like bait. "Come on, sweetie, I can pay. Get in."

"Fuck off, creep, or I'll call the cops."

"Bitch!" he screeched as he peeled out down Sepulveda. He wasn't the last. A cable television installation van went around the block twice before the Hispanic driver was able to get through the traffic and into Lyle's parking lot. But by then it was too late. The overcrowded bus pulled up, and Amy was able to squeeze in. Barely.

Most Californians have no idea what cold is. So, when the temperature drops into the sixties, as it had that April morning, they are all convinced they will freeze to death, so they dress as if they were arctic explorers and crank the heaters all the way to bake. The bus was stifling hot and packed to the gills. An aroma not unlike sweat-soaked polyester with a dash of Jane Austen's dirty litter box hung in the air like mildewed laundry on a humid day. Every seat was taken, and the aisle was standing room only. Amy stood among her new intimate friends near the front of the bus where the first four seats behind the driver on each side faced inward to accommodate the aged and infirmed instead of facing forward like all the rest. That made the aisle a tiny bit wider.

The bus lurched forward into Sepulveda traffic, and all of the standing riders were jerked back and forth. Amy was caught off guard and nearly fell. When she regained her balance, she realized that the man standing behind her had moved closer to her. He was a big guy, a little taller than she was and about five times as wide. On the bench below them, three compact Hispanic men dressed in elaborately embroidered western shirts, jeans, Charlie One Horse straw hats, and comically pointed cowboy boots glared up at the big guy. All but the one with the feathered hat band sitting in the middle. All of his attention was glued to Amy's chest. He didn't even have the courtesy to look away when she caught him staring at her. Usually, she would call guys out on that, but something about the intensity of his stare unnerved her. She tried to turn her back on the little guy but that meant switching hands on the safety rail overhead. She heard him say something like *"¿Son tus grandes tetas reales?"* and the other two *paisanos* broke out laughing.

Still smiling, the one on the left said *"Apuesto a que es una puta,"* to the one in the middle. Encouraged by his *amigo's* support, he made eye contact with Amy for the first time.

"¿Me chuparás la polla por diez dólares?" he said with a grin that would have given Peter Lorre the shivers.

"Lo siento, no hablo español," she said with a forced smile and tried to turn away. As she had said, she didn't exactly speak Spanish, but she had lived in LA long enough to know *"puta"* was not a term of endearment. But under the circumstances, she didn't want to push a confrontation. After all, this was their world, and she was the intruder.

She switched hands on the rail and turned her back on the *paisanos* as best she could in the limited space. This left her facing more or less forward and practically nose-to-nose with a well-fed black woman in a bright orange and yellow *Dashiki* dress and matching *Kente Kufi* hat with a face like a Pit-bull with kidney stones.

The bus bounced through an intersection, and all the standing passengers bobbed about trying to keep their balance. Amy used the opportunity to move back a few inches away from the angry black woman but bounced off the big guy's doughy body behind her.

She closed her eyes and tried to endure the ride. After all, it was only three and a half miles. All the bodies in the small space and the bus's overactive heater were not helping matters. The metal underwire in her bra felt like a garrote tightening around her lungs and the wool of her sweater felt like Brillo against her damp skin. Trickles of perspiration were inching their way down her back. The Pillsbury Doughboy was pressing closer to her.

How had her life come to this? When she and Ted had moved to L.A., he was going to be the next Michael Anthony, and she was supposed to be the next Elle Macpherson. They would be the golden couple on every magazine cover. But L.A. is full of Michael Anthony and Elle Macpherson wannabes. All talented and beautiful, and all competing for that one-in-a-million shot at the gold. If they're lucky, the Michael Anthonys wind up playing in dive bars and doing manual labor in the day or peddling drugs to pay the rent. Most either give up or get strung out on coke, or worse. The Elle Macphersons that don't wind up waiting tables for the rest of their lives only get discovered on the casting couch. Some get lucky and grace the pages of sleazy magazines or become stars of the home rental market in blockbusters like *Schindler's Lust* or *Forest Hump*.

The bus plowed over a pothole the size of the San Andres Fault and sent a six-point-seven-magnitude quake through the passengers. The Pillsbury Doughboy used the opportunity to press closer against her. Amy tried to move away, but the woman in the *Dashiki* was not about to yield any ground, especially to a blue-eyed, blonde, white girl. The bus shuddered again as it crossed an intersection. The Doughboy was almost suffocating her, which was strange because he was the one with the labored breathing. She had been wrong, it had gotten worse.

The Doughboy was getting bolder now, and he pressed against her, almost forcing her to lose her balance. It was no accident. He was not being forced in her direction by other people. No longer in rhythm with the bus's vibrations he was rubbing against her, and that was definitely not a roll of Certs in his pocket. Not that he didn't need one.

Amy let go of the handrail with her left and buried her elbow in the Doughboy's soft gut. At the same instant she drove the heel or her right foot down on his Dr. Scholl's sandal. It was the first time in weeks she regretted not wearing heels.

The Doughboy made a wet gasping noise from the back of his throat. His roll of Certs melted, and he collapsed in slow motion onto the *paisanos*.

Apparently, the Three Caballeros didn't like being touched by the Doughboy any more than Amy did. Unfortunately, they lacked her self-restraint. The woman in the *Dashiki* was apparently well acquainted with the Doughboy's antics and began loudly cheering the Three Caballeros. Everyone else within punching range of the ruckus surged away from the altercation like British Soccer Hooligans. At the sound of pointy boots impacting on fleshy ribs, the bus driver slammed both feet down on the brake pedal and made an unscheduled stop, blocking two lanes of traffic. All of the standing occupants of the bus, including the pugilists, were tossed forward and heaped on the floor in a damp pile of bodies and squirming limbs.

As soon as the bus stopped rocking, the driver threw open the doors and called for the police on the dispatch radio. Amy herself had been tossed onto one of the seats vacated by one of the combatants. She did not want to spend the rest of her afternoon making witness statements about the Pillsbury Doughboy and his roll of Certs. The way her luck had been going lately, she would probably be charged with assault for elbowing him in the gut and inciting a riot.

Before anyone else could untangle themselves from the dogpile on the floor she pulled herself up and around the safety-pole at the end of the bench and slipped down the stairs. She heard the bus driver yell something after her about not wandering off, but she had no intention of sticking around.

Once she was off the bus she inhaled deeply, savoring the fresh smog. Even what passed for air in L.A. smelled good after the rolling sweat lodge she had just escaped. After the confined heat and dank reek of the bus, the cool sixtyish degree breeze cut through her damp sweater and made her shiver. The bus had already crossed Sherman Way, and it was just a few more blocks to her shop, so she decided to take advantage of the cool day and walk the remainder. But walk quickly, after all it was still Sepulveda Boulevard, and with at least half a dozen no-tell-motels between her and the shop she would stand out like a sasquatch wearing an Oxford school tie.

Other passengers were beginning to find their way off the bus, and she did not want to stand around talking with them about whiplash and which ambulance chasers could get the best payday from RTD. She set off at a good pace, not exactly hurrying, just...brisk. Straight down the center of the sidewalk, not too close to the curb or too close to the storefronts along the busy street. She ignored the horns and shouted offers of passing vehicles. When cars pulled to the curbside and offered her rides, or business opportunities, she just kept moving. She didn't quicken her pace, that showed fear, but she didn't slow down or tell them off either. Interaction would only lead to conflict.

It was ironic that strutting along a catwalk, in nothing but designer underwear, she didn't get cat-called. But walking down a public street in a crewneck and loose slacks, and these idiots were screaming like football fans at the Super Bowl. This was even worse than the bikini contests she and Rachel had done. At least when she was parading around on stage in a string bikini in front of drunken frat boys, she was getting paid, if she won. Besides, there was always a bouncer or two between her and any overly amorous admirers.

The bikini shows had been easy money back home. But here in L.A. one had to do more then look good in a bikini. "Wardrobe malfunctions" were expected. If tops didn't pop open or string bikinis didn't come undone on stage the only way to win the prize money was to "take care" of the judges and the promoters before the show.

To be paid or not to be paid, that is the question. Whether 'tis nobler in the mind to suffer the slings and arrows of the casting couch. Or to take up arms against a sea of perverts and oppose them by keeping your knickers on.

She went on hundreds of auditions and try outs. There were thousands of really beautiful women just like her from all over the world all trying for the same parts. At least six out of ten were willing to do nude scenes on camera, and eight out of ten were willing to do nude scenes off camera.

She didn't have any moral objection to nudity. She didn't have any problem with the idea of doing a nude scene in a movie if it was dramatically significant to the film. The

229

only real objection she had about doing a nude scene or posing for naked pics was how it would impact her career later on. If she went topless in some B-movie, or posed nude in a men's magazine now, the pictures would resurface years later when she became famous. That would taint her public persona the way it had with Vanna White or Suzanne Somers and even prevent her from being taken seriously as an actress and getting the kind of parts she really wanted.

The odd truth was she didn't feel anything at all about being naked in front of total strangers, or even a lover. She understood that men got some sort of sexual exhilaration from seeing her naked. She knew that some women, like Rachel for instance, got a thrill from titillating men, but not her. It went both ways too. The sight of a naked man did nothing for her. Whether it was Richard Gere or Ted, the effect was the same, nothing, unless they were wearing black socks. That always made her laugh out loud. There was nothing funnier than a naked man in black socks.

She had nearly chucked the whole acting thing a year ago when her so called "agent" Daniel Cline booked that last audition.

"It's a local late night TV show called *Fright Fest*. It'll be perfect for you," He said over the phone. Daniel was always on the phone. In the two years he represented her she had only ever been in the same room with him once.

"What is the role exactly? And don't even bother telling me if it involves taking my shirt off." He had sent her on more than one audition for parts like Sexy Sorority Girl or Blonde Cheer Leader in cinematic masterpieces like "Zombie Co-eds from Planet Nympho."

"Amy, Babe," (he called everybody 'Babe') "Have I ever asked you to do anything you didn't want to?"

"Yes. Almost every time you call me. So, what's this part? Am I playing the topless teen girl that gets chased around lover's lane by a slasher in a catcher's mask after banging the jock?"

"No, no, it's nothing like that at all. You'll be the hostess for a late night horror show. You'll introduce some old creature feature, tell a few factoids about the movie, and do a couple of gags in the bumpers. You know, like the old *Seymour's Monster Rally* back in the seventies or that *Svengoolie* guy out of Chicago."

"I never heard of Seymour but I remember staying up late to watch *Svengoolie* when I was a kid. But they're men, isn't that sort of a boys club?"

"The station is looking to do something a little different. They want a sexy Goth chick, like the original *Vampira Show* from way back in the fifties. They want a cross between Morticia Addams and Pamela Anderson."

"Oh, I see. Is that the kind of image we're trying to promote? I mean, I don't do the dumb blonde thing."

"That's why I thought of you for this, babe. You won't be either. Your character is supposed to be sexy, with attitude. Sort of sassy and sarcastic. But not blonde."

"What?"

"It's all part of the Morticia Addams-Lilly Munster-goth-girl aesthetic they're going for. You'll need to dye your hair black. Jet black."

"No way, I can't do that."

"Do you want the part or not?"

"Can't I just wear a wig or something?"

"You know what a really good wig looks like? It looks like a really good wig. Look. Amy, baby, this is six weeks of paid work, for sure. With an option for three years if the

231

ratings are there. If you pull it off, they are talking syndication, and residuals for reruns. So, you need to show them at the audition that you're willing to commit to this show."

"Okay, okay. But aren't you worried about me getting typecast as a vampire chick?"

"You can't get typecast as anything unless you get cast as something."

"Yeah, but…"

"You know who cries about being type cast? Nichelle Nichols. She cries about being type cast all the way from her mansion in Beverly Hills to the bank to deposit her fat residual checks for work she did twenty-eight years ago."

"You know if I'm the only blue-eyed blonde to show up they'll notice me more." Amy hated the idea of dying her hair. One of the things that made her unique among other models was she was a real blonde. An honest to God, dyed in the wool, natural blonde. That was why she was so adamant about never playing the dumb blonde roles. It was the bleach blondes that were so stupid. But they gave the real ones a bad reputation.

"No. They'll just think you're either such a diva that you won't follow instructions or you're so stupid that you came to the wrong audition. Dye your hair and wear something black and slinky. We can worry about you getting type cast after you have the part."

That's just what Amy did. Daniel had been right about the wigs. After three days of sifting through every costume shop in Hollywood she and Rachel found some temporary black hair dye and did the dirty deed. She borrowed a backless (and nearly frontless) black cocktail dress from Rachel, bought a pair of spider web stockings, new black pumps with heels so high they almost gave her a nosebleed and went to the audition.

She didn't get it. She could have lived with that, if it wasn't for who did get it.

She sat in a room full of hopeful vampire girls in skintight black sheath dresses, demonic tattoos, red contact lenses and even a few with actual fangs. While she waited a bottle blonde with plastic prosthetics as overdone and unconvincing as Dick Van Dyke's cockney accent, flounced in wearing a gauzy white lace and satin peasant dress. The only thing about her that struck Amy as being genuine was her utter stupidity.

Needless to say, the synthetically stacked bleach blonde got the part because of her "innovative interpretation of the part."

Amy was furious. With herself, with her agent, with the blonde bimbo, with the casting director, and with acting in general. But most of all she was angry that she let Daniel talk her into changing herself to get a part against her better judgment. It was insult to injury that the part went to someone else that not only used her idea but was badly imitating her real look.

Even more frustrating, the temporary dye was not as temporary as the package had promised. After washing her hair over and over again the ends of her prized platinum locks remained black. She finally had to have an inch trimmed off the end to lose the dark tips. It still hadn't grown back to where it was.

An air horn and a woman's voice snapped her back to reality. Amy was surprised to see she had already crossed Vanowen. A Tonka-truck-yellow Jeep with the top down, the doors off, and a Confederate flag painted on the hood had run an over-sized off-road tire up on the curb. Sitting at the wheel was a woman, well sort of a woman. She had a John Deere baseball cap pulled over a neon red mullet, camouflage army pants, tan work boots and a white wife beater that showed off the tattoos up and down her burly arms. One hand was resting on the wheel, with the other she tapped the ashes away from the butt of a Swisher Sweet. She smiled lewdly and cocked one unplucked eyebrow at Amy.

"Hey, babe, wanna take a walk on the wild side?" the woman said.

Amy rolled her eyes and kept walking.

Rather than continue this conversation she turned into the used car lot at the corner to take a short cut to the back door of her shop.

"Breeder!" The woman flicked the still burning butt in Amy's direction and bounced back into traffic.

In the back row of the lot, glittering in the sun like a diamond engagement ring was a gigantic white Chevrolet truck that took her breath away. It was a thing of beauty. White shoe polish on the windshield proclaimed "1993 Chevy crew cab! $19,999.99 No Money Down!" It would be a perfect replacement for the van, but with her current finances it may as well have been six million dollars and include Lee Majors as a chauffeur. She paused for just a moment to admire the truck.

"What a beauty!" a man's voice intoned from behind her. He wasn't talking about the Silverado. Amy braced herself for the crude advances of yet another Don John on the make and tried to ignore him. He was in his early forties, dressed in imitation alligator loafers and a counterfeit Armani suit with what was left of his thinning hair pulled back in a ponytail. At first glance, she thought he was a pimp trying to recruit her into his stable. But on closer inspection she realized he was something even lower, he was a used car salesman. He was definitely on the make but he was not looking to buy, he was looking to sell.

"I'm just looking," Amy blurted out in an attempt to divert him before he started a sales pitch. But those words to a used car salesman were like blood in the water for a shark.

"Of course you are, and so am I." He leered over the tops of his Ray-ban knock offs, trying hard to look like Tom Cruise in *Top Gun* but coming off more like Jack Nicholson in *Terms of Endearment*. Amy rolled her eyes and tried to squeeze between the Chevy and a Ford Bronco with oversized off road tires. Because she had to do a sort of limbo to get under the protruding side mirrors of the two trucks the salesman was able to head her off by going the long way around.

"I couldn't help but notice you were admiring this Dually. Does your husband or boyfriend have a boat, or a camper?" he said trapping her between the two trucks. Amy stopped and prepared to drive her knee into his soft groin if he came any closer. But he kept his distance, and after a moment of awkward silence, she realized he only wanted to ravage her wallet, not her.

"No, I don't own a boat or a camper. I was literally just passing through your lot, I don't want to waste your valuable time." She took two more steps toward him in the narrow space, making it clear she was not going to back down.

"Then what do you want that big gas guzzler for? You'd never be able to get it in a parking space at the mall anyway. A gorgeous babe like you'd be a lot happier in this cute little '89 VW Cabriolet convertible right over here. Just eight thousand with no money down, depending on your good credit."

"I'm not looking for a car, and even if I was, my credit is worse than your plastic shoes. Now, would you just get out of my way so I can get to work?"

Showing sudden good judgment the salesmen stepped back to let her by, but in his line of work it was never a good idea to let a potential customer escape completely. As Amy passed briskly by him he held out a business card.

"Well, if you change your mind, I'm Dave Collines. Give me a call and I'll put you in your dream car."

Amy glared at him but took his card. She was in sales too, and they were neighbors after all. She took his card and stepped over the cable divider that separated the car lot from the alley behind it. The next building over was the strip center that held Dresden Antiquities.

She skipped the keypad for the burglar alarm just inside the back door because the security company was one of the bills that were past due. But the power bill was one she had paid, so she plugged in the electric kettle on her work bench and filled the tea caddy with yesterday's still damp tea leaves. Or were they from Sunday? It didn't really matter what day they were from; she had to use them anyway because they were the only tea leaves she had left.

She switched on all the lights, cut through her cluttered workroom and went out to the sales floor. Usually, the sales floor was an Aladdin's Cave of wondrous treasures, but today it was just a junk shop of moth-eaten old furniture and broken odds and ends. Why did she even bother? Nobody wanted any of this old crap. It just sat here gathering dust and taking up space she could no longer afford to pay for. Then again, nobody could come in and buy anything if she didn't unlock the door.

There was no mad rush to get in as she slid open the scissor gate across her front window and door. But she had formulated a plan to at least get the van running, for the moment, and there were things to do.

She took a plain jewelry box from the back room and for the next hour she sorted through the jewelry she kept in the center display cabinet. She chose the most obviously valuable pieces to take to a pawn shop to hock. That would at least get the van running and provide eating money. That would give her a little breathing room to figure out what to do next. But what would she do next? The only thing that came to mind were the words of the late great Scarlett O'Hara, "I'll think about that tomorrow."

Would it really be so terrible if she had to close down the store? Why was the store so important to her anyway? It's not like she had always dreamed of hustling used furniture her entire life. She certainly was never going to get rich and famous doing it. The only real benefit of the store was it was the only thing that kept her here in L.A. But why was it so important to stay in L.A.?

She didn't have any friends or family outside of Rachel. Dawn and Rusty had moved to Florida when they retired. Ted had gotten custody of most of the fair-weather-friends they had made as a couple in L.A. Not that that was any loss.

She had only gotten into the antique business as a way to pay the bills while she and Ted waited to be discovered after Brain-Dead-Ted had gotten her fired from the Family Fitness Center by storming into the women's locker room

237

and accusing her of having an affair with the gay owner. None of the ladies in the locker room at the time found it the least bit amusing. Neither did the owner, or his boyfriend. So Amy cut her losses and counted herself lucky that she wasn't being sued and Ted didn't end up in jail.

With no other way to pay the rent, Ted on probation, and of course not working, she took a part-time job in Dawn Moorehead's North Hollywood antique store. Working the counter and helping out with restoring things in back. Dawn and her "friend" Rusty Lyons had been regular members of Amy's aerobics class and were sympathetic with her situation.

Amy was grateful to have a job, any job. Especially one working for a woman so Ted could not accuse her of sleeping with the boss. The job was perfect for her because Dawn gave her the freedom to come and go for modeling gigs and auditions, and it gave her a chance to put some of her Art History degree to good use.

When the owners of the North Hollywood strip center where Dawn had her shop raised her rent from the ridiculous to the impossible, Dawn decided not to move the shop again. Rusty had her twenty-five in with the L.A. School system and was ready to retire anyway, so they sold the house and bought a condo in Miami.

With the last of her savings, Amy bought out most of their inventory. What she couldn't afford she took on consignment, found a new location and opened Dresden Antiquities.

That night, she stayed open until nine to make up for the late start that morning, but to little avail. She only had a handful of customers, most were just lookie-loos. She did manage to get rid of those dreadful Bradford Exchange,

Princess Diana collector plates, but the customer paid with plastic. That meant Amy wouldn't see a dime of the five hundred for at least two weeks. Not that she was sad to see them go. They weren't exactly antiques and in her humble opinion, Diana Spencer was nothing but a gold digger.

After she closed, up she thought about crashing at Rachel's. But without a car the logistics would have been difficult. Rachel worked nights at a men's club on Sunset. She had probably already gone into work, anyway. And it would have been awkward to ask about staying there after what had happened the last time. Not that Rachel would ever turn her away. Amy loved Rachel like a sister, and Rachel had made it abundantly clear the last time she stayed there that she loved Amy too, but not exactly in a sisterly sort of way.

After enduring the ham-fisted advances of Rich Wang, the assistant night manager of the grocery store across the street, she got a wilted green salad and spent the next two hours leaving messages on interior decorator's answering machines about all the bargains she had in the shop.

She considered calling that liquidator Dawn bought from all the time. But he wasn't really interested in buying, only selling. Besides he was such a flirt when they talked, if she called him, he would try and ask her out, again.

And why not? What was wrong with him? He was tall and handsome, he looked a little like Ted Danson, he had a good job, and best of all he didn't play in a garage band. But he just didn't do it for her. No one did. Not even Ted really. With Ted, it had always been about what he could be, or what she could make of him. Ted had been a project to her, a fixer-upper, not a lover.

It had always been that way with her. She was different from the other girls somehow. She didn't exactly know why but she was. Everybody around her knew it too, no matter how she tried to fit in. It was the eight-hundred-pound gorilla in the sitting room that nobody ever talked about. Except that weird kid back in grade school.

Ethan or Evan, or was it Ivan, she couldn't remember now. He was always more interested in playing Barbie dolls and baking in his Easy Bake Oven with the girls than anything the boys were doing. That was fine with her because she was usually with the guys riding her skateboards or playing baseball (hardball, never any of that sissy softball crap). One day in gym class Ivan took a brutal dodge ball to the face and broke out in tears, much to the amusement of everyone else.

"Why don't you ever pick on Amy? If I'm a girl in a boy's body, than she's a boy in a girl's body. It's like aliens switched our brains or something!" he blurted out at his tormenters before he ran off to cry under the bleachers in his humiliation.

The Christmas before last, when she and Ted went home for the holidays her sister told her that Ian, that's right, that was his name. That Ian had dropped out of school and spent a year in Copenhagen. He plucked his eyebrows on the way back, shaved her legs and then Ian was Diane. Now she's a roadie for the Grateful Dead.

She yawned and stretched her aching back. She had been sitting in the office chair hunched over the phone for too long. She needed sleep if she was going to get everything done tomorrow she needed to. It would be at least an hour each way to the pawn shops on the bus. She needed to turn in.

To do that she would need a place to sleep. She swept a spot of the concrete floor in the back room as sawdust-free as she could make it. As much as the smell of sawdust reminded her of her father's shop, she didn't want to sleep in it. Especially without being able to wash her hair in the morning.

She got the polar bear skin rug from its hiding place and laid it out. She kept it hung over a rail in the stockroom covered with a tarp to protect it from the dust and to cover its creepy glass eyes that seemed to follow her around.

Even though the rug was very valuable, she didn't dare put it on display in the front room. The California Department of Wildlife kept a close eye on the sale of any bear parts in the state. The bureaucrats tracked the sale of bear parts closer than the DEA tracked crooked doctors writing bogus prescriptions for pill-popping celebrities.

More than the Fish and Game people, Amy was worried about the PETA fanatics. She was afraid that if she put the rug in the salesroom some animal rights nut would go off in her store and start throwing red paint all over the place. The rug was worthless if it was covered in paint stains, not to mention any other merchandise that got hit in the crossfire. On the other hand, a bunch of protesters picketing her store over the rug could get her some much needed publicity. But in California's shallow reactionary climate, she didn't dare risk looking like a fur-wearing, animal-killing, Cruella de Vil. Although she couldn't help but wonder how the crazy-little-Asian-woman-from-the-gun-shop-next-door would react to a bunch of hippies marching up and down the sidewalk in front of their businesses. Gun nuts and vegans are natural enemies.

She made a final walk through of the sales floor, killed all the lights, and double checked the locks on the front door and sliding gates before she retired to the back room for the night. As a last ditch obstacle to any intruder she took a heavy enamel-coated wrought-iron statue of a hawk and blocked the swinging door with it. Even with the door blocked she could still hear the never-ending traffic from Sepulveda Boulevard outside.

She didn't want the only work clothes she had with her to look as if they had been slept in the next day, so she changed into an old paint-splattered Chicago Bears jersey she used as a smock when she did restoration work. She hung her sweater and slacks over the rail where the bear lived and used the dusty tarp as a blanket.

She was completely exhausted, but sleep was elusive. She laid there on the floor in the semi-darkness and watched the irregular patterns of light from passing cars flash through the frosted window of the swinging door make eerie Rorschach images on the back wall and ceiling. Even at this late hour, she could hear people on the street outside.

All she wanted was to sleep. Just close her eyes and wait for the fresh new hell that being broke in L.A. would bring with first light. Light, too much light. If she could just put out those streetlights.

The dim glow of the building security lights illuminated the thin drapes across the front window and the constant haggling of the teenage entrepreneur bickering over the price of his goods made Amy toss and turn on the fold out sofa bed. To call this thing a bed was more than generous, it was barely a sofa. As far as being a bed, it was more like laying on a slab of cold concrete then a bed. Of course, if she didn't like it, she could always double up with Rachel in her room.

With a soft click a new light was added, but at least it was in the other room. When it was clear it was going to stay on, she opened her tired eyes. The radiance from Rachel's bedroom illuminated the hallway to the bathroom. At least she hadn't turned on the hall light, thank God for small mercies. But it was more than enough for Amy to see by. Amy waited for the light to go out, prayed for the light to go out. The light didn't go out. It seemed like it was taking Rachel an awfully long time to go to the bathroom.

"Rachel?" she called out when she couldn't stand it anymore. "Are you okay?"

Rachel swayed into the rectangle of light emanating from the hallway and posed. The glow of the bedroom lamp shimmered in her jet-black hair. That wasn't right, Rachel was a redhead this week. She hadn't been a brunette in over four years.

She just stood there and stared at Amy with a wicked smirk on her pretty face.

"Time to pay your rent, honey," Rachel said and swayed to the end of the bed.

"What are you talking about? You know I don't have any money."

"There's more than one kind of currency." Rachel's nightgown became more transparent the closer she got until it faded away completely and left her stark naked.

"What are you doing?" Amy gasped and pulled the blankets up to her chin. Rachel leaned over and began slowly pulling the blankets down. Amy was paralyzed. Her limbs felt like lifeless lead weights.

"You know what they say, sweetie, 'gas, grass or ass, nobody rides for free.'"

Amy sat bolt upright and gasped. Her body was covered with a patina of cold sweat and sawdust. The doorway out to the sales floor was lit by the flashing headlights of non-stop traffic on Sepulveda Boulevard. She was not in Rachel's apartment, she was safe in her own shop. She was not naked, well not entirely, and her best friend was not trying to rape her.

She didn't know if the sobs that came out of her chest were from relief or grief at what she now knew she would have to do.

She pulled her knees to her chest and hugged them until the wet, gasping sobs had passed, and she was able to breathe again. Her muscles ached from trying to sleep on the cold concrete floor and she felt grimy. That was somehow appropriate for what she had to do next.

She only had two options left now. She couldn't bring herself to give up and go back to Chicago. That would be even more humiliating than the only other option. The dream wasn't a psychic premonition or some sort of vision. It was her subconscious trying to tell her something. Telling her what she had to do.

When she had regained her composure, she got up, pulled on her dirty slacks, got a drink of water from the bathroom sink and went to the front counter. After thumbing through the Rolodex by the till for almost five minutes, she found the number she wanted. She glanced at one of the three grandfather clocks she just couldn't sell. It was three-nineteen in the morning. That was just fine with her. She didn't want to talk to any real people anyway. The answering machine would be just fine for her purposes.

She dialed in the number and waited patiently through the greeting. After the beep she said, "Hi, Daniel, this is Amy Dresden," she spelled out the last name, and gave her pager number. "I was just calling to let you know that I have changed my mind about doing art shoots. Well sort of. Within limits at least. I'm never going to have an image to worry about and in the meantime I need the money. So if you have any paying shoots coming up, call me. Er…I'll only do stills, no video, and only solo. No boy/girl or girl/girl stuff. Not even simulated. And no tonsil shots. Just glamour swimsuit or lingerie, you know like Esquire, not Playboy or Pent…" The line went dead. She hung up the receiver and thought about calling back to finish her rant about what she would and would not do for money but decided against it. She already sounded desperate enough, no need to make it worse.

She stood there staring at the phone for five full minutes without moving. The next call would be the hard one. She took a deep breath and put the receiver to her ear. The dial tone buzzed loudly. She didn't have to look this number up, she knew it by heart. Just like she knew her party would still be out at three-twenty-eight in the morning. Again, she waited through the bubbly greeting and the beep.

"Hi, Rachel, it's me, Amy. I changed my mind. I want to take you up on your offer…"

***

Wednesday, April 6, 1994

It wasn't long before Rachel got back to Amy. She was one of the most popular dancers at the Wild Cat. She got the plum shift, six to closing. At twenty minutes past four she called back to the shop with the news that it was all arranged. Amy could come to the club at eleven and audition for Goldie.

After Amy explained her predicament with the van, Rachel agreed to come and get her. She would be there around seven or seven thirty and they could go swing by

Amy's apartment to get some clean clothes and cosmetics for the audition and rescue Jane Austen. That would also give them a little time to work out a routine for Goldie.

To keep herself from thinking too much for the next few hours Amy did busywork of tidying the sales-floor and putting the bear back up on the rail. It was the strangest thing, it seemed to be grinning at her before she covered it with the tarp. Something about the way those dark, lifeless eyes stared at her made her skin crawl. A horrible nineteen-fifties B movie played out in her imagination. To get revenge against the American Army for performing a nuclear test on a remote Alaskan glacier, an evil Eskimo shaman cast a spell on the glowing remains of an irradiated polar bear. Its skin got shipped back to the states where on the nights of the full moon it became *the ghost-bear!* Its reign of terror began by eating an unsuspecting blonde antique dealer. It could only be stopped by teenage rebels Steve McQueen and Michael Landon when they chased it off the cliff at Make-out Point in their hotrods.

Amy was snapped out of her half-doze, half-daydream by the sound of tires screeching in the parking lot behind the shop. She glanced at her watch, eight forty-seven. That was Rachel all over; she would be late to her own funeral. She grabbed the jewelry box for the pawn shop and dashed out the back door. But Rachel's silver CR-X was not there.

The crazy-little-Asian-woman-next-door was leaning into the driver's side door of her little blue sports car, fastening the latches that held the top closed. Bending over in such a short black skirt was not exactly ladylike a pose. Embarrassed, and oddly ashamed for looking, Amy turned her back and slammed her metal shop door loudly enough to let the other woman know she was there.

She heard the other woman's high heels scrape on the asphalt and a distinct metallic clank.

"Oh...it's only you." When Amy turned back the little woman's eyes were completely concealed by a pair of mirrored aviator glasses. She tipped her head slightly to let her glossy black hair cover half her face. She held her shoulders square and tight with both hands together directly in front of her, below the edge of the open car door, deliberately out of sight. The stiff posture coupled with the almost military cut of her bright red blazer reminded Amy of the guards at Buckingham Palace.

"You startled me." What little of the woman's face Amy could see had turned almost as red as her blazer. "I didn't think you were here today because I didn't see your van."

"Sorry." Amy smiled at her unsurely. "I heard you pull in and thought you were my ride."

With an obvious force of will the woman relaxed her shoulders, stood a bit straighter and let her hands fall to her sides. But she still kept her hands behind the car door. She looked around, obviously trying to stall.

"Come to think of it, I didn't see your van yesterday either. It didn't get stolen, did it?"

"No, I'm not that lucky. No one else would be stupid enough to want it anyway. It's in the shop, again."

"That's a Ford for you, 'Fixed Or Repaired Daily.'"

"Yeah, that's what my Ex always said. This is the third time this month it's been in the shop. It's the last Ford I'll ever buy."

With her keys in her left hand the woman stepped out from behind the car door and shut it, without rolling up the window. She was clearly trying to hide something in her right hand. She walked almost sideways to keep her willowy body between whatever she was hiding and Amy. She looked like a six-year-old caught raiding the cookie jar. No—that was wrong. She was clearly embarrassed, but she was not child-like. Perhaps she really was shy, and the barely there miniskirt was a concession to a husband or boyfriend's fetish. Regardless of her size and her shyness, she had…presence.

As she reached the back door of her shop she shifted whatever was in her right hand around her thigh to keep it out of Amy's sight. With the awkwardness of her off-hand she scrabbled the key into the lock then froze for an instant as if thinking something over. Leaving the keys hanging from the lock she turned back around, careful to keep her secret behind her back. One dark eye peeked around the black curtain of hair and over the top of her impenetrable sunglasses. It seemed to see more than it should. Now it was Amy that felt exposed under its direct gaze.

"With your van on the fritz, I could give you a ride if you need one." It wasn't what she said but the way she said it that made Amy uncomfortable. It was, after all, just a neighborly gesture, but seemed to imply something more.

"Er… yeah…I mean no…I mean…" Amy began to stammer but she was saved by the bell, or the horn. Rachel's Silver Honda bounced into the parking lot at just that moment. "Thanks for the offer but my ride's here. I gotta go."

The little car stopped perpendicular to the blue one. It vibrated with a muffled bass beat from inside. Rachel leaned across the seats and opened the passenger side door for Amy and let Dire Straits pour into the parking lot.

"Thanks anyway," Amy shouted over the *Sultans of Swing*. "That's very kind of you." She slithered down into the tiny car and waved as she slammed the door. The little woman stood there as still as a statue watching Rachel make a three-point turn and peel out of the parking lot.

"Who was that?" Rachel asked Amy once she was in the car.

"Just the crazy-little-woman-next-door. She owns the gun shop or at least works there. Cute little thing, isn't she?"

"If you say so. That red coat makes her look like a garden gnome if you ask me."

"Can we swing by my place first to get some clothes and feed the cat before the interview?"

Rachel stepped on the gas and made a left onto Sepulveda that made a truck driver question whether or not her parents had been married or merely business associates. As they drove, Amy filled Rachel in on her situation with the van and rent and bills. After flatly refusing a loan of any kind they came to a working agreement. Until she got the van out of the shop Amy would stay at Rachel's apartment. That way, Amy could use the Honda during the day, as long as she had it back before Rachel had to start her shift at the club.

After a covert raid on Amy's apartment they retrieved a suitcase full of clean clothes, Amy's make-up case, a Sherpa bag containing an annoyed Jane Austen, and twenty-seven eight by ten color glossy photographs of Amy in string bikinis on the hood of Ted's Corvette to be used for Lyle's advertisement, all without being seen by the landlady or her daughter.

The next two hours they spent at Rachel's apartment working out what songs to play, what to wear, and more importantly, what not to wear for Amy's audition for Goldie at the Wild Cat Cabaret.

***

They were only fifteen minutes late for the audition. At a quarter past eleven in the morning, the club was a hive of activity getting ready to open for the day. Rachel led Amy in through the back door and down a side hallway to Nancy "Goldie" MacGill's private office and tapped lightly on the door. After a moment of silence, they heard a voice made deep by cigarettes and too much coffee.

"Come."

Rachel pushed open the door and guided Amy in with her. Goldie sat behind a cluttered desk with a black Virginia Slim in a long holder clenched between her teeth in the corner of her mouth. She was in her middle thirties. The harsh light from a green glass shaded desk lamp reflected up from the stack of invoices, work schedules, and ledgers spread over the blotter and highlighted every line on her face. Her hair was shock white, not gray from age but white as snow. Her skin was anything but white. It was so deeply tanned that it matched her coffee-brown eyes and had the texture of very expensive leather.

She continued writing and did not look up at them as they came in.

"You're late, Tiffany. Again. Is this the new meat you were so excited about last night?" She tossed her pen down on the blotter and leaned back in her chair. She was pretty or had been not too long ago. The inverted bobbed blonde hair and way she clinched a Lucite cigarette holder in her teeth made her look like the love child of Carol Channing and Hunter S. Thompson.

"Well, come on now honey, don't just stand there like a department store dummy, let's have a look at you. Lose the jacket and give us a spin. Let me see how you move."

Amy slipped off her denim jacket, revealing a little black strapless leather dress with the zipper all the way down the front. Amy hated that dress, but Rachel had insisted it would be perfect for the audition. Ted had bought it for her before they left Chicago. He claimed if she wore sexy rock-n-roll chick outfits like that to his shows, it supported his "stage persona." Being with the hottest chick in the place was good for his professional image and had the added bonus of showing the groupies he was taken. She thought he just liked her to dress like a slut. Whenever she wore it, she spent the entire time pulling the front up and the back down. It was an impossible tug-of-war. The worst part of it was Ted constantly trying to pull the zipper down more and more, as if she didn't already have enough on display.

She didn't exactly shake her bootie, it was far more subtle than that, and all the more effective for it. With her spine straight and shoulders back, Amy did her best runway spin and turned on her thousand-watt smile. Dozens of the photographers she had posed for had shown her how to show off her long legs to best effect. Years of aerobic training had taught her how to move without the awkwardness so common in statuesque women. After completing the slow-motion pirouette she struck a pose somewhere between "come and get me" and "I'm way too good for you."

"Good God the woman's an Amazon! What are you six, six-one?" Goldie said.

Never breaking character, Amy did a slight hair toss and flashed a flirtatious smile. "Oh no. I'm not that tall, it's the shoes. I'm barely five-nine. Really closer to five-eight and three-quarters."

Goldie turned to Rachel and in a high-pitched sing-song voice said; "I'm *barely* five-nine." Switching back to her regular speaking voice "Makes you want to climb up a step ladder and strangle her pretty, long neck."

"Yeah, or punch her in the knee-cap," Rachel said with a smile.

"Well, you've got the looks for the job, but can you dance?" Goldie said turning all her attention back to Amy. "Have you ever danced before? This is a grueling job. You'll be on those heels for a solid eight hours, nonstop. And when you're not shaking it on stage, you'll have to be on the floor waiting tables. You think you can handle that?"

"I'm used to being on my feet all day, that's not a problem. I've never danced professionally before. I have done a lot of runway stuff and some car shows and bikini contests. So, I'm comfortable with being on stage. As far as the physical demands go, I used to work as an aerobics instructor. I did four classes a day, five days a week, so I think I can handle this."

"Well honey, this ain't "Sweatin' to the Oldies." The audience won't be a bunch of Volvo-driving-soccer-moms trying to lose a couple pounds to get back the attention of their bored husbands. There's a big difference between being on stage in a bikini and doing a lap dance for some beer-bellied truck driver. You have to make the smelly bastards think you actually like it. Really sell it. Can you do that?"

"If I can convince over-privileged middle-age *hausfraus* that the eight-hundred dollar designer jeans I'm modeling on the runway will look as good on them as they look on me, I can convince horny guys that I'm into them when I'm naked."

"Now that's the spirit! Keep that attitude and you make us both a fortune." She handed Amy a job application. "Fill this out while I make a copy of your Driver's License and Social Security Card. Then get out on stage so I can see what you can do. Tiffany can show you the way backstage." She plopped the form down on the desk in front of Amy and hustled out, leaving the room feeling suddenly empty without her.

The application was a generic form from an office supply store. It asked questions that had no bearing whatsoever on nude dancing. She didn't see how any of her real-world vocational experience could apply to being an exotic dancer. When she got to the box marked "job skills" she wondered if she should include her measurements, bra size and that she was able to do the *Pasini Mudea* yoga pose.

After she had finished the application, Rachel ushered Amy out of Goldie's office, past the men's room to a door off the narrow hallway. It led into a tiny anteroom with heavy black imitation velvet curtain over an archway into the dressing room.

"Are you sure Jesus wants' me to do this? I mean, doesn't it seem wicked to you, Cindy-Bare?" The voice was an adult, but its insecurity made it sound childish.

"Of course he does! Didn't Larry tell you so himself?" The other voice was reassuring and authoritarian. "If you're going to be a fisher of men, you need to use the gifts God and the family gave you to lead sinners back to the true way of the Lord. Anyone can save a soul seeking redemption, they are already on the path. But we seek out the lost souls that do not know they need to be saved. We must use the gifts God gave us to bring them to Jesus. How could God's own work be wicked?"

Rachel pushed the black drape aside and directed Amy into a trapezoidal room. A young woman with copious amounts of espresso brown hair teased in every direction, and ridiculously augmented breasts sat at one of three places at the makeup table, staring into the reflection of her enormous gunmetal blue eyes. All she had on was a blue sequined G-string and more makeup than Gene Simmons. To her left was a Farrah Fawcett wannabe dressed in a skintight white spandex mini-dress, white stockings, and a nurse's cap. The blonde was only one or two years older chronologically, but centuries older emotionally. There was something almost matronly about the way she watched the other girl. The instant Rachel and Amy barged in the conversation stopped dead and all of the blonde's attention was on Rachel.

"Tiffany, what are you doing here at this time of the morning? I thought you only worked nights." The blonde's cheery voice was betrayed by a hardness in her cold blue eyes.

"Oh, hi there, Cindy-Bare. My friend is here for an audition. I came along for moral support," Rachel said.

"Tiffany?" Amy said giving Rachel a sideways glance.

"Stage name. It's best if you just get into the habit of using it whenever you're in the club."

"It comes in handy if a mug sees you in real life." Cindy-Bare said. "If some weirdo comes up to you on the street and calls you by your working name you know where you know him from."

"I see. So, I guess that makes me Joan then." Amy said and stuck out her hand. The blonde shook it with a firm grip and an aggressive stare.

"I'm Pat...er...um...I mean...Hillarie. I just know we're going to be friends," the brunette said as she turned around, nearly sweeping all the cosmetics off the counter.

"You certainly are," Amy said with a wink. Hillarie frowned.

"I don't get it."

"You know, HILL-arie, like hills," Amy said, cupping her hands over her own humanly proportioned breasts. Hillarie's eyes widened and her face burned red through the heavy layers of makeup. She turned to Cindy-Bare "Is that why Larry changed my name after the operation?"

"Better than Tit-tania," Rachel said as she grabbed Amy's shoulder and led her to the stage. "There's your first song now, hurry, get out there."

Amy climbed up the three steps to the stage platform and waited for the synthesizer riff that led into ZZ Top's *Legs* to end and for Billy Gibbon to start singing.

How had she come to this moment? Was she really about to strut out there and take off her clothes in front of a room full of strangers? She wasn't just stepping on stage, she was crossing a line. Once she crossed that line there was no turning back. How much further would she go? How low would she let herself sink?

Her cue came and she strutted out on stage high-stepping and proud. She made the first lap then spun around the pole at the end proving that she did in fact have legs and she did in fact know how to use them. That part was easy.

255

The whole first song was easy. All she had to do was gradually peel off Ted's horrible little black dress. That left her in her black lace bra and panties. That wasn't too bad.

The second song was the real barrier. She started out in her underwear with Sting demanding his MTV. It was just like the bikini shows she had done with Rachel. But when she got to Mark Knopfler's driving guitar riffs the time had come. This was the turning point.

Time stopped as if Rod Serling himself had pressed the fob on that infamous gold watch of his. Every detail and nuance was imprinted in her memory with the permanence of blood stains on a wedding dress.

She was at the pole near the end of the "T" shaped stage. Goldie was at the rail, a Virginia Slim in its cigarette holder clenched between her artificially white teeth. The domino mask of untanned skin her sunglasses left around those appraising brown eyes made them look like black holes sucking all the light and life out of the universe. Two rows behind her a pear-shaped Hispanic woman in baggy jeans and a Maggy Maids T-shirt was moving chairs out of the way as she vacuumed the cheap gray carpet. At the bar, a topless woman with a fire-engine-red mullet was more interested in checking drinking glasses for water spots than anything on the stage. Not even the DJ was interested in what Amy was or wasn't wearing.

They didn't understand that this was an auspicious moment. A turning point in history, like Neil Armstrong's first steps on the moon or the day the Beatles appeared on the Ed Sullivan Show. This was the grand unveiling. The first public appearance of Amy Dresden's magnificent mammaries. But to them it was just another day at the office. Just another average ordinary every day set of boobs.

It was more humiliating because they were so unimpressed. At least if they were cat-calling and jeering they would be paying attention. But none of them even cared that she was about to bare it all. It meant nothing to anyone but her.

She opened the French clasp on her bra and tossed it behind her. She tried to remember that dancing wasn't just about getting naked, it was about charisma too. Goldie wasn't interested in seeing yet another set of big tits, she was looking for entertainers. Just flashing her knockers wasn't enough; she had to flirt with the audience. That would have been easier if Goldie had been a man, or even looked remotely interested in what she was seeing.

After the longest four minutes and thirty-eight seconds of her life, Sting's demands for his MTV began the fade and she was able to return to the relative safety of the dressing room. At least for a few seconds. Rachel was actually jumping up and down and silently clapping her hands together.

"You look great out there, you're killing it. Go on now, just one more song. And don't forget, look her in the eyes and *emote*," Rachel said.

"She's okay, I guess." Cindy-Bare said, but she didn't look too impressed. She had been watching from the wings with a face like she smelled rotten eggs. Hillarie was still more concerned with troweling on the war paint than with anything Amy was doing.

Drums began to pound. Amy took a deep breath, burst through the curtain and struck a pose as Joe Elliott declared "Love is like a Bomb." Steve Clark's power cords began and carried her up stage to the pole with swinging hips. She did a couple of spins and dips. All the while tugging and stretching the elastic of her panties. After a full minute, that seemed to last only a second, she turned her back on Goldie as Def Leppard broke into the tender, romantic chorus of "Pour Some Sugar on Me." Amy slipped the black lace down her thighs and let her last remaining garment, and her last remaining self-respect, drop to the floor.

Her father always said, "If you're going to be a bear, be a Grizzly Bear." So, she didn't hold anything back. Rather than just kicking the panties to the side of the stage she bent all the way over to pick them up. Far enough that she was able to look Goldie straight in the eye between her knees. Finally she had Goldie's attention.

She picked up the knickers, stood slowly, and tossed them to the back of the stage before she did her final reveal. For the next three and a half minutes she strutted, squatted, crawled and writhed around on the stage. No one could accuse her of being bashful.

With the song's finale she ended on her knees at the edge of the stage, thrusting her hips in time with the last drumbeats. A dance step she most definitely did not do at her senior prom. The music ended and the ambient sounds of the vacuum cleaner and rattling glass returned. She froze trying to catch her breath. Goldie clapped her hands three times, slowly.

"Not bad. Not bad at all. Not exactly great, but not bad. Like I said before, you've got the looks, but your dancing needs work. Nothing we can't fix though."

"So, I've got the job?" Amy said as she got to her feet. Without the spell of the music she suddenly felt very naked and desperately wanted to make a beeline back to the dressing room to get something on. But Goldie clearly wanted her to stay. Standing there in the center of the room

258

naked as a jaybird and carrying on a conversation was as much a part of the audition as the dancing had been.

"I'm not quite sure. I need to know something about you first. What are you doing here?"

"What? I don't understand. What do you mean 'what am I doing here?' I'm…I'm looking for a job. That's what I'm doing here."

Goldie took a long drag from her Virginia Slim and sent a string of smoke rings drifting up to the stage. "Yes, of course you are, honey. But why *here?* Why stripping? Why not waiting tables in a straight restaurant?

"You're too old to be in college, so it's not about tuition. There's no stretch marks so you not to trying to support a kid on your own. And you're with Tiffany so you're not supporting some loser boyfriend…"

"Rachel and I are just friends, we're not…."

"Yeah, right, whatever you say. It's not drugs either. You've got too much energy to be shooting smack. Your teeth are way too good to be a tweeker, and you're not thin enough to be on coke.

"So what's the story? Is it some weird sex thing with Tiffany? Why are you willing to strip?"

"Rachel is not my girlfriend!"

"Yeah, that's just what Rock Hudson used to say about Gomer Pyle. I don't care one way or the other. What you do, and who you do it to, is no skin off my back. As a matter of fact, the mugs will pay double if they think two girls are into each other. So, what is it that makes you desperate enough to show your pussy to strangers for money? It's okay, honey, I've heard 'em all over the years. There's literally nothing you can say that I haven't heard. What kind of monkey do you have on your back?"

"Antiques." Amy said dryly. Goldie blinked three times and the tip of her cigarette holder drooped.

"The music must be affecting my ears. Did I hear that right, did you just say 'antiques?'"

"Yes."

"As in old furniture?"

"Yes."

Goldie slapped the stage and began to laugh out loud "Well all-righty then! That's a new one. I've seen Chippendale dancers before but never seen a dancer for Chippendale."

"I do have a 'straight' day job. I own an antique shop over in the Valley but I'm having a little bit of a cash flow problem right now. I have more merchandise than customers. If I don't pay some bills the repo man will come a-knocking on my back door."

"Well, we can't let that happen, can we?" Goldie smiled like the Cheshire Cat coming upon all three blind mice. "I can relate to your problem. I have too much 'merchandise' and not enough 'customers' too. The last thing I need is another blonde that can't dance. But seeing as you're Tiffany's friend I guess I can give you a shot.

"You have a great look. But. What you need is a gimmick. With your sweet face and that all-natural look, you should go for the school-girl thing. You know; a school uniform, knee-high socks, some braids, maybe come on stage with a book bag or a teddy bear. Play up the whole wholesome and innocent thing.

"Lose the black leather and lace, it's way overdone. Work out a couple of routines with Tiffany. You know, the innocent little schoolgirl seduced by the hot teacher. Or bad-girl good-girl stuff. The mugs will pay through the nose for that."

"Rachel and I are not together."

"Yeah, exactly, play up that whole 'in the closet' thing too. The mugs hemorrhage green over lesbi-friends. Especially if they think they might see some real action. And whatever you do don't shave that natural blonde bush. Guys will cough up their union dues for a glimpse of a real blonde bush.

"But…you're not a good enough dancer to put on nights, yet." Goldie flipped open a pink leather-bound day runner and flipped through the pages. "I can put you on three days a week starting next Monday. Eleven to five to start. That will give you some time to work out your stage persona and get some experience dancing. After that, we'll see about some better shifts. Will that work for you?"

"Yeah…sure."

"Right, eleven o'clock on Monday morning then. Be there or be square.

"Tiffany can go over the house fees and how tips and all that work, and any other rules you need to know about." She began to scribble in her book. 'Oh, one last thing, what's your stage name going to be?"

"Joan? Like Joan Jet, or how about Stevie. I just love Stevie Nicks."

"No, those are both too butch for you. Especially with you and Tiffany."

"Rachel and I are not a couple. I'm not gay!"

"Yeah, right, okay. Whatever you say. I'll play along as long as you want, but you're not fooling anybody."

"You need something more 'girl next door.' Oh I've got it; Stacy. It's perfect. Short, cute, easy to remember. There's a Stacy on every cheer-leading team."

"Right, fine, I'm Stacy. I'll see you on Monday."

Amy made a show of walking slowly back to the dressing room in spite of how frantically she wanted to get her clothes back on. Just as she came off the stage the first chords of "Calling on You" by Stryper began blaring and Hillary bounced out on stage in a blue sequined mini-dress.

Before she could reach her clothing, Rachel had her in a hug.

"Congratulations! You really impressed Goldie out there." Amy squirmed out of Rachel's embrace. Goldie was already convinced they were lovers, she didn't want to substantiate the rumor. Amy was uncomfortable with displays of affection, especially when she was naked. Not that she thought that Rachel would ever try to force anything, but it was just...awkward.

"Yeah, I got the job. Now, let me get dressed and get out of here so I can go do my errands." Amy didn't feel too good about it, but she proceeded to get dressed and tried to keep up appearances. It was more difficult because she couldn't honestly tell her best friend, her only close friend really, how dirty she felt. After all, Rachel had been dancing for almost three years now, how could she tell her only friend how degrading her job was?

"Looks like we're gonna see a lot more of each other." Cindy-Bare said, watching Amy appraisingly.

"I don't think it would be humanly possible to see any more of each other than we already have," Amy said as she stepped into her panties.

"No, not *humanly* possible. But you know what? Jesus can see everything. He can see things humans can't, like what's really inside people's hearts."

Amy stopped struggling with the French clasp on her bra, dumbfounded.

"I know that look," Cindy-Bare said. "You think I'm some sort of Jesus freak, and I probably am. But the Savior is the answer. I have seen a lot of lost girls come through here with a lot of different problems—drugs, abuse, poverty—and the answer to every one of their problems was the same thing, our Savior, Jesus Christ."

"Well, the Lord helps those that help themselves." Amy finished fastening her bra and picked up her dress. "The answer to my problem is money. So, unless your humble carpenter can loan me ten grand I don't think he can help me."

"Money is just an illusion. Even if you win the lottery tomorrow and had ten million dollars, it would not fill the empty void in your soul that leaves you questioning the meaning of life."

"The only thing in my life I am questioning right now is how to pay my rent."

"Let me take you down to Croydon House to meet Larry. He can explain it all and make you see clearly for the first time. He can show you what is really important in life and help you find the way to inner peace."

"I have all the inner peace I can use right now, Cindy, but thanks for the offer." She zipped up the front of her dress abruptly. "Come on, Rachel, I have a lot to do today." They hurried down the hall and out the back door.

"Sorry about her," Rachel said as they got into the car. "A lot of girls in this line of work are on the edge like that."

"I can see why." To put an end to the conversation Amy cranked up some Iron Maiden on the radio.

***

Amy dropped Rachel off at her apartment and took the borrowed Honda to make her rounds of pawn shops to unload some of the jewelry. She only got about two-thirds of what she expected, before going back to her own shop.

As she let herself in the back door of the shop there was a muffled buzz from her bag. It had to repeat itself three times before she realized what it was. Her pager. She only used it for modeling and acting jobs, and it hadn't buzzed once in the last six months. A quick glance at the number told her it was Dan, her agent. *What could he want?"*

Ignoring the light switch she trudged through the cluttered work room out to the sales floor to use the phone by the cash stand. Dan's assistant picked up on the first ring and put her straight through to the man himself.

"Amy, baby…" He called everybody baby. "Tell me that wasn't a drunk call last night. Tell me you really mean it."

"I mean it. I need the money. But…"

"Fantastic! I already have a gig that would be perfect for you."

"Now, Dan, I meant what I said last night about what I will and won't do. I'm willing to do artistic shoots, but no porn!"

"No porn, right, gotcha. Have I ever steered you wrong?"

"Yes. Almost every time."

"Well this one is a cream puff. It's perfect for you."

"I've heard that before. How much, and what do I have to do?"

"You'll be posing for an old client of mine, Henry DeCesare."

"Oh, I remember him. He was on some dumb cop show in the eighties. My sister had his poster in her bedroom. What does he want me to do?"

"Well he's kind of retired now, lives up in Beverly Hills somewhere. He's decided he wants to be an artist. You know like that Star Wars guy does."

"Okay, but what does he want me to do and how much is he going to pay me?"

"I'm not exactly sure, it's all artsy-fartsy stuff. He said he needs a platinum blonde with fair skin because he wants to use body paint to make you look like a rock or something. I've sent a couple of girls out there before, and they didn't have any problems. Said he was always real professional and a total gentleman. No pervy stuff. He says he has a certified make-up artist for the girls and a legit studio set up in the basement of his house. He is offering three-hundred an hour."

"For three-hundred bucks an hour he can paint me green if he wants to."

"So you'll do it? I can count on you?"

"After what I did today, it will be a step up."

"How's nine tomorrow morning for you?"

"The sooner the better."

As they swapped contact information and ironed out the last details, she saw someone stop at her front windows. Even though it was still gray and overcast there was enough sunlight shining in the display windows to backlight the potential customer.

As soon as she could hang up the phone she grabbed the keys and rushed to open the door but stopped short just a few feet shy of her intended goal. The woman outside was not a customer. It was one of the working girls that plied their trade up and down the Sepulveda Boulevard stroll. She had only stopped to check her reflection in the window. From her side with the sun reflecting in the glass, the interior of Amy's shop was pitch black.

Amy was hypnotized by the stranger as she stood there primping her hair. She was probably the same age as Amy but life had used her hard and she looked at least twenty years older. Skinny legs with scabbed knees stuck out of baggy cutoffs. A too small crop top only accented her emaciated shoulders and sagging breasts.

Unaware that she was being observed the hooker examined her bleeding gums and few remaining teeth in the reflection. When she moved closer to the glass to better see a blemish she saw Amy standing there watching her.

Before Amy could turn away the hooker shouted something. Amy couldn't exactly make out what she said through the thick glass but it involved Amy doing something with a grizzly bear that the ASPCA, and the bear, would not approve of. Before the hooker could make clear exactly what the bear was supposed to do with the electric eggbeater, an '85 Chrysler Lebaron with fake wood side-panels pulled to the curb and picked her up.

Amy watched them disappear into traffic. Was she any better than that…thing out there, or did she just have a better product to peddle in a more upscale market?

It was a long, tiring day in the shop for Amy. It was far more exhausting to sit around waiting for a customer and having nothing to do than it was to be overrun with too many customers. The day seemed to drag on forever. When four-thirty finally came she decided to close early. After a quick stop at a grocery store to get some supplies she headed back to Rachel's apartment to make dinner and hand off the car.

When she reached the apartment, Rachel was packing a gym bag with her "work clothes," but Amy was able to persuade her to hang out long enough for grilled chicken and a salad with no dressing. As they ate, Amy filled her in on the modeling job for Henry DeCesare.

"It's through the agency so I won't see a dime of the money until the first of the month. But it should be enough to catch up on my rent," she said over the last of the dry chicken.

"I don't know about this one. It's the sensitive artists that are usually the perverts. The creative types are the ones that give models a bunch of bullshit about you being their muses to get you into bed." Rachel said.

"Dan was pretty vague about this body paint stuff. What do you suppose he wants me to do?"

"A lot of them want to paint clothes on you. I knew one girl that had a photographer paint jeans and a t-shirt on her, then made her walk through a Walmart naked. There was this one artist who wanted to cover me in paint and have me roll around on a canvas like a big Rorschach test. But he was a painter not a photographer. You never know. At least in the club if some mug tries something there's always a bouncer around to put him in his place."

"There won't be any bouncers at Henry DeCesare's." Amy poked at the salad with a fork. "Do you think I should back out?"

"How about I go with you? If 'Officer Cisco' tries anything funny we can just walk. Like we did that time at the Harryhausen."

"That would be great, thanks," Amy leaned over and hugged Rachel. It was intended to be a sisterly gesture. But it didn't feel sisterly at all. Suddenly very self-aware Amy sat back and awkwardly pushed the last bits of chicken around on her plate.

"Shit, I'm running late. Goldie is gonna kill me if I'm late again." She grabbed her bag and car keys and ran for the door. She stopped in the threshold and looked back at her friend. Amy's face was beet red but she was trying hard to look natural. She was failing.

"I'll be back around three, Sweetie. Hold that thought till I get home." Before Amy could answer Rachel shut the door and was gone.

Amy was not sure what, if anything at all, had just happened. All she was sure of was it was uncomfortable. No longer interested in her meal, she piled the dirty dishes in the growing heap in the kitchen sink.

Hoping to take her mind off whatever that was, she changed into a pair of light gray sweatpants and a comfy old T-shirt and curled up on the couch with Jane Austen to do some channel surfing. They finally settled on a dumb action picture about Keanu Reeves and Sandra Bullock being trapped on a bus. They drove all around L.A., unable to stop.

It was so hot on the bus that Amy could barely breathe from the heat. But the smell was all wrong. Not exactly bad, but still wrong. Instead of armpits and assholes it smelled of incense and perfume.

She could feel perspiration running in rivulets down her back and puddling under her breasts. She hated when that happened because it

268

always got soaked up by her bra and made it chafe. Good thing she wasn't wearing a bra today. But the downside of that was the wetness would make her top stick to her chest and become transparent. Good thing she wasn't wearing a top then.

Wait—what was she doing on a crowded bus with no clothes on? She looked franticly around. Outside the bus was nothing but burned out buildings and rubble. No sign of Keanu Reeves or Sandra Bullock anywhere. Sitting on the bench below her was her ex-boyfriend Ted, her agent Dan, and Rachel's ex-boyfriend Derrick; all three were staring up at her like hungry animals. She turned toward the front of the bus to get away but Goldie was blocking her path. She felt a warm body press against her from behind. She twisted and squirmed to get free from the groping Pillsbury Dough boy, but there was no escape. Her feet were magnets stuck to the steel floor of the bus.

"Not bad. Not bad at all," Goldie said soothingly. "You guys are 'friends' right? You should work out some routines together."

She felt the groper press against her from behind and nuzzle her neck. This time his breath was clean and instead of stale sweat and Blue Star Cream he smelled of Estee Lauder. The groper's hands came around her and cupped her breasts. Not with the bloated, sausage-like fingers from before, but nimble slim fingers ending in elegantly manicured French tipped nails.

"I know you want me. You've always wanted me." Rachel's voice was husky in her ear.

"Get some baby! You know that slut wants it," Derrick shouted from below.

"Go on, you little tramp, you never really wanted me. All you ever wanted was her," Ted said.

"When you're done playing I have some girl on girl work for both of you," Dan said.

269

"Go on now, the mugs hemorrhage green over lesbi-friends. Especially if they see some real action. So go for it! It's not like you're not into it or anything," Goldie said.

"Everybody always knew you were a dyke. You were just using me to get to LA. Just like you use everybody else to get what you really want," Ted sneered at her.

"I was right about you all along," Rachel whispered. *"I always knew you'd like it if you tried it."*

"Just make sure they all get a good look. Let the mugs back in the cheap seats see how wet she's making you. Wet bush always gets the biggest tips."

Amy screamed and sat up straight. Her heart was pounding so hard she thought her chest would burst open.

Rachel screamed back. She was just coming through the front door six feet away, and fully clothed.

"What!? What's wrong? Amy, what's happening?"

Amy's huge pale blue eyes darted around the room. She was on the couch in Rachel's living room in sweatpants and a t-shirt, not naked on a bus driving through a bombed out city. Still too breathless to talk she waved Rachel off and shook her head.

Between gasps she said "Sorry…bad…dream."

Rachel closed and locked the door and flicked on the living room lights. The sudden glare hurt Amy's eyes but it was also a relief.

"I tried to be quiet so I wouldn't wake you when I came in. Did you think I was a burglar or something?" Rachel tossed her bag on the dining table.

"No, no. Nothing like that. Just a stress dream. You know the type; you have to take a test you haven't studied for."

"Must have been a hard test to make you scream like that. What was it?"

"I can't remember exactly what it was about. It's all getting fuzzy now." She lied. She didn't want to go into any of the vivid details with Rachel about the dream. There would be no going back to sleep now, so she switched off the TV and headed into the kitchenette to put on a kettle of water.

"Are you sure you're okay? You scared the daylights out of me with that screaming. I'll bet the neighbors think I'm murdering you in here."

"I'm so sorry; I don't know what got into me. Would you like some coffee while I'm in here?"

"Good God no, it's bedtime for me. Just a quick shower to get rid of the glitter and I'm off to dreamland."

"I hope you have a better trip than I did."

"I should sleep like a rock. I didn't get much yesterday with your audition and all."

"Oh, I'm so sorry, I forgot you do the vampire thing because you work nights. How was work tonight? Did Goldie give you any grief about being late?"

"No, not Goldie. But I had a little grief with a Japanese salaryman."

Amy was still puttering around the kitchen waiting for the water to boil when she noticed the dark spot on the crotch of her sweatpants. She pulled the front of her T-shirt down to hide it. Her first thought was the nightmare had frightened her so badly she had wet herself. But that was only half right. She had wet herself, but it wasn't urine, it wasn't from fear. That was even more mortifying. Particularly because she had always had a problem in that area. When she was being intimate with Ted, even at the

271

height of her arousal she couldn't manage to do that. Much to her embarrassment, and Ted's annoyance, they had had to rely on store bought lubricants to make things work. The last thing in the world she wanted now was for Rachel to see. Who knows what she would think? Before her tea was ready she sat down at the dining table and crossed her legs to hide her shame.

"What's a salaryman?" she said, trying to sound at least half normal.

"A Japanese businessman. First time in the states. He could hardly *speakie the Engrish.*"

"So what did he do?"

"Well, at first it was going pretty good. I guess he had a thing for redheads. But after seven table dances he tried to play a little 'Tune in Tokyo.' So Ivan took him out in the parking lot and tuned him in."

"Oh, that's terrible. Does that sort of thing happen a lot?"

"No. Not often. The bouncers are real good at making their presence felt in the club so most customers behave themselves. Ironically, there is less trouble in nudie-bars than in regular bars because there's no booze to make guys artificially stupid.

"I gotta get this glitter off me, I'll be right back." Rachel disappeared into the bathroom and the shower started. Amy closed her eyes and took a deep breath and held it, relieved that her friend hadn't noticed her 'accident.' She was about to let it out when the tea pot began to whistle shrilly. She jumped out of her seat, took the pot off the stove and put some loose leaf Chamomile in the tea caddy to steep. With a quick peek around the corner to be sure the coast was clear she changed into some dry panties and a clean pair of jeans. She had just made it back to her seat at the table with the milk when the sound of the shower stopped.

As she poured first the milk then the tea into her cup, Rachel swept into the room with all the subtlety of a twister in a trailer park wearing nothing but an imitation red silk kimono she had bought in Little Tokyo. Vigorously drying her imitation red hair with a bath towel, she plopped into the chair next to Amy's.

"Yuck, I will never understand how you can put milk in tea."

"It tastes better than coffee, and it's not nearly as bad for you."

"Well there's no accounting for taste."

"Rachel, just out of curiosity, what did you tell Goldie about me?"

"Oh, just the usual."

"The usual?"

"Yeah, you know, the usual stuff a boss wants to hear about a potential employee before she hires them."

"What exactly does the owner of a strip club want to hear about a 'potential employee?'"

"Well, obviously that you're gorgeous. You have to admit that's true. But even more important she wants to hear that you're reliable. She wants to hear you're not too nuts and you don't have some wacko jealous boyfriend that's going to bust into the club and start fights with customers for looking at you."

"You mean like Ted did at the gym?"

"Yes, like Ted did at the gym. So I told her you don't have a boyfriend."

"Did you tell her I had a *girl*friend instead?"

"Why would I say something like that?"

Amy shrugged and stirred her tea. "What did you tell her about us?"

"Not much, just that we're old friends and we did some modeling jobs together and we had been roommates for a while. Why?"

"Goldie is convinced we're a couple."

"A couple of what?"

"You know. She thinks we sleep together."

"So? What's it to her?"

"Nothing—it's not..."

"Not what?"

"It's...she thinks I'm a lesbian. There's nothing wrong with being gay or anything...just that...I'm not...I mean...I don't like girls."

"The lady protests too much, methinks."

"Come on, Rachel, give me a break. I'm just not into women. To tell you the truth, I'm not all that interested in men."

"That would certainly explain what you saw in that pretty boy Ted."

"Pretty boy? What the hell are you talking about? He looked just like Eddie Van Halen."

"Eddie Van Halen? More like Valerie Bertinelli. That guy was just one spa day away from being Boy George."

"Come on, Rachel, are you trying to say Ted was gay or something? I did catch him in bed with another woman, well a girl at least. She may have been underage but she was definitely a she. He was totally masculine. If anything he was too masculine."

"Ted was *macho*, but not masculine. There is a big difference. Ted made David Bowie look like Clint

274

Eastwood. That's why he was constantly trying to prove it. He was always trying to compete with the other guys. He had to be with the hottest babe in the club. The girl nobody else could ever get. You were just a status symbol to him. Just like the Höfner bass and the Fender amplifiers he just had to have. That's why he needed that ridiculous sports car too. Why do you think he was so sensitive about his height? It's got to be tough to be tough in four inch heels. And like all the other guys, all he cared about was getting his rocks off as fast as he could. That's the difference between being with a man or a woman. It's like apples and oranges. There's no comparison."

"More like cucumbers and oranges."

"The point is being with a woman is nothing like being with a man. Guys only care about two tits, a hole, and a heartbeat."

"I've met a few that would settle for two out of three. But as repugnant as guys are, at least I know what they want to do to me. I wouldn't even know what to do with another woman. I mean what *do* you do? Does one of you take turns being the guy? Are there power tools involved?"

"You've seen too many porno movies. It's nothing like that. With guys, foreplay is just something to get out of the way before the main event. They're only interested in one thing and what hole they can stick it in first. Once that's done they just roll over and pass out like a beached whale, usually pinning your arm to the mattress till it goes numb in the process.

"But with us it's not just about getting off. It's about your entire being, body and mind. Not just your pussy. It's about exploring all of your senses. It is so much more than lick this and stick that in there."

"But I don't like foreplay either. I never even saw the appeal of kissing. The idea of someone sticking their tongue in my mouth, or anywhere else, just grosses me out."

"That's because you've never had the right person do it. You told me you have only ever been with Ted, and that one time with the guy in the back seat of his Mustang at your prom."

"His name was Shane, and it was a Camaro."

"Whatever. The point is neither one of them was exactly what you would call a 'sensitive' lover. Did either one of them ever even try and give you what you wanted or needed, or did they just want to fuck?"

"Ted did. At least he tried. That was even worse than just doing it with him. At least when he did that, we could get it over with and go to sleep. But when he tried to be 'sensitive' it was unbearable. I don't know which was worse, him trying to twist my nipples and poke at me with his fingers, or him slobbering all over me. It was just embarrassing…and sticky. Afterwards, I never felt completely clean, no matter how hard I scrubbed."

"With women it's not dirty. With the right woman it's…it's like a million butterflies fluttering all around you."

"Ick, bugs." Amy rolled her eyes.

"What I'm trying to say is, with a woman, it's not just about the physical part. It's more than just getting each other off."

"That's good because the thought of licking someone's thing is disgusting. Ted talked me into kissing 'Little Teddy' a couple of times and that was bad enough. But it was even worse when he tried to return the favor. I couldn't bear to kiss him for at least a week after. I kept thinking his lips were like toilet paper. It was so degrading." Amy shivered at the memory. "The very idea of putting my mouth on another woman's–you know—is just repulsive. I can't imagine me kissing some woman where she pees. It's just nauseating."

"I don't know, you might like it."

"Oh don't give me that 'how do you know you don't like it until you try it' shit. I had a drama teacher back home that always said that. She used to make me read love scenes with her as the guy to get me to kiss her.

"What is it about me that makes everybody think I'm a dyke. I'm not exactly butch or anything."

"Well, you do always wear sensible shoes."

"That's just because I'm so tall. Men are intimidated enough by me when I wear flats. And it's not about looks, anyway. I mean just look at you. I would never even suspect in a million years that you're...er...one, by looking at you. You don't exactly look like Eleanor Roosevelt or anything, I mean... And

how do you know a girl is...is...well you know?"

"I don't *know*. Not for sure. I can't quite put my finger on it, its intuition. You just...*know*. The only thing all gay people universally have in common is we're all individual people. We don't all look and act the same, or even like the same things.

"I know some girls that are totally into the butch types, but me I like tomboys. Some girls are totally into femmes and others like boy-babes. And almost any combination in-between."

"So how do you find each other?"

"The same way straight people find each other, trial and error. Sometimes you have to take a risk. Of course, with us it's scarier because you never know how somebody will react. Sometimes you tell a person how you feel about them and you get lucky, and they fall into your arms. Other times they are offended and try and break your arm. It's really scary when it's somebody you truly care about."

"So you just guess?"

"Yep, that's about it. I'm usually pretty accurate. I've only ever been completely wrong once."

"Really? With who?"

"Some dumb blonde I met at an audition."

"All right, I deserved that."

"Speaking of blonde, I was thinking of going blonde again, myself. I could get it to match yours. We could do a sister act."

"Yeah, but the collar wouldn't match the cuffs." Amy regretted saying it even before the words were out of her mouth.

"What are you, a method actor? With the two of us doing the bump and grind do you think the mugs would pay any attention to what color my bush is?"

"I would imagine that it would be their center of attention."

"I suppose I could dye it too. Like Dana Plato did that time she posed for Playboy. Or I could just shave it all off."

"No, I don't think that's a good idea." Suddenly unable to look Rachel in the eye, Amy glanced down into the dregs of her tea. Doing the naked lesbian *Lambada* in front of a crowd of horny frat boys and businessmen felt a little too much like her nightmare.

"After all, Goldie herself said she has too many blondes already." Her pale blue eyes jumped back up flashing as only a model's eyes can. "Why don't you try something totally different? Like green or blue."

"That would be different. Maybe a little too punk rock for the club though. I might be able to pull off white or maybe light pink." Rachel remained perfectly still and composed as she watched Amy look at everything in the room except her and exploited the awkwardness of the silence. When Amy felt so trapped that she was about to get up and start straightening the kitchen, Rachel stood up as if nothing had happened.

"Well if we're still going to Officer Cisco's for your photo shoot I'd better get a little beauty sleep. I still have to work tomorrow. Wake me up when it's time to go."

Amy sighed heavily. She had always been rather casual about undressing in front of other people. Even back in high school she had never been the least bit bothered about using the girls shower after gym class or changing clothes with other girls in the locker room. As an actress, it was not unusual for women and men to be rushing around backstage in various states of undress between costume changes. She and Rachel had seen each other nude hundreds of times, and it had meant nothing to her. But after Rachel had told her how she felt, that had changed. She would not just be nude at this photo shoot, she would be naked. Amy just could not endure Rachel seeing her that naked.

"Rachel, you know I was thinking about it and maybe it's better if you don't go. It is an agency shoot so I really doubt he'll try and pull anything. Besides, that way I can go straight to the store after the shoot and you can get some sleep for your shift tonight. Last thing you want to do is show up to work with bags under bloodshot eyes. Goldie will think I'm not letting you get any rest."

"We wouldn't want that to happen. If you're okay with going alone, I could use a couple extra hours sleep. See you tonight then," Rachel said and walked into the bedroom with a knowing smile that made Mae West look like Mother Teresa.

***

Thursday, April 7, 1994

While it is true that nobody walks in L.A., it is equally true that nobody knows how to drive in L.A., especially on the rare occasions that it rains. The extraordinary phenomena throws drivers into a county-wide panic in which they either refuse to exceed fifteen-miles-per-hour even on the freeway, or to drive any slower than sixty-five on narrow side streets and school zones. After all, it is a scientific fact that a car going through a puddle at speed will not get wet.

Amy didn't like driving Rachel's CR-X, it was way too low to the ground for her liking and it handled like a go-cart compared to the Detroit Iron she usually drove. The manual transmission made negotiating the winding switchbacks and twisting side roads of the Hollywood Hills even more tiresome. The light but steady rain made the combination of searching for the entrance to Henry DeCesare's house while working the CR-X's clutch and dodging kamikaze soccer moms in BMWs nerve racking. And Amy's nerves were already near the breaking point.

Even though the rain was fairly light she ran across the street to prevent her hair from getting too wet, but in her haste she splashed through a cold puddle at the base of the stairs that flooded one of her flats and left her foot freezing. The path up the steep steps led through a dense tunnel of foliage, then across a narrow lawn to a second set of steps up to a small landing and an elaborately carved hardwood front door with enormous ornamental brass hardware. She rang the bell and stood close to the wall to try and stay out of the rain as much as she could. But nothing happened. After what felt like an eternity, she tried the bell again. Still nothing. Growing up with the harsh Chicago winters had made Amy more tolerant of cold weather than most Angelinos but the flooded shoe made her wet foot feel as if it was encased in a block of ice. Her hair was getting soaked, and goosebumps were beginning to erupt on her bare legs. After all her preparation that morning, she was sure she looked like a wet cat. She pressed the bell a third time, still nothing.

She glanced at her watch and decided she must be at the wrong address. Maybe there were two paths from the gate and she missed the other one in her haste to get out of the rain. The instant she turned her back to leave the front door jerked open abruptly.

"Yes? What?" demanded he most beautiful man she had ever seen. He was not just handsome, he was Michelangelo's *David* in a pale blue, paisley, Eton Egyptian linen shirt.

"Well? What do you want?" His blue eyes sparkled and his perfect nostrils flared as if he smelled something foul.

"I'm Amy Dresden," she said.

"How nice for you."

"I have an appointment. Daniel Cline sent me for a photo shoot with Henry DeCesare."

"You mean you *had* an appointment. You're half an hour late"

"I'm sorry about that. I had trouble finding the house hidden back here like it is."

He sucked his teeth as he looked her over. When Amy was sure he was about to send her packing he threw the door all the way open and gestured her in.

"Well, I suppose you had better come in then. Better late than never."

"Thanks, I'm getting soaked out here."

"Yezz. Do try not to drip on the floors. We just had them refinished. I am Andrew Zavacká, Mister DeCesare's personal administrative assistant." He did not offer to shake hands. "While I let Henry and Rui know you're finally here you can fill out the 'model release' forms. I will also need to make a copy of your driver's license as proof of age for Henry's files. As if anybody would ever think *you're* seventeen." He shoved a clipboard of paperwork at her, took her ID, and left Amy alone in the ominously silent chamber.

The cavernous living room was Hollywood's approximation of an upscale hunting lodge from the 1880s, or at least a thirteen-year-old boy's idea of one. All around the room disembodied glass-eyed animal heads stared down at her. An actual stuffed mountain lion crouched at the foot of the stairs ready to spring on any unsuspecting deer that happened by. All of the furniture was upholstered in wild animal hides. A fantastic late nineteenth century German oak breakfront gun cabinet displayed the polished walnut and gleaming blue barrels of half a dozen sporting arms. The room was clearly the result of a mathematical equation; two equal parts ego and testosterone, multiplied by unlimited disposable income, minus good taste.

But the one thing that most dominated the space was a gigantic fireplace. It was almost as large as her entire apartment. Over the stone mantel was a larger-than-life oil on black velvet of the fading star in his glory days. He leaned over the handlebars of a Police Model Harley Davidson Electra Glide with his uniform shirt open to the waist showing off enough curly black chest hair to weave a Navaho rug.

"Hi there! You must be Amy. I'm Henry DeCesare." She had been so engrossed in the painting that the convivial voice almost made her jump out of her skin. She spun around and came face to face with the man himself. DeCesare was dressed in his photographer's costume: brand name khaki cargo pants and a matching utility vest over a gleaming white silk shirt open just far enough to display two gold chains as thick as the Queen Mary's anchor lines.

He was ruggedly handsome in spite of having the most perfect skin she had ever seen on any real person, man or woman. Even though he was nowhere nearly as beautiful as the bronze god that had let her in, he had something more than just good looks that Andrew lacked. A raw animal magnetism that made him the center of attention. What the fan magazines of the silent era used to call "it." Sure he was an aging, macho, egotistical fop in a silly outfit and bad rug, but he was an astoundingly charming, aging, macho, egotistical fop in a silly outfit and bad rug.

"Oh…uh…hi. Sorry about that, you sort of startled me. I'm Amy Dresden. Daniel Cline sent me."

"That's okay, I have that effect on a lot of women your age. I bet you were a big fan of Motor Patrol when you were in middle school. No need to be so star struck, you'll find I'm a regular person just like everybody else," he said holding out a hand.

She took it and tried to ignore the vain assumption that she was impressed by his presence. In a strange way, it was refreshing to meet a man that was making a fool of himself over his own appearance instead of hers. But she had been caught a little off guard and tried to stall.

"What an amazing room. It must have taken you ages to find all the perfect original pieces for it."

"Thanks. Andy's friend did most of the work. But the ideas were all mine. All that's missing is a bear skin to go in front of the fireplace. But it's almost impossible to find a real one." Amy heard cash registers ringing in her ears. All of her insecurity's about being caught off guard and the shoot vanished like a lawyer's ethics.

"Well isn't that lucky! I have a beautiful bear skin." She gave him her best let's make a deal smile.

"I'm sure you do," Henry said laughing out loud. "But you won't really be bare in the photos. Rui, my make-up-girl, is going to do a complete body paint on you. From head to toe."

Amy shut her eyes and pinched the bridge of her nose in frustration. *And they say blondes are dumb.* "I mean, I have one for sale." His face went completely blank. *Oh shite, he thinks I'm trying to sell something else.*

"When I'm not modeling, I work in an antique shop, and I have a genuine polar bear rug for sale. It's almost nine and a half feet long. It's just gorgeous." As she spoke she pulled a business card from her coat pocket. "I have all the paperwork to prove its provenance too. All nice and legal."

It took him almost as long to read her card as most people took to read War and Peace. Finally he looked back up at her.

"I'll pass this on to Andy and have him take a look. If it's as good as you say you might just have a sale. In the meantime, let's get you into character."

He ushered her down a flight of stairs into an enormous, finished basement full of high end professional photographic equipment, backdrops and props. Andrew was standing at the doorway to a bathroom chatting with a tiny bleach blonde Filipina in white yoga pants and fluffy pink sweater.

"Amy this is Rui Santos. Rui this is Amy Dreadsone, from the modeling agency." Rui stuck out a tiny hand and Amy took it. It was warm and soft.

"Nice to meet you, Amy."

"You and Andy have already met, of course." Andrew rolled his eyes and kept his hands in his pockets, which made Amy suddenly aware she was still holding Rui's hand. She began babbling to hide her embarrassment at the *faux pas*.

"My name is pronounced Dresden actually, like the city in Germany."

"If all the pleasantries are out of the way," Andrew said as he pulled her driver's license from his pocket and handed it back to her, "we had better get started with hair and make-up. We are already running late." He pushed open the door to the bathroom and gave Amy a hard look. "Ladies, if you please."

Rui led the way into a bathroom twice the size of the one in Amy's apartment. A stool covered with a fluffy white bath towel stood in front of a marble countertop, strewn with cosmetics, applicators, eyelash curlers, hairbrushes, curling irons, blow dryers, spray bottles, aerosol cans, an airbrush with a miniature compressor, and a couple of items that looked more like medieval torture devices than beauty products to Amy.

Andrew pushed past the women and perched on the side of the bathtub with his arms folded across his chest. The way he stared at them reminded Amy of an English teacher she had in high school that made no secret of his belief that he was the next Hemmingway and teaching to pay the bills was a waste of his precious talent. Amy stood awkwardly looking from Andrew to Rui not sure what to do.

"Have a seat, sweetie." Rui smiled at her and gestured to the stool. "Don't worry about him; he's just mad because he couldn't get Streisand tickets."

Amy hesitated, "Should—should I, er. Should I get undressed or something?"

Rui giggled like a teen-ager at a slumber party. "No, that's not necessary. Not yet anyway. I need to do your hair first, then your face. Unless you're worried about getting make-up on your dress."

Now it was Amy's turn to laugh. But the sound was somehow manic. More like the way that same English teacher laughed when he got rejection slips in the mail. She squatted on the stool with her arms folded across her chest. This was far more difficult then she had anticipated.

Rui took the curling iron from the counter and began wrapping strands of Amy's long platinum locks into tight ringlets and in spite of herself Amy began to relax. She would never admit it to anyone, but Amy loved to have her hair done. Yes, it was vain and shallow, but she just loved it. It made her feel pretty and special. It was one of her guilty pleasures, like hiding under her heavy quilt and eating an entire box of chocolates while reading trashy romance novels. She closed her eyes and let herself drift along while Rui did her work.

"You seem pretty nervous," Rui said as she worked her magic on Amy's tresses. "It this your first 'art shoot'?"

"Yeah. I'm not real comfortable about it. But I really do need the money."

"Well, just relax and you'll do fine. I've worked with Henry on a couple of these shoots and he's a real pussycat. He won't ask you to do anything nasty and he won't make you look slutty."

Andrew harrumphed.

"As a matter of fact," Rui continued throwing an icy stare in his direction, "you'll be able to let your boyfriend or even your parents see these photos when I'm done with you."

Amy dropped her eyes at the thought of her father seeing naked pictures of her.

"Does your boyfriend know you're doing this?"

"I don't have a boyfriend to know."

"That's hard to believe. As pretty as you are I bet you have your pick of the litter."

"The trouble is the entire litter grows up to be dogs," Amy said, and both women began to laugh. Even Andrew smirked at that.

"Your hair is just the perfect color," Rui said.

"Even the roots?" Andrew asked.

"Even the roots," Rui repeated, glaring at him as she got a loose plastic shower cap from her kit. "We won't need to color it at all."

Amy stole a quick peek in the mirror before Rui could cover it with the plastic. She had done a magnificent job. Amy's hair floated around her head in an intricate cloud of braids and curls. Amy was quite pleased with the outcome, and for the first time began to feel a little better about the shoot.

Rui poured a bottle of grayish-white goop onto an artist's palette and began trawling it onto Amy's eyelids like spackle. As a rule, Amy usually went light with make-up but Rui was piling it on like Earl Scheib. Amy could not bear to look.

After what felt like an eternity Rui finally stopped slathering on the paste and switched on a mini-air compressor. Amy steeled herself and snuck a peek in the mirror. Thick white circles enclosed her eyes making the pale blue stand out like beacons. Chalky white streaks crisscrossed her forehead and radiated out from her nose to the edges of her lips. Her usually full lips were hidden in the same dead white color. She gasped at the sight.

"I look like a wicked old witch!"

"I'd be careful how you spell that, sweetie," Andrew said.

"Don't panic, Amy," Rui turned around with an airbrush in her hand. "We're not done yet. That's just the undercoat."

"Undercoat?" If you put on much more I'm going to look like Marcel Marceau in drag."

"More like Marcel Marceau *out of* drag," Andrew said.

"At least Marcel Marceau could keep his mouth shut. Don't pay any attention to Andrew; he's been in a tizzy all week because he came in third place in the Cher impersonator contest at Oil Can Harry's. Don't worry, you won't look like a mime. It will be more like Kabuki makeup when I'm done. Trust me, you'll be just beautiful. Now close those baby blues," Rui began to spray liquid make-up with the air brush first along Amy's scalp line then down across her forehead.

After covering Amy's entire face and neck all the way to the collar bone, Rui finally took a step back and admired her work. "That's good. Time to start the body work. Can you get undressed now please?"

Amy was suddenly acutely self-aware. "Is he supposed to stay in here?" she said gesturing to Andrew.

"Oh, get over yourself, honey." Andrew tilted his head like a barn owl. "You haven't got anything I want to see."

"Just because you don't want to see it doesn't mean I want to show it to you."

Andrew glared at her, rolled his eyes and sashayed toward the door. "I suppose Henry could use a hand in the studio."

Amy stood up and slipped out of her dress. Unsure of what to do with her hands she made a show of meticulously folding it and laid it on top of the toilet tank.

"The bra too please," Rui said. She dipped a foam rubber applicator in her palette again as Amy removed her bra.

"Wow, you have almost no tan lines at all," Rui blurted when she turned back around.

"With my complexion getting a tan is almost impossible. After two minutes in the sun I look like a fire engine."

"Well not having any tan lines today will save us some time. I won't have to try to hide them. I was working on this awful horror movie once—*Sharkman of Blood Beach*—you know, one of those horrible drive in B-movies where a guy in a cheap rubber monster suit runs around killing half-naked teenagers in gory ways.

"Sit, sit." Rui gestured to the stool and Amy obediently complied. Rui compared three bottles of concealer against Amy's chest and went on with her story. "So there was this one girl that was as brown as a berry. I mean the brownest white girl I have ever seen. She must have spent every spare moment in the tanning bed."

"Yeah, I know the type." Goldie's face danced through Amy's mind. "Their skin ends up looking like saddle bags by the time they're thirty."

"Well the Sharkman was supposed to attack her in the shower. But when she took her top off they were so white they looked like spotlights. I mean she could have replaced Rudolph on Santa's sleigh. It took me hours to make them match the rest of her, and I had to touch them up for every take."

As she prattled on, Rui turned back to the counter and began mixing another batch of concealer. As she leaned over the counter Amy could not help but admire her hindquarters. There was a subtle difference between Asian butts and European butts. The Asian butt is less rounded and lower down on the torso. Also the crack does not come up quite as far as Caucasians. The inward curve of the lower back is less pronounced causing less side-to-side sway.

In spite of that, the action of stirring the makeup was not only moving Rui's delicate shoulders, it was telegraphing a minute wiggle down her spine and causing an almost imperceptible sway in her narrow hips.

Amy realized she was staring at a woman's ass. And that woman could see her doing it in the mirror. She couldn't look away without being obvious about it. So she closed her eyes and tried to think about something else, anything else. She tried to think about basketball. The

Lakers would be playing the Denver Nuggets later that evening. But rather then pondering their chances of victory all she could imagine was Rui jumping up and down on the sidelines in a yellow and purple Laker Girl uniform.

"Amy...Amy!"

"What? Oh, sorry."

"Did you doze off on me there?"

"No. I was just thinking about the Laker's game tonight. Do you like basketball?"

"No. My boyfriend is a big fan, but I just don't get it. What's so interesting about a bunch of overgrown men playing a kid's game?" As she talked, she casually cupped her left hand under one of Amy's breasts, as if grabbing a strange woman's boob was a normal thing to do and lifted it to dab concealer along the crease under it.

"No implant scars to hide either. I can't tell you how many times I've had to try and cover some bimbo's implant scars for topless scenes. Like everybody can't tell she had a boob-job. Those things are about as convincing as a politician promising to lower taxes."

Unable to answer Amy clenched her teeth and tried to hold still. Rui's touch was so...so...Amy didn't know what exactly. Maybe it was because she wasn't trying to squash or bite it, Rui's touch made her skin tingle. Ever since high school, Amy hated it when guys tried to squeeze and prod at her boobs like they were kneading pizza dough. All the twisting and yanking didn't turn her on, it just hurt. Ted was no better. For some reason that completely escaped her, he thought that twisting her nipples excited her. In fact the opposite was true. Ted's fingers, while very dexterous, were covered in hard, coarse calluses from years of playing guitar.

They felt like rasp files poking and twisting at her tender flesh. But Rui's fingertips were soft and warm and gentle.

It took all of Amy's will not to shiver as Rui dabbed the cool makeup along the underside of her breasts. Amy's heart was pounding. Was it because Rui's touch was so business-like that it affected her so much?

"The only thing worse than trying to cover implant scars is hiding tats, I can't tell you how many tramp stamps I've had to cover up," Rui prattled on. Maybe if she just grabbed one and gave her a good old fashioned titty-whistle the unnatural tension would be broken and Amy would be able to think clearly again. But Rui didn't do that. When she was finished with the undercarriage and up into her cleavage she did something even worse.

After refreshing the supply of product on the soft applicator Rui began patting it around the outer edge of Amy's areola. Amy's breath shortened. She could feel her nipple hardening at Rui's touch.

"Hey, are you okay?" Rui asked pulling back and staring into Amy's eyes.

"I'm fine."

"Do you have asthma or something? Cuz you're breathing kinda hard. Do you need to get an inhaler?"

"No, I don't need an inhaler." Amy shut her eyes and tried to think of an excuse, any excuse for her reaction. "You just startled me is all. The make-up must be cold." She knew it was a lame excuse but it was the only thing she could think of.

Rui looked at Amy's swollen nipple. "It's not that cold" she muttered in Tagalog. She switched back to the pale gray and began to define Amy's rib cage. By the time she was through her ribs stood out like a concentration camp survivor's.

Amy focused all of her concentration on her breathing, or at least she tried to. But even the breathing exercises she had learned in her yoga classes only covered the symptoms. The separation of mind and body did not completely distract her from the physical reality of Rui's touch. Every square inch of her skin was suddenly hypersensitive to the slightest sensation.

Rui's closeness did not help matters. The scent of her Vera Wang perfume was making Amy tipsy, and it was only by clinging to the stool with all her strength that she was able to keep her hands to herself. She had not felt anything even remotely like this in years. Not since she and Ted had left Chicago, and hardly ever then.

It was like those rare snowy Sunday mornings when Ted was too exhausted, or hung-over, after the gig the night before to wake up. She would snuggle up to him under the heavy comforter as wild, frigid wind clawed at their apartment windows. Those precious few hours, before he was sober enough to wake, where the best times for her. She cherished them even though they almost always ended up with her flat on her back trying to think of other things wile Ted did his business on top of her.

Rui was droning on about all the tasteless tattoos she had to cover as she finished Amy's ribs and began to trace the muscle definition on her abdomen. Amy worked diligently at keeping in shape. Her stomach was hard and flat but the definition Rui was adding made her look like a body-builder. When she was finished painting on the six-pack she switched to an oversized cotton swab and began working on Amy's navel.

Amy had an involuntary muscle contraction, she felt her stomach, and other things, tighten suddenly and was unable to suppress a gasp and a shiver. She had an overpowering urge to run her fingers through Rui's hair. She desperately wanted to touch Rui's face, but she didn't dare. She clung to the stool to keep her hands in check but she could no longer look away. She stared down into Rui's light brown eyes and swallowed. Rui jerked back, rocking on her heels. She stood slowly, never breaking eye contact with Amy. Now her golden skin turned as pink as her sweater. She tried to say something but couldn't, cleared her throat and tried again.

"Hey, look, Amy, I'm really sorry," she dropped her eyes. "I'm flattered really. But I'm not... I mean I have a boyfriend."

Amy's hands covered her face and she gasped again. She could feel her cheeks burning so hot she was surprised the makeup didn't melt off.

"I mean whatever you're into is fine with me. It's none of my business really. Whatever floats your boat, right? I don't have anything against it, but I'm just not into it, okay? No offence or anything."

The words hit Amy like a slap in the face. "Why does everyone think I'm a lesbian? I'm not gay."

"Whatever you say," Rui said, "Doesn't matter to me one way or the other. Just try and control yourself, okay. Try and act like a professional."

"I am a professional."

"Fine then," Rui plucked the swab out of Amy's navel and tossed it into a waste basket. She replenished an applicator, moved behind Amy and began to work on her spine and shoulder blades. Outside of giving simple direction like raise your arm or lean forward, she didn't speak to Amy again until she had finished all the highlights and sprayed on the topcoat with the airbrush.

Rui's pretty face had become a blank, unreadable mask as she worked. The friendly, chatty demeanor was gone. She covered Amy's skin from her hairline to the tips of her fingers all the way down to her waistline. When she turned her back on Amy to mix another batch of makeup her narrow shoulders where rigid and her eyes had become hard and hostile.

This time when she turned back around she would not look Amy in the eye. "Give me your foot." She sat down on a step stool in front of Amy and began the process of first highlighting details around her toes, ankles and knees then sprayed her long legs with the airbrush.

"Look, Rui, I'm sorry if I said or did something that offended you."

"You didn't say anything," Rui replied coldly without looking up. "Don't worry about it. It's not like you're doing it on purpose."

"Doing what?"

The steady spray of the airbrush stopped. Rui seemed to study Amy's left kneecap for a moment and clenched her free hand into a fist. Then resumed her work without saying another word.

"No seriously, what did I do to make you think that?"

Rui glared up at her. "Just because I said you're pretty doesn't mean I'm into you. Now I know you can't help getting excited but this is real life, not a porno movie. Just because you like me doesn't mean I'm suddenly going to turn lesbo."

"Like you? What are you talking about? I'm not—"

"I'm not some naive FLIP. I know you kicked Andrew out so you could get me alone but it isn't going to work."

"Rui, really I don't know what you're talking about. I'm not trying to—"

"Drop the innocent act, I know what you're doing. And you know what you're doing. And I know that you know that I know what you're doing. So can we just get this over with?"

Rui turned her back again. She began fussing with the airbrush and mixing the body paints without turning back around or looking at Amy's reflection in the mirror.

"Take off your panties." Amy didn't know why it surprised her when Rui said it. It wasn't like she didn't know it was coming. But she really didn't want to do it. This was even harder than doing it at the club in front of a room full of strangers. At least they had only been disinterested. Rui was offended by her body and Amy couldn't fathom why. So she thought of the money, and how much she needed it and complied.

Rui turned back around with the air brush ready and pulled a frown like Amy's second grade teacher when she caught a student preparing to shoot a spitball when her back was turned.

"What?" Amy said.

"Why didn't you shave today?"

"Shave?" Amy truly had no idea what she was talking about.

"You were supposed to be shaved. I can't paint over…*that.*"

In the mirror behind Rui Amy saw her reflection. Rui and done such a good job of making her skin look like white marble that she almost blended into the bathroom's decor.

Her unpainted bikini area made the triangle of silver blonde hair glimmer like neon on a dark desert highway.

"I didn't know I was supposed to. I'm sorry, nobody said anything about shaving. He just said they wanted a blonde."

"Have you ever seen a Greek statue with a bush? This is a fine art shoot, not a centerfold for a titty mag." Rui turned her back and started rummaging through her make-up.

"I've never posed nude before, how was I supposed to know."

"Yeah, whatever you say." Rui pulled an electric razor from her kit, switched it on and off to test the batteries and held it out. Amy just looked at it in her hand and Goldie's' words echoed through her head: "And whatever you do, don't shave that natural blonde bush. Guys will cough up their union dues for a glimpse of real blonde bush."

"Well?" Rui said snapping her back to here and now. Amy looked away from the razor.

"Okay, fine," Amy mumbled. Rui didn't move.

"You don't honestly think I'm going to do it for you do you?"

"What? Oh, no, of course not." Amy took the razor from Rui and sat down on the toilet.

"Do you need me to leave you alone?" Rui asked her voice still hard and cold. Amy switched the razor on. It was the same kind her father had used to trim his sideburns when she was a little girl. The sound made her think of him, and that did not help with what she had to do. She took a deep breath and went to work. Tufts of silvery hair fell into the water below. The vibration of the blades made her skin quiver. Was this finally the bottom? How much lower could she go?

"Come on, we don't have all day." Rui said. "I still have to finish painting you."

Freshly shorn, Amy handed the razor back to Rui and returned to her seat on the stool. Rui didn't waste time covering the last remaining bits of Amy's most private places and was packing up her equipment even before the last coat was dry.

"When you're done shooting, you can use the shower in here," she said over her shoulder as she disassembled the air compressor. "The body paint is water-soluble and will come right off with regular soap and water, but you may have to scrub a little." Amy knew that Rui really meant was she would not help her remove the paint from all those hard to reach places. For some reason she didn't understand, that disappointed Amy.

Amy took a deep breath and went out into the studio. The room was almost pitch black now, only illuminated but the muted glow of modeling lights in the soft boxes. Henry and Andrew were adjusting the power setting on one of the strobes as she walked the last mile to the set.

"Wow, Rui did a fabulous job," Henry said when he got a good look at her. "You look like a real Greek goddess."

"I suppose she'll do," Andrew muttered.

Henry approached her, looking her over. He walked around her to see every side. Oddly, this felt normal to Amy. It wasn't as if he was inspecting a side of beef, but more like a fashion designer appraising the outfit he had put on her just before sending her down a runway. Her usual confidence began to return. She didn't feel the least bit exposed or embarrassed about being nude.

Henry led her to a low plinth in front of a huge dark brown Old Masters Canvas Backdrop. He stood on the plinth holding a large plastic urn painted the same colors as she was and demonstrated the first poses he wanted her to take. She was surprised that anyone so very male could strike such a feminine pose. She supposed it was his years as an actor that enabled him to so easily to step out of his own gender role and into another. None of the poses he asked her to do were particularly provocative, and he was so charming and supportive that she completely forgot she was naked.

It was only when Rui was asked to touch-up the body paint when it had been smudged or smeared from her moving that she was reminded of that fact. Much to Rui's annoyance and Amy's amazement, she found herself pointing out spots at the slightest signs of wear.

The actual shoot took only two hours. In that time he shot one roll of medium format film for each of four different poses. All the poses were reminiscent of classical Greek statues. The hardest ones were with the urn. In those, Amy was standing with the urn under one arm, pouring its contents into a basin beneath the plinth just out of shot. The difficulty was that after each shot Andrew would have to run up and replenish the urn's supply of water for the next exposure.

The tipping point came on the final pose. From a coffee table book of classical Greek art, Henry showed her photographs of several statues all in a similar pose entitled "Crouching Aphrodite." It was by far the most modest of the shots. She was kneeling on the balls of her feet, with one knee down almost touching the plinth and the other razed to cover most of her chest. In some variants, she was to cover her breasts with her hands while in others she was more exposed.

The trouble started after she had rested her forearms across her knee while covering her breasts. Before she could do the more open pose, she called on Rui to touch-up a smudge she had made on her upper thigh.

Rui rolled her eyes but hurried over to the plinth and crouched down in front of Amy. Amy held up her forearms, showing the back sides where they had rubbed on her thigh as she had leaned over her knee. Amy's throat was dry, and her heart was pounding so hard she was sure Rui could hear it.

Once her forearms were done she leaned back on her hands for balance and, staring directly into Rui's big brown eyes, opened her knees to give Rui access to the smudge on her thigh. Fixing the smear was her only cognizant intention. She even believed that herself at the time.

Amy could not tear her eyes away from Rui's and the pounding in her ears was so loud now she was sure she couldn't hear it if anyone spoke. As Amy's eyes widened, Rui's narrowed then dropped along Amy's torso. They paused fleetingly on her swollen nipples then darted south for a split second. Unconsciously, Amy spread her thighs infinitesimally. That was the last straw for Rui. Much is said about the famous Irish temper or infamous hot-blooded Spaniard's rage or even the fiery temperament of redheads, but none compare to an angry Filipina.

"Bitch, get it through your fucking head I'm not going down on you." Rui sprang to her feet so abruptly that Amy jerked back, lost her balance and toppled off the plinth onto her shoulders with her feet sticking straight up in the air.

Henry handed off his Hasselblad to Andrew like a baton and dashed onto the set to separate the ladies while they could both still be called ladies. He caught Rui's wrist just as she wound up to throw her palette and applicators in Amy's face. Unable to get to her feet yet, Amy crab-crawled back across the background to escape.

Rui spun on Henry like an angry cat and would have clawed his face if he hadn't caught her other wrist in the nick of time. She struggled wildly to get free, but he was easily twice her size, and in spite of being well into middle age he hadn't quite yet gone to seed.

"Easy there, little lady, before you do something you'll regret," Henry said in a smooth, even tone.

"Anything I'll regret? The only person that's going to have any regrets is that *puta* when I get through with her."

Amy managed to get to her feet but kept her distance. "I'm really sorry you're so upset, but I don't know what I did that offended you."

"Don't pull that dumb blonde shit with me! Nobody's buying it bitch."

"What did she do?" Henry asked. "What could have been so bad?"

"What could have been so bad? How would you like it if Andrew was walking around with a hard-on?"

"What's Andrew got to do with this?" Henry bit his lower lip and his eyes darted from person to person.

"Leave me out of this one, honey. I'm *so* not involved," Andrew said.

"You think so, fairy-cakes?" Rui snapped at him, "Then you do this bitch's make-up, I'm done with it! I'm not some dyke bitch's fucking fluffer." She pulled her wrists free from Henry's hands, stormed into the bathroom, and slammed the door hard enough to shake the soft boxes.

"What got into her?" Henry said with a slack chin. "I've never seen her lose it like that before."

"More like *who's* got into *her*, right Amy?" Andrew threw Amy a lewd wink.

"I wasn't coming on to her," Amy insisted.

"Coming on to…her?" The gears in Henry's head were still grinding. None of this made any sense to him.

Rui stomped out of the bathroom with her makeup kit and an expression on her face that could curdle milk. No one dared speak as she marched past to the stairs. She stopped, suddenly turned back, and glared straight through Amy.

"When you take the body paint off, use cold water. It doesn't make any difference to the makeup, but you could definitely use a cold shower." Her angry footsteps could be heard echoing up the stairs and through the rooms above. After the front door slammed above them, Andrew looked at the Hasselblad in his hands.

"Henry, this roll is almost done. There's only two more exposures left. Why don't we just call it a day?"

Henry shook his head like a dog and looked at Amy standing by the background. For the first time since the shoot started, Amy felt naked. She tried to cover herself with her hands. It was then that she realized what had so offended Rui. Amy was wet. She tried to hide it by turning a hip to the men and covering herself. But her awkward attempts only drew their attention to it.

"I think you're probably right, Andy," Henry said, his eyes now locked on Amy's obviously erect nipples. "The mood is spoiled anyway. Besides I'm sure I've got shots enough to use." To Amy's relief he tore his gaze away from her and looked at the camera. "Why don't you show her where she can clean up?" He took the camera and headed toward the stairs.

"Come on, Sappho, time to hit the showers," Andrew said.

"I wasn't coming on to her!" Amy's voice was frantic.

"Who are you trying to convince, me or you? The shower is this way." He led her back into the bathroom and laid out a pile of fluffy white towels.

"No, seriously, Rui is nuts. I wasn't coming on to her."

"Whatever you say, sweetie." Andrew opened the shower stall and turned on the water. "It has a Power Spray hand-held shower head so you can get all those tough to reach nooks and crannies. Take as long as you need."

"I'm not gay. I'm not interested in women. I like guys!" Amy repeated franticly trying to get him to believe.

"If the shower head doesn't do it for you, you can always take matters into your own hands." Amy was so insulted by the suggestion that she was left speechless. He flittered by her but stopped at the doorway and called out "Oh, and do try not to drip on the floor."

Once she was in the shower, Amy was grateful for the high water pressure, not for the vulgar reason that Andrew implied but it covered the sounds of her sobs. After she had a good cry she, discovered that Rui had been wrong about how easily the paint would come off. It took her almost half-an-hour to get rid of most of it. But even with aggressive scrubbing, it stuck in crannies and creases. It would eventually take two weeks to get it all out from under her fingernails and the lines in the palms of her hands.

When she had finished and dressed, she found Andrew was still in the studio dismantling one of the soft boxes. The room seemed much smaller with the overhead florescent lights on, and all the props that were left out looked fake, giving the room a nightmarish, surreal ambiance.

"Did you get everything off that you needed to?" Andrew tossed the speed ring on the floor and rolled up the body of the soft box.

"Most of the paint is gone, if that's what you mean."

"Yessss, of course it is. Henry has taken the film to the lab himself, so I will show you out." Amy was surprised and relieved that she was spared the humiliation of him searching her to be sure she hadn't tried to steal the bath towels and soap. She was even more surprised that he let her leave through the front door instead of the servants' exit. But her relief was short-lived when she found a parking ticket on the windshield of Rachel's Honda.

She tried not to cry as she drove back to Van Nuys to open her shop but was not entirely successful. Not being successful was something she was getting used to. She was sure that once Henry told **Daniel** what a fiasco the shoot had been, he would never send her on another job. Not even porn.

So this was it. Her dreams of a career in modeling and acting were as dead as disco. They had died like the King of Rock and Roll, face down on the bathroom floor. Her shop would go under in a month or two, leaving her so far in debt that she would have to work double shifts at the Wild Cat just to eat. She had finally sunk so low that she was no better than the working girls on Sepulveda.

The rest of the day was no better. She managed to get the shop open around one, but she didn't have any customers. Not real ones anyway. Richard Wang, the assistant night manager of the grocery store on the far side of Sepulveda made his usual Thursday afternoon stop. He usually got off the bus early for his shift and killed the extra time by coming into her shop and trying feebly to flirt with her. He had no interest in antiques at all, most likely because there was no room for them in his parent's garage, but like a lot of Asian guys he had a fetish for tall blondes, another thing that would not fit in his parent's garage. He hung around wasting her time for the better part of an hour asking inane questions about random items and trying to determine her zodiac sign.

Around three-thirty her pager beeped. It was Daniel Cline. She was sure he was only calling to tell her that Henry had complained about her behavior in the shoot and that she should not quit her day job. It was better to rip the band-aid off all at once rather than peel it back a little at a time, so she called him back just to get it over with.

"Amy, baby, how did the shoot go?"

"Not great I'm afraid. The make-up artist threw a hissy fit because she thought I was coming on to her."

"Were you?"

"She is a woman!"

"Yeah? So were you?"

"*Gottverdammt!* I'm not a lesbian. I wasn't hitting on anybody."

"You're not gay? Really? I always thought you and Rachel Langdon lived together."

"We were roommates after I dumped my *boyfriend* for cheating on me. Rachel and I are not lovers. Not then or now or ever."

"Could have fooled me. You two just put out that kind of vibe. Live and learn. Anyway, the real reason I paged you is I have another gig for you. Have you ever heard of *Lions Art Magazine*?"

"No. What is it, some kind of wildlife thing?"

"Not exactly. They specialize in art nudes. You know the stuff. Black and white with dramatic lighting. That sort of stuff."

"Dan, I don't think…"

"You would be working with a woman photographer named Shangee, or Sangee, or Shan Gee. Something like that, I never get those Japanese names right."

"Daniel, I can't…"

"What they want is a really pale-skinned, white girl and a really dark-skinned, black girl posing together with all the artsy-fartsy back lighting. I've got Nyakim Moore to pose with you. She is about as black as they come. The two of you will look great together."

"No! Absolutely not! I'm not doing any lesbo shoots. Especially after what happened today. No way."

"It's not a 'lesbo shoot,' babe, its fine art. You won't be doing it with Nyakim; you'll just sort of be there, together. Just to show off the contrast between how light you are and how dark she is. It's a message piece about how unfair it is to hold women of color to white beauty standards."

"No it's not and you know it. It's about two women licking each other so some pseudo-intellectual pervert can whack off to it and still claim it's not porn because it socially relevant high art. No matter how you dress it up is still just dirty pictures."

"They're paying five grand for just one day's work. If they like what they see, and what's not to like, it will lead to more layouts. Once you get your name out there I might even be able to get you a *Playboy* centerfold. Those start at twenty-five hundred. With your looks, you could go all the way. Playmate of the Year maybe. That's a hundred grand and a car!"

"And all I have to do is go down on Nyakim in some smut mag. No. I'm not doing it. Not for all the money in the world. I don't care how broke I am."

"It's not like we're talking *Easyriders* or *Hustler* here. Amy, baby, don't go all prude on me now. Not after we've come this far. This is your last chance to make some real money. Its either this or go back to Sunday supplements and car shows for chump change."

"Let me see if I understand exactly what you're saying here. If I don't do this shoot, you won't get me any other work. Is that what you're saying?"

"Well, babe, look at it from my side. What is the point of trying to find you jobs if you turn them all down?"

"So, if I don't get it on with Nyakim, you're going to drop me as a client. Yes or no?"

"Come on, babe, don't be like that. We could make a lot of money together."

"Yes or no?"

"Babe, you're not giving me much of a choice here."

"Then let me make the choice for you. I quit. If the only way I can make any money in this business is to peddle my ass like a common street hooker turning tricks than I quit. At least I'll have some self-respect left."

"Okay, fine, if that's the way you want it. But there's no turning back this time. You're burning this bridge. Just

remember, Amy, you can't pay the rent with self-respect."
The phone went dead, along with the last of her dreams of
stardom. All that was left now was the shop, and dancing.

Seeing no point in keeping the store open too late she
locked up at five and headed for the barn. Even with the
rush hour traffic she managed to get back to Rachel's by six,
well a quarter past six anyway, which left no time for small
talk about their days. Rachel had to hustle in order to be on
time for her shift at the club. They barely had time to say
hello and pass off the car keys.

This was fine with Amy. She didn't want to talk about
her decision to give up on her career. It was too big to say
out loud to anyone at this point. Amy thought of the old
joke about the stable hand in the circus. He went to a bar
every night and complained about having to clean up the
elephant's excrement in the big top three times a day.
Someone asked him, "If it's that unpleasant why don't you
just quit and get another job?" and the stable hand said
"What? And give up show business?"

The last thing in the world she wanted to do was tell
Rachel, of all people, about Rui. Or even to think about Rui
herself. To take her mind off of the pretty little Filipina she
ran a hot bath. Even after the long shower at Henry's, body
paint was still turning up in embarrassing places. All she
wanted to do was get the last of it off so she would never
have to think about Rui and this day again.

But the bath was little help. When she got in, the water
turned a milky gray as it dissolved the remaining makeup.
Now mixed with glitter residue from Rachel's shows, it only
redistributed over her body as a sticky gray film. Instead of
emptying her mind, the hot water only allowed it to review

every last detail of the day's events, or to wander into places she desperately did not want it to go.

After another good cry, she dressed in sweats and turned in for the night. She slept a black, dreamless sleep, which seemed appropriate to her at the time because she was now fresh out of dreams.

**

Friday, April 8, 1994

At four-thirty when Amy heard Rachel come in, she pretended to still be asleep. She played possum until she was sure Rachel had gone to bed and was fast asleep. She put the kettle on and watched the morning news in utter despair as they reported on the suicide of Nirvana front man Kurt Cobain.

A heavy metal purist, she was never a big fan of grunge rock, but this morning of all mornings she really felt his loss. It put the end of her dreams of fame into perspective. Her modeling career was over, but not her life. That was no reason for despair. There is more to life than being a model or an actress. She had to get off her pity pot and get her tight little ass in gear.

So, she would never win an academy award or be on the cover of Vogue. There was still tomorrow, and she still had to eat. There was the shop, and she would make that work. Now that she was no longer distracted by trying to have two careers, she could concentrate all of her attention on one.

The first thing she had to do was get the van out of the shop and to do that, she had to take Lyle his bikini pictures today. That was it! Lyle was right, advertising was the answer to all her problems. She had been so busy trying to promote herself that she never thought about promoting the shop. She could do some local TV spots. Something stylish and classy, her in a smart business suit, like the ones the crazy-little-Asian-woman-next-door wore, but with a longer skirt of course. And if that didn't work, she could do something wild like the late night discount barns do. Maybe cutting grandfather clocks in half with a chainsaw wearing a bikini. That would get her store some attention.

But commercials cost money, and she didn't have any. But she would. It was unpleasant, it was embarrassing, but she would just have to suck it up and do what she had to do. Dresdens weren't quitters. She would strip for a few months with Rachel at the Wild Cat. She would do the sister act, she would flirt with other girls on stage to get better tips. She would show off her natural blonde bush—after it grew back—and make the perverts think she's into them. She would be the best stripper Goldie had ever seen—for the time being.

In the meantime, she would make the rounds of all the health clubs, fitness centers, and even the rec-centers and find gigs as a freelance aerobics instructor or even a personal trainer. Without having to rush off to auditions on a moment's notice she would be able to make and keep appointments with paying clients. If things didn't pick up at the store within two or three months at least she could quit show business for good.

She finished her tea, had a shower, dressed in her black pencil skirt, stole Rachel's red cashmere sweater from her closet and went to the store.

***

By lunch time, she had not made any sales for the day. But she had tracked down a video guy she had worked with on a fashion show. He would be able to shoot the TV spots for her at a reasonable price and would not expect her to sleep with him as part of the deal. He still wasn't cheap, but she needed quality if she was going to get the audience she wanted. She had managed to get some prices from local TV stations too. It was a lot more than she expected. It meant she may have to shake her money maker for a year or more to get the cash she needed but at least she had a goal.

Not entirely disappointed with the morning's work she slipped into the back room for a bite. She started a fresh pot of tea and unwrapped a couple of rice-cakes. She wished she had a little bit of honey to put on them, but she was all out. She had just bitten into the first one when the shop's doorbell rang. A customer! A real, live, flesh and blood customer.

A giant was standing near the cash stand, admiring the three grandfather clocks she had not been able to shift in almost a year. The guy was big enough to use one of the clocks as a pocket watch and had shoulders wide enough to use as billboards. Which was strange, because he had a purse dangling from one. Even though there was nothing particularly feminine about it, it was definitely not a messenger bag or a brief case with a shoulder strap, it was a purse. It even matched his shoes.

"Hi there." Amy never said, "Can I help you?" because that put potential buyers on guard. He looked away from the clocks and smiled warmly. He was ruggedly handsome with leading man good looks, which made the curled eyelashes a ridiculous non sequitur.

"Quite a selection of grandfathers you have here," his voice was soft and slightly slurred. "What are you asking for the large one?"

"I couldn't let it go for less than five-thousand. It was made in London around 1860 by J.C. Jennens & Sons."

He opened the cabinet, carefully and examined the weights.

"That's just a little pricey."

"It *is* a hundred and thirty-five years old."

"I don't suppose you have a dealer's price?"

"We could work something out if you have a wholesale license."

"I see. Well that's really neither here nor there, what I'd really like to see is your bear skin."

"What?" The words hit Amy like a blow to the stomach. Instinctively she took a step backward and balanced on the balls of her feet ready to defend herself. "Get out of my store before I call the cops, you fucking pervert."

His face hardened and he turned away from the clocks to face her straight on. Just as suddenly, he began to laugh. "Andrew was right; you really are a natural blonde. I want to see your *polar bear* skin. I'm Jeffrey Pike, Andrew Zavacká sent me to look at a polar bear rug you have for sale."

"Andrew? Oh right, of course." Amy began laughing too. "Whatever was I thinking? I'm so embarrassed. You must think I'm some sort of crazy woman. I keep it in back, right this way." She led him into the back room and pulled the tarp off the hide. He sucked his teeth and made a face like he had just had a bite of her plain rice cake.

"That's the most horrible thing I have ever seen. 'Why grandma, what big teeth you have.' Its eyes are like something out of a horror movie, aren't they? Henry will just *love* it! You do have all the proper paperwork? We wouldn't want the Fish and Game Department kicking in Henry's front door now, would we?"

"It's all right here." Still mortified about her outburst, Amy sounded too anxious. She dashed to a filing cabinet and pulled out a manila folder full of paperwork. "I've got all the provenance you'll ever need. I have an affidavit here from the hunter that killed the poor thing, verifying it was shot in 1970. That's two years before the Marine Mammal Protection Act of 1972. And a second one signed by his guide. Plus a photo of them with the bear in Alaska right after he shot it."

"How much?" he asked stroking his neatly trimmed goatee and staring into the bear's lifeless black eyes.

"Uh...It is almost nine feet long and in amazing condition. I'm asking thirty-five for it." Amy gave the high-end price for a bear skin with a head of that quality, expecting him to haggle her down to around twenty-five thousand.

"Well, it's Henry's money."

He took an ostrich skin checkbook from his bag and walked to the cash stand. While Amy was engrossed in ringing up the best sale she had made in the last three months, Jeffrey drifted back over to the three clocks.

"You know," he said almost to himself, "this clock would be perfect in Henry's library." Amy stopped working the register and looked up at him, holding her breath. There was no way he would buy the clock too, that would be asking for too much. "Not that Henry has ever been in his library—there's not any comic books in it. I doubt that he

313

can even tell time anyway. Would you consider four and a half for the clock, along with the bear?"

"Sold!" Amy was barely able to contain herself over the turnaround in her business. But she did her best to hide her glee. Jeffrey sauntered over and began writing out a check with a gold Montblanc pen.

"You have a lot of lovely things here."

"Thank you. I'm careful about what I buy."

"You certainly have a good eye for it. I think we will be doing business again. As long as you promise not to call the cops on me for looking at your bare skin."

Amy looked at the check, that was a lot of zeros. Then she saw the company imprint and logo. Pike and Associates Interior Design of Beverly Hills. Her jaw dropped. Pike and Associates were the decorators to the stars.

"My installation team will come by around three to pick up the rug and the clock," Jeffrey said.

Amy watched Pike walk out of her shop, get into his BMW, and pull away. She took the check out of the till and stared at it, contemplating all those zeros. The store was saved. She could get the van fixed, she could pay rent, and with what was left over she could even eat.

Amy closed at four that day, so she could get the check into the bank before the weekend. She was excited to be able to pay some bills and maybe sleep in her own bed again. Rachel was a sweetie and she loved hanging out with her, but that convertible sofa was torture.

After the bank, she went to Lyle's to give him the photos so he would get started on the van. But the news was not good. Expecting her to be as good as her word Lyle had started work early, only to discover it was not just a blown head gasket. It was terminal, she had cracked the block. The Econoline was not worth fixing.

With the van on its way to that great traffic jam in the sky, Amy was still dependent on the Honda for the time being so her next stop had to be Rachel's apartment.

Rachael squealed with glee when Amy told her about selling the bearskin rug. She was truly happy for her. But the first intelligible words out of her mouth seemed so disconnected that Amy had to make her say it twice before they had any meaning.

"I guess this means you won't be going to the club on Monday?"

"Oh, the club."

"It's okay; I know you weren't real happy about dancing. I was just looking forward to working together."

"I'm sorry about that part," Amy said over the Chinese takeout she had brought home. "I like working with you. Just not working with you naked."

"That's fine; your heart was never in it anyway."

Amy spent one last night on Rachel's convertible. Saturday morning, she put on the black leather dress she had worn to the audition at the club, packed her bag and took a cab to her shop before Rachel was up for the day. She had a lot to do, and not a lot of time to do it.

She dropped her bag off in the store and walked back to the car lot on the corner. The 1993 Chevy crew cab was still there and so was the same sleazy salesman. When she took off her denim jacket and revealed the little black dress she was able to make the salesman take off an additional thousand dollars. Once the papers, were signed she went back to her store and changed into work clothes for the day like a reasonable person. She was determined that would be the last time she would use her looks to make her living.

A month later Henry DeCesare held a show in a Beverly Hills gallery selling signed and numbered Giclee prints of his photos of Amy and six other girls for five thousand dollars apiece. A local television movie hostess was so impressed with Henry's images that she fell for the artist. When she moved into his house with him, she didn't make him remodel, but she did convince him to move all of the guns from the case in the living room to a safe in the basement and to replace the vanity shot of Henry as Officer Cisco with one of the prints of Amy with the urn over the fireplace.

While Amy never worked as a model again, she did continue to profit indirectly from that shoot. Andrew Zavacká's partner, Jeffrey Pike, became a regular customer, buying sometimes two or three pieces a week to place in the homes of the rich and famous. Pike's word of mouth spread and within two years Amy's credit cards were paid off and Dresden Antiquities was actually making a modest profit.

About the Author

The Book of Jobs is the second published novel to escape the twisted mind of M.L. Grider. In addition to writing, Grider is a professional photographer. He is busy at work on the next adventure in the Helen Wu series among other wild and warped stories.

More Fascinating Fiction from
Thursday Night Press
An imprint of DX Varos Publishing

M.L. GRIDER
BITTER VINTAGE

SOURDOUGH JACKSON
TORPEDO JUNCTION

A.M. JORDAN
MCGUIRE'S LUCK
WEIRD CANYON
SASQUATCH LOVE CALL

KAREN A. MORRISSEY
FISHER KING: PERCY'S DESCENT

NONFICTION:
SOURDOUGH JACKSON
THAT OLD SCIENCE FICTION

ELISABETH L. MORRISSEY
IT'S NOT ALL ABOUT YOU

CPSIA information can be obtained
at www.ICGtesting.com
Printed in the USA
BVHW090319110922
646701BV00001B/6

9 781955 065542